St. Helens Libraries

NLW

Please return / renew this item by the last date shown. Items may be renewed by phone and internet.

Telephone: (01744) 676954 or 677822
Email: centrallibrary@sthelens.gov.uk
Online: sthelens.gov.uk/librarycatalogue

Nov

2 9 JUN 2019

1 8 JUL 2019

2 2 APR 2022

3 0 JAN 2023

WITHDRAWN FROM ST HELENS LIBRARIES

STHLibraries   sthlibrariesandarts   STHLibraries

Take   ST HELENS L   D1614790

ST.HELENS COMMUN

3 8055 01287 9615

Take-Away-Tea Books
https://nickybondramblings.blogspot.co.uk

Publisher's Note: This is a work of fiction. Names, characters,
places, and incidents are a product of the author's imagination.
Locales and public names are sometimes used for atmospheric
purposes. Any resemblance to actual people, living or dead, or
to businesses, companies, events, institutions, or locales is
completely coincidental.

Cover design by Portal - Design & Illustration
Book Layout © 2016 BookDesignTemplates.com

Carry the Beautiful/ Nicky Bond. -- 1st ed.
ISBN 978-0-9956574-0-3

For Bessie and Casper

CONTENTS

"Though we travel the world over to find the beautiful, we must carry it with us or we find it not."

RALPH WALDO EMERSON

At the time, the significant, meaningful moment being experienced isn't realised. It's just a moment, the same as any other, like all the moments before and all the moments that will follow. The sunrises at dawn, the all-night chats, the love made and shared with ease. Without giving any thought, or considering the alternative, it's clear there will be a limitless future filled with just as much emotional importance, and feeding one's soul with joy. The mixture of youth, optimism and a liberal dash of naivety make clear that this is the way it will always be, that this is *the way life is meant to be.*

But time passes. At some point without having given it conscious thought, the moments that brought such satisfaction at the time, have become stand-alone experiences. They were never bettered, simply left behind with nothing that followed coming close to competing. The moments are isolated in the past, slipping their moorings and floating away, transitioning into memories of a different time, of a different person. And as more time passes, what was gently bobbing on the water has mostly washed away, with little else to cling to as little else has followed. Those isolated moments from way back when have disappeared, leaving an ache for the loss of innocence and the end of potential.

There was no understanding there would be no more. And when the realisation dawns, you are dead inside. The lack of moments that *don't* follow, eat away at

what was once so hopeful. You mourn what didn't happen. You mourn the life you assumed you would have,
that never materialised. And the best way to cope with
that loss is to choose never to look back, never to remember. You push it out of your head and leave no
room for it to creep back. The past is boxed off. The lid
is closed, pushed into the back of your mind. Into the
dustiest and most concealed of attic corners. Your soul
never once has to accept that it hasn't felt joy since it
watched the moments drift away on the tide. It can fool
itself as it makes lunch. It can fool itself as it drives to
the office. It can fool itself as it watches television. It
fools itself that the closed box in the mental attic is buried. Forgotten. Nothing to be concerned with anymore.
A different lifetime, a different person. As if it never
happened.

Until the day you open the box.

CHAPTER ONE

Tilda. Friday 7th October 2016. York.

The woman sat on the bench and ran through the lie in her mind. She was alone yet surrounded by people. Legs strode past her, bags-for-life swung, buggies trundled by. No one asked her if she was all right, no one stared and wondered what she was thinking, no one registered her at all. A plain woman, glassily concentrating on an indeterminate spot in front of her. She was nothing significant or diverting to distract from their busy lives. She wasn't causing a scene and she wasn't seeking attention. She was invisible.

The immediate area around her was one of appropriate bustle. It was 5pm so last minute shoppers mingled with city-centre workers en route to car parks, bus stops and the train station. A group of greenly-uniformed teenage girls had commandeered a neighbouring bench. Some were sitting, some were standing, others were using it as base camp for their bags as they window-shopped nearby. Their proximity to Claire's Accessories was unlikely to have been left to chance. With shrieks of laughter they were cocoond by their adolescent ignorance of the world around them.

In the opposite direction, an elderly gentleman on an identical bench scattered pieces of bread from his pockets, feeding the pecking pigeons at his feet. They nipped at his fingers and seemed to bring untold pleasure as he watched them strut and grab. Equally unaware of the scene around him, he was fully engrossed in his task.

The schoolgirls were still predictably self-absorbed. The lone woman in the middle remained unnoticed.

Tilda, for indeed the lone woman had a name, stayed seated and unmoving. Her knees bent at a right angle, her hands clasped tightly on her lap. If anyone *had* paid her attention, they might have noticed her eyelids flutter and her lips move slightly - as if she were rehearsing a speech in her head. They might have spotted that between rehearsals, her gaze kept settling on the red door across the square. The one with the brass plate and external intercom. But no one noticed, so no one realised, and Tilda was left to worry and wait undisturbed.

Muffled sounds of Bob Dylan rang out from her handbag as the immediate impulse to silence him jolted her into movement. She answered her phone.

"Hello?"

"Darling, it's me. I couldn't wait. How's it going?"

Tilda's anxiety was punctured with a stab of relief. She smiled at her friend's impatience. It reassured her. It provided a sense of normality about proceedings that were anything but.

"I spoke to you less than ten minutes ago. Nothing is *going* yet, it's still too early."

"Are you primed? Are you ready? Are you worried?"

"I'm fine. I'm sitting here, just waiting."

"And you know what you're going to say?"

"Yes. I have it clear in my head."

"And do you know what you're going to do if he doesn't remember?"

"Yes, I think so. I'll play that by ear and see how it feels. By then I should have worked out if I need to make a speedy exit."

"I'll leave you to it then. Good luck. Ring me."

"I will, definitely. It will be all right."

Tilda's composure lasted a second more as she ended the call and returned the phone to her handbag. She noticed her hand shake, but forced the incriminating evidence of nerves out of her mind. Now was not the time to accept she might be having a wobble. She really had no way of knowing it *would* be all right, in spite of her calm reassurances to her friend. What would she do if he didn't remember? What would she do if he wasn't there? Even more daunting, what would she do if it all went to plan?

She checked her watch. Fifteen minutes and it would be time to move. She leaned back, feeling the metal slats against her spine. Fifteen minutes and then she'd know.

Tilda stared at the red door and rehearsed the lie one more time.

Part One

A MONTH EARLIER

CHAPTER TWO

The Solicitor. Saturday 10th September 2016. York.

As misunderstandings went, it simply wasn't possible for the error to be *all* his fault. He followed her around as she gathered belongings and played her 'Outraged and Offended' card. He wished she'd stay still and start behaving. Silly cow.

"I'm *not* treating you like a prostitute, for Christ's sake. I just thought you might need the taxi fare." He continued to pace as she searched for each item. What couldn't she understand?

"I'm being fucking nice, here. I wasn't offering to pay you for...the *other* stuff."

Nina dressed hurriedly. Her face, that only minutes before had contorted into expressions of the utmost pleasure, was now rendered repulsed by his ill-thought out, post-coital small talk. It was a face clearly saying *'Get out of my way and never contact me again, you arse hole.'*

The man began to tire of attempting to appease her. She'd served her purpose, after all. So *what* if she was being ridiculous because of a misunderstanding. He stopped following her around and instead began to pick up the scattered pillows by his feet. The unmade bed and strewn clothes did little to disguise the opulence on show. Egyptian cottons, the embossed flock of the carefully selected feature wall, the leather-bound headboard - not his own handy work, of course, but rather an indication of the excellent recruitment skills he exhibited when insisting on his PA's employment a decade before. Rosie had excellent taste. *Well done me!*

He allowed a moment of self-satisfied basking before remembering he had been accused of something that was untrue. Like the adept solicitor he was, he continued to argue, even when stopping would have been the far easier option. He was being slandered and by someone who had suddenly chosen to take the moral high ground when it came to accepting cash. This was not on. It was time for Nina to hear a few home truths. He changed his 'I'm so sorry if there's been a misunderstanding' face to a 'Don't you dare take that tone with me, Young Lady' expression. The visible change was not immediately clear, but the tone of voice was. He was angry.

"Stop this, Nina. Now. Do you hear me? It's not as if you've refused to take my money before, is it? You've never had a problem being plied with dinner and drinks, have you? I don't recall having to *force* the copious amounts of Slimline and Bombay down your throat in the past. And you certainly seemed to enjoy the wide variety of five star accommodation I personally funded - those weekends away in the Lakes? All I've done is offer the taxi fare home after a perfectly charming evening and you're treating me like some kind of bastard. I want to make sure you get back safely - it's a good thing about me. I'm being a non-bastard, here. You should consider yourself lucky."

The defence rested, smugly awaiting the verdict. *Not guilty. It should never have come to court. I'm sorry, my mistake, you were wonderful.*

A muffle came from beneath the black chemise currently being pulled over her head. It continued to be largely inaudible as her face reappeared, the under-her-breath mutterings appearing to be the best way to focus on avoiding a blazing row that would certainly halt the speed of her exit. In the end, it was no use. It seemed she had to speak. Speak or shout - she was unable to control the delivery. He saw it was coming and steeled himself for the onslaught. It seemed the prosecution had something to say.

"You are unbelievable! Did you know that? Bloody unbelievable. I knew this was a mistake, I knew it and I came anyway. What is wrong with me? I must be self-destructive. I must have a death wish or just be bloody stupid. One phone call in five years and I come running. What was I thinking? I must truly hate myself."

It appeared the case was still wide open. It was just not immediately apparent to him, why. Blouse half buttoned, coat and bag in hand, Nina wiggled her feet into her shoes as she walked them out of the bedroom. He followed her. She was definitely pissed off. Maybe it was time to turn on the charm again. He tried to soften his voice although he often felt this could be misinterpreted as sounding whiny. He did it anyway. He was clutching at straws.

"Seriously Neens, stay if you want to. If that's what this is about. I was only thinking you'd want to get back to... Peter, is it? All I said was I didn't think you'd be free for the whole night. It was the taxi fare I was offering, not your fee, for fuck's sake."

This comment elicited a stare of such hatred that he physically shrank back. She opened her mouth as if to respond but thought better of it. Marching to the apartment door instead, he followed her, continuing to attempt to smooth things over. The same situation could easily happen again in the future. When the usual late-night friends were out of the country or unable to answer their phones and he'd find himself calling a blast from the past for an old time's sake shag, he wanted to know whether hers was a number he should keep.

"Nina, I didn't mean *free of charge*, I just meant... well you *know* what I meant. You've got commitments. I've not forgotten that, and I didn't want to be selfish by asking you to spend the night here. I would love nothing more than to cuddle up all night and cook you breakfast in the morning, but we're both realistic. We know that we can't get away with that. You've got to go home and I just wanted to make sure you were going to get there in one piece. That's all."

He stroked her arm and pulled her towards him, the protective nature of his embrace underlining the altruistic concern he hoped was evident for her safe departure. In his arms, she allowed herself to be held, just for a few seconds, softening her rigidity and relaxing slightly. But it was no use. Seconds later he witnessed the screaming voice in her head rear up once more as her face changed, breaking through the thickly daubed layers of bullshit and forcing her to pull away and share a fraction of what was going through her mind.

She stepped back and took a breath. Noting the physical change, he too took a step back. What was her problem? Something else was upsetting her. It couldn't all be him, surely? Hormones? It was definitely *not* her time of the month. The antics of the previous half hour had made that more than clear. Christ, not the menopause? Was this the age range he had unwittingly entered? He was only just in his forties and yet the women around him were becoming downright unshaggable due to their time of life craziness. Keeping their figure, looks and sense of adventure in the bedroom was one thing, but acting like fucking divas the minute they'd cum was something else. Sod this. Maybe it was time to instigate an under forty rule. On second thoughts, under thirty. You could never be too sure.

His inner monologue ceased just as Nina managed to find the words to express her mood. He waited, wondering if he would feel a hot flush from where he was standing.

"Your concern is appreciated. No, really. It's touching..." - the sarcasm dripped off her every word - "... but if you cast your mind back through the mists of time, you might remember that back in the day, when - as you so romantically reminded me - you got me drunk, took me out to dinner and shagged me in FOUR star lakeside hotels, I left my husband for you. My fucking husband."

The silence was brief. Then his face crumpled as the realisation hit. Oh Jesus Christ. Jesus Christ on a sodding bike. She was *that* Nina.

The immediate moments that followed had not been pretty but they were quick. A small hole in the wall was all that was left to show of the stiletto shoe hurled his way. He'd seen it coming, of course, so managed a fairly standard dodge. Still, it had hurt. Not the impact - he was no stranger to a well-timed duck - but rather his sense of pride that he had messed up his social life with the schoolboy error of a forgotten detail.

Bloody Nina De Granges. He remembered it all now. The promises, the plans, the last minute panic and finally the running away when it all got too real. It was a lifetime ago so how was he supposed to remember every little thing that happened to him?

This was happening more and more frequently these days. A small but important missed detail, causing him the need to charm his way out of a situation that shouldn't have existed in the first place. Last week, a misplaced file had caused a short delay in an open and shut case. He'd been able to blame it on the work-experience kid but it had still been sloppy. Then a few nights ago he'd opened his gym bag to find his finest silk black office socks rather than the white toweling sportier version he'd needed. He'd assumed it was his cleaner's fault. That's what he told himself anyway. He didn't pack his own bag *every* time.

Dismissing these oversights as stress-induced or more realistically, evidence of a malignant brain tumor, he poured himself a drink. From his aerial view floating over the rainy reality below, he looked down as he watched the taxi containing the very angry woman pull away and out of his life. Maybe age was creeping up on him, too. That was probably all it was. But if so, it was really shit.

It was as he scribbled a note to maintenance explaining the stiletto hole that he remembered the job he'd been putting off for weeks. It was still there on his desk looking up at him. A page-long list of names, websites and numbers, neatly compiled by Rosie and awaiting his attention. He hadn't paid a bill, answered an invitation, or laundered his own clothes in years. Why was she insisting he did this mundane task himself? Particularly, when it was exactly the sort of thing at which she excelled. She liked practical matters - all that boring reality stuff he could never muster enough enthusiasm in order to deal with. It was only a matter of whittling out the unsuitable options, choosing one or two to interview and then awarding the lucky winner the job. And it wasn't as if they were going to be employed for long. As far as he could make out, it would be a short-term contract - a couple of months at the most.

Silently contemplating reducing Rosie's Christmas bonus, he pulled up a chair and stroked the mouse into life. The list appeared to be alphabetical so he started at the top.

He didn't let it take up much of his evening. Minutes later he had clicked on the staff profiles of the first company, reassured himself by the fact there were some attractive people he may one day meet - although that also felt unlikely; his involvement after this point would be financial only - and decided he'd done enough research. The gig was theirs'.

The matter warranted no more of his time and he did not intend to let it take up any more. It was far more than the old bastard deserved, anyway.

CHAPTER THREE

Tilda. Monday 12th September 2016. Stockport.

"And with the time coming up to sixteen minutes past five, here's Debbie with the travel. How're those roads looking, Debs?"

"Thanks, Dave. The M60 is..."

"Hey, Debs, did you hear about the woman who crashed her car whilst applying mascara?"

"Um, no?"

"She got whipped lashes. Whipped lashes!"

"That's funny Dave. So, the M60 is down to one lane just past junction..."

Tilda slowed to a stop at the lights and let the radio wash over her. She didn't bother groaning. What would be the point? Drive Time Dave couldn't hear her, and as his ever-increasing audience percentage was shared regularly in the press, it seemed as though he was getting away with it. She listened to this section of Drive-Time with Dave every day. A brief snippet of a much longer programme. It would be unbearable if she were a long distance lorry driver, for instance, or if her commute consisted of the M25 for two hours each day. But for this little window, Drive Time Dave would continue to do. Mindless chat and recognisable tunes were all she could cope with. She could save her discernment for a time in the week when she was less tired.

Her phone rang. A couple of hands-busy seconds to make her fully hands-free and she heard the voice. It boomed around the car.

"Darling, it's me."

"Hey, Bea. What do you want? I only saw you..."

...she quickly calculated the time it had taken since leaving the office...

"...eleven minutes ago. What did you forget?"

"Just a teeny tiny smallish favour, really. No biggie but I never got around to mentioning it today. It's just that you could really help me out."

"Go on." She indicated left as she waited to hear the request.

"I'm going to a party at the weekend - you know, Posh Myles in Payroll? I was wondering if I could borrow that cardy you wore last week. You know? The beige-y one?"

She cast her mind back. It was an oatmeal cable knit poncho style affair with decorative toggles. Warm? Definitely. Stylish? Absolutely not. And certainly nothing like Bea's usual wardrobe choices.

"Bea, I don't understand. Your clothes are colourful and vibrant and...sexy. Why do you want my old cardy?"

"Oh sorry, darling... I didn't explain. It's a Murder Mystery Party - I know, how banal! - but I've been told to dress as Miss Marple and so I thought of you. Please let me borrow it. Please?"

Tilda ended the call. She knew no offence had been meant. It had made her laugh more than anything. She'd wash and dry the cardigan that evening and take it into work first thing. The thought of radiant Bea Charleston wearing Tilda's dowdy clothes was an amusing thought. It kept her smiling as she drove, and drowned out the voice from the radio that continued to whitter on.

"Thanks for that, Debs. Sounds busy tonight, stay safe out there, drivers. So, Debs, did you do anything good this weekend?"

"Just a quiet one, Dave. I pottered round the garden. Did a bit of clearing up before the Autumn sets in."

"That's great Debs. It's funny you should mention that because on Saturday, I spent hours watering my herb garden. You could say I did over-thyme. Over-thyme! Here's a golden oldie for you. Gina G. *Ooh Aah... Just a Little Bit*. It's nineteen past minutes past five.

Tilda's key turned easily, but needed the obligatory hip-shove in order to open fully the door to her house - the cosy Stockport semi that had been home for nearly half her life. She expertly barged the swollen door out of its frame with minimum effort and stepped into the hallway. For perhaps the third or fourth time in recent weeks, she noticed that the mint green carpet was looking a little grubby. Maybe it was time for a steam clean? She would dig out the yellow pages at the weekend. Whilst appreciating the regularity of her weekday routine, come the weekend, all bets were off. She had time to be spontaneous and take the opportunity to relax her usual highly organised stance. This weekend she had no plans whatsoever, so sorting out her hall, landing and stairs carpet would be perfect. She smiled to herself with the mental plan now in place. Weekend plans. Excellent.

Wiping her feet on the mat, she hung her bag on the bannister and removed her rain mac, placing it on the white wooden orb that topped the post. It hadn't rained after all, despite the early clouds that morning. It was always better to be prepared, though. Pulling the bobble from her still-neat ponytail, she massaged her scalp whilst shimmying her feet around the floor until she located her slippers. Systematically losing the trappings of the working day, she untucked her shirt, opened the next button down to expose a hint of clavicle, and walked through the snug lounge into the even snugger kitchen where the kettle, mugs and teabags waited.

This was her favourite time of day. The only time she could have complete silence. No phones ringing, no emails waiting, no bosses demanding, and no colleagues bantering. It was bliss. Just the bubbling of the kettle and the rise and fall of her own breath. She sniffed the milk. It would last another day, maybe two, but certainly not four as the date on the carton suggested. She poured the boiling water, waited the exact number of seconds until the teabag had stewed to the strength she preferred, and topped up the steaming liquid with a splash of skimmed milk. She took her drink into the living room and sank into her armchair. A creature of habit, she always sat in the same place. Over the years, it had molded to her body, and now it just felt wrong to leave it. Curling up somewhere else would be akin to a betrayal. Carefully placing her hot mug onto a perfectly matched coaster, she rested her head on the cushioned chair back and soaked up the tranquility.

Elsewhere, far away from the coaster, the table and the armchair, a man was packing a bag. Quickly moving around the bedroom, his lightness of movement made him appear younger than he was. From a distance, he could pass easily for late twenties, with just the salt and pepper stubble distinguishing him from this misconception. He rolled up a couple of t-shirts, a jumper or two and a faded pair of jeans before stuffing them into his canvas holdall. His movements were fluid and carefree. Tall and lithe, his knees bent easily as he packed his bags. The usual aches and pains of encroaching middle-age still seemed a long way ahead as he continued to arrange his belongings beside the camping equipment. Clearly not a chore, he added more items whilst maintaining his relaxed demeanour. A small notepad, a sketchpad and a tin of watercolours were slid into a side pocket, cushioned against an old grey fleece and a basic spongebag. A range of paintbrushes softened from use, and a bundle of pencils were added. The man was smiling to himself, humming under his breath as he organised his belongings. A quick check to see if he'd missed anything and he paused, rooted around the drawer in the bedside cabinet, and pulled out an old Biro. Squishing it through the zip, he stopped and threw himself back on the bed. The smile widened as he lay with his hands behind his head, the dark curls nestling in his palms. The next few days were going to be wonderful.

A sudden noise caused Tilda to stir with a jolt. A louder, firmer hip-shove alerted her to the fact that the front door was opening. Her nerves on fire for an instant, she soon realised what was happening and calmed down.

It was only him.

The peace shattered and her nap over, the jangling keys and the heavy tread were accompanied by an, 'I'm home!' yell, which was wholly unnecessary yet repeated daily. There was no one else it could possibly be. With half a mug of tea un-drunk, she was loath to move, but it was no use. The routines established many years ago, and without her informed consent, whirred into action. She took a last swig, heaved herself out of her chair and walked into the kitchen, flicking the kettle back on as she passed. He followed her, a stray leaf and smudge of mud accompanied him and marked his territory as he strode into the home they shared.

"I'm gasping, love. What a bloody day." He pecked her cheek as he passed her, just as she removed the milk from the fridge once more.

"Tea?" she said.

"Thanks love," he said.

Seventeen years ago, Tilda Willoughby had become Tilda Rudd and moved in to the house in which she now stood. She was young to be married at twenty-three but it had felt like the right thing to do. Mike Rudd was kind and reasonably attractive. He had made her feel safe and his open face smiled easily.

They had met eighteen months earlier. Tilda's friend, Freya, had been staying for the weekend and so as evening came, they headed to the pub for a cheap dinner and a bottle of wine. Now that University was over, they pretended this would play second fiddle to a night of Mancunian clubbing, yet both were secretly relieved. A quiet night in the local, with audible conversation and a comfy seat, was perfect.

It had been Freya's fault that Tilda and Mike got together. After she selected *Live Forever* on the jukebox, a Noel Gallagher lookalike turned round from his position at the bar and spotted the girl that had chosen his favourite song by his favourite band. Complete with shaggy hair and Manchester accent, he was practically exotic in the dull surroundings of The Crown circa 1998. Freya had started to chat to him, but as soon as his polite conversation became overt flirtation, she showed her hand and explained she was in a relationship. This was not strictly true but she *did* fancy a guy from her graduate scheme and had already decided on a five-point game plan to make him hers. She was currently at point two, which was to display abject indifference to his presence at all times. It was only a matter of time before he succumbed to her efforts, she could tell.

Just as she was explaining this to the nice man by the

jukebox, Tilda returned from the toilets and appeared just in time for Mad-chester Mike to save face. He turned to the new blonde on the scene and gave it all he'd got.

"If you're not single either then tell me now 'cos I might as well go back to me pint".

This opening line to the woman he eventually married, made her simply laugh. He responded with a relieved smile and an offer of a drink. The rest was history.

Some things about Mike never changed. He was not a fan of refreshing and rejuvenating his life. Fads and trends would come and go, passing him by completely. He liked consistency. Almost twenty years on and he still sported the same scruffy hair and professed an undying love of Oasis that had been clear that night in the Crown. He continued to work for the same paint company, albeit in a promoted role, and he bought an updated model of the same Vauxhall every four years. There was nothing he loved more than his weekly takeaway of chicken kebab and chips and when Tilda said "Tea?" at six o'clock every evening, he uttered exactly the same words, day in day out.

"Thanks love."

As tonight was a Monday, chicken kebab and chips did not feature on the Rudd household menu. Chicken kebab and chips was a Friday or Saturday night meal. Monday night was something quasi-healthy and well-intentioned. The excesses of the weekend were behind them and a new week of good healthed-aspiration lay ahead. Tilda's weekend hadn't included excess at all, and Mike's usual Friday night four-pint limit was hardly cause for concern, but the routine was set. It had been set for as long as she could remember. Monday night was something plain and simple. Tonight it had been cod fillet, boiled potatoes and salad. It wasn't as insipid as it sounded. Tilda had added a dressing to the rocket to liven it up and they had eaten it happily enough. After her efforts of preparing dinner, Mike cleared the plates and washed up. He also put the kettle on as she made the sandwiches for the next day. It was teamwork. There was a clarity to their roles. Everything ran smoothly. It was always the same.

The carefree man with the backpack strode towards the mud-spattered 4x4 and threw it, and the rest of his luggage in the back. Looking up at the sky and feeling the last of the day's sun on his face, he smiled contentedly before pulling himself into the driver's seat. In a retro move that indicated his own personal vintage, he selected a cassette from the glove box, and slotted it into the dashboard. Bob Dylan's recognisable mumble filtered through the speakers as he pulled out of the drive and towards the open road. The answer, it seemed, was blowing in the wind. The latest adventure had begun.

With a couple of hours to go before they called it a night, Tilda and Mike settled down to watch television. This was the one area of life in which Mike's routine *had* evolved over time. The invention of the iPad had given a very modern twist to their post-work evenings and benefitted them both more than they'd imagined. Rather than spend ten tense minutes of passive-aggressive disagreement about which channel would win the battle that evening, the iPad came along and stopped it all. Now, there were no debates because Mike had made a change. This was a big deal.

These days he was more than happy to don headphones and stretch on the sofa. He could balance the tablet across his thighs, as he watched any number of sports matches, films and police-chase-based programmes that Tilda would never have been interested in even if she were being paid. The smaller screen did not bother him in the slightest. Not when it meant never missing a Champions League match again. A couple of metres away, a happy Tilda would be in sole control of the television remote allowing her to gorge on nightly editions of whatever season's nature programme was dominating the schedules that week.

Tonight however, Autumn was still a few days from being watched so it fell to a box set of well-worn travel documentaries. She squatted as she swiftly removed the one she wanted and slid it into the DVD slot. Minutes later, as a head-phoned Mike continued to grin at the exploits of a hapless US motorist flagged down by a gun-toting cop, Tilda was lost in her own travels. She sank back in her chair, transfixed as she heard the gravelly BBC voiceover, its reassuring gravitas whisking her away, on this occasion, to the West Coast of Scotland. The rocks, the sea, and the light... such beauty made her head swarm. Sliding into a mental bubble bath, she let herself be submerged by the streaming Scottish sunlight on screen. Her own surroundings disappeared. The magnolia walls, the pale green carpet, the remnants of the leaf and mud smudge all fading into the background until they were no longer there. The crick in her neck melted and her aching shoulders became weightless as she travelled to remote islands by boat, climbed jagged rocks high above sea level and lay back on grassy cliffs with rosy cheeks and panting breath. She felt the sun on her skin and heard the waves crash beneath her, far below her elevated position with the stunning panoramic views. It was utterly wonderful.

When the disk whirred to a stop, Tilda came back. The aches returned, the mud stain was visible, and to her right, Mike was gently snoring. She turned off the TV and the DVD player, checked the backdoor and switched off the lamps. Giving Mike's leg a gentle shake as she passed, she left the room and walked upstairs.

The end of another day.

CHAPTER FOUR

The Solicitor. Tuesday 13th September 2016. York.

The next day, in a magistrate's court on the opposite side of the country, the suburban cosiness of Tilda's home was nowhere to be seen. White institutional blinds were drawn, but over the years had become uneven, and hung badly - largely ineffectual in their attempts at hiding the late morning sun. Long shards of light were seeping through, illuminating haphazardly-spaced shafts of dust as the unfortunate case was heard. It was a sparse room. Devoid of comfort or tenderness, it echoed the feelings of approximately fifty percent of the people that entered.

Now that it was over, two of the key players strode outside, giving the warmth of the weather the chance to compete with the glowing satisfaction of inner victory. Standing on the pavement, they shook hands. Two grey-suited men of similar middling age, repeating a scene that, that particular section of street had witnessed, many times before.

"I can't thank you enough. You certainly showed her. I had my doubts last week, but you played a blinder today. Had me going, I can tell you!"

The client kept pumping the hand of the solicitor. He had certainly earned his fee. It would be a hefty amount of money but nothing compared to what it could have been had he not bought the action. Being several inches shorter, the client had to hold his head back at a significant angle in order to converse face to face. The sun was burning his ever-widening bald spot and his cheeks were increasing quickly from a rosy glow to a red-faced sweat.

It didn't matter. He had won.

The man opposite appeared untouched by the warmth. He carefully disentangled his hands, so that they fell to his side once more. He didn't especially like to be touched. Not like that, anyway.

"It was nothing. Really. A relatively simple case. As I said last week, there was nothing to worry about at all. The outcome was never in doubt."

His greying hair was cut short and the goatee that perched on the bottom of his slim face was neat and precise. He looked in full control of all aspects of his appearance including body temperature - an admirable feat in the morning's climate. His professional demeanour allowed a small smile for the gratitude expressed but nothing more. In the position that the men stood, the tall man seemed to have a dazzling halo of sunshine surrounding his head. This was highly apt, as far as the client was concerned. He had been sent from heaven to make all his problems go away. He continued to spout enthusiastic gratitude, whilst repeating himself over and over again.

Behind the men the imposing courtroom stood tall and proud. Decades of justice had taken place within these walls - unfairness countered, criminality challenged, guilt exposed. The worn stones underfoot had been witness to whoops of elation and tears of despair. Ruined and desperate souls had slunk away in shame, whilst elated vanquishers had back-clapped, bear-hugged and praised their higher power of choice. Justice was a black and white issue, and everyone that emerged from behind the heavy doors belonged on one side or the other. It was always clear to see.

As the two men neared the end of their conversation, the courtroom doors were pushed open once more. This time however, there were no accompanying whoops of triumph. No one marched through with justice and righteousness feeding their demeanor and instilling a sense of pride about their day's endeavours.

Shakily at first and then with a sudden jolt, the door swung open. Looking behind him, the client saw a pair of wheels emerge cautiously then more assuredly as they were followed by two more, as a woman he had come to loathe navigated a cumbersome double pushchair through the exit of her local magistrates court. Once outside she paused, looking for a non-existent ramp that might aid her descent. With a concerted effort amidst a truly child-unfriendly environment, she had to settle on lowering the wheels down each individual step, whilst jolting and unsettling her children inside. One of her babies began to cry half way down, so once on the ground she rooted around a giant bag slung over her shoulder and produced a dummy. As if on cue, his brother decided to insist on equal attention. As he opened his lungs to scream, she rummaged once more. This baby was rewarded with the remnants of milk left in a bottle from an earlier feed. She held the teat to his open mouth and continued to breathe, whilst at the same time wondering exactly when the bailiffs were going to arrive, and when they did, where would she go?

Spotting the men hadn't taken her long. And once she'd seen them, she couldn't stop herself. She marched, or rather *assertively pushed,* the buggy over to where they stood, unsure what was about to pour out of her mouth, but knowing it was essential it did. She faced the client. Her now ex-landlord.

"Feels good does it? Feel like a big man, do you? You

make me sick! There was damp all through that house, and you did nothing about it, nothing! And then you have the cheek to throw me out because of missed payments when I was ill. I don't know how you sleep at night."

She could almost taste the venom in her mouth. *Short arsed, stupid bastard.* She turned her ire onto the solicitor.

"And as for you! Well, I'm glad you've both got so much to smile about. I see the situation rather differently, as I'm sure you can imagine, what with me having just been evicted, and not having a clue where my babies are going to sleep next week.

The solicitor managed to remove his smile, although in all fairness to him, he'd put on the show of positive feeling in order to extricate his hands from the sweaty grasp of his client. He wasn't feeling smug or happy at all. He was indifferent as usual. Feelings made no sense at all.

The woman continued.

"But don't let me kill the mood. Please. After all it was really clever of you to leap on that procedural error in order to win. So *fucking* clever. Stupid me, wasting my time working out a fair and reasonable repayment plan, when you've got legal skills like that. Well done. Your wife and kids must be so proud."

He stiffened and she sensed it.

"Oh, what's that? No wife and kids. Hardly a surprise. Well then I hope you enjoy telling the cat all about your day. And now, if you'll please excuse me, I've had just about as much as I can stomach of both of you. You absolute *wankers*."

One minute later and the drama was over. The woman's words had rolled off the shoulders of the short man, only temporarily pausing his widening grin. She had pushed her babies, bags and what was left of her pride, down the road and in search of a bus.

"Goodness, that was unbelievable. Does she really think she's been hard done to? The days I gave her to find the money. Bloody ridiculous."

The solicitor barely gave her a second look before cooly replying.

"I am always baffled as to why people bring children to something like this. The sympathy vote never works. No judge falls for it."

The client laughed hard, as if it was the funniest thing he'd ever heard.

"Sympathy vote! Ha ha ha. Yes, that's exactly it. It didn't work out the way she wanted, and now she has to get that pushchair on a bus. Ha ha."

Wiping his eyes, he offered a final vow of thanks and another vigorous shake of the hand before walking away in the direction of the multi-storey car park. That left the tall, sunlit solicitor.

He was very good at his job. He had won another case. He would make the firm proud. No. He corrected himself as an afterthought. He would make *his* firm proud. That still didn't come automatically, no matter how much time had passed. And as much as the reddened landlord had stressed about it, the case had not been a difficult one. In fact, it had been incredibly easy. He should have passed it to someone else. A junior member of staff could have learnt from that and enjoyed the buzz of the win. He never really felt the glow of victory anymore. He didn't feel much at all, except one thing.

Hunger.

He looked at his Breitling. Quarter to one. He had finished earlier than expected. It made sense to have lunch in town and then head back to the office later. Time for sustenance.

One thing did bother him a little bit, though. As welcome an outcome as today had been, it hadn't seemed right. There was no point winning when you had an unfair advantage. Being the fastest in a race can't possibly feel as satisfying if your opponent's legs are tied together. He remembered the woman's face when the judge had refused to suspend the possession warrant. It showed utter despair. She had been given bad advice and was now homeless. The babies, not even six months old, were evicted from their first home. Someone on her side had not done their job properly.

His hunger pang ached some more.

Pushing it out of his mind, he began the short walk to the prettier part of town, where he would be spoilt for choice. The middle-class eateries of the old Roman settlement were charming to look at on a bright day like this. There were dozens of colourful hanging baskets dangling from wattle and daub fascias as far as he could see. The jauntily placed chalkboards lining the pavements gave him a clear indication as to what was on offer. His mouth watered involuntarily. Despite this, the man was a creature of habit. He appreciated the choice available and was glad to see the town he had lived in for four decades looking so welcoming in the September sun. But, just as he'd always planned, he turned a sharp right and paced determinedly towards the shabbily painted, gloomy exterior of the Lamb and Lion. Another working day, another liquid lunch. It might help him forget the woman's face.

CHAPTER FIVE

Tilda. Friday 16th September 2016. Stockport.

Tilda's skills of tuning out her colleagues were being tested to the limit. She kept her eyes on the screen but found herself reading the same sentence over and over. Si and Alex - as Bea would say - were getting on her tits.

"Oi, cock breath! Put this on the Sign Off pile for me."

Si, a man-boy in a shirt and tie made an attempt to throw a bulging file at his similarly immature colleague across the desk. The colleague had tried to compensate for his own youth with an attempt at a beard. An attempt but nothing more.

"Piss off. I'm not going that way."

"So, make a detour," said Si, renewing his hold of the file.

"I'm going to the machine, I'm not going anywhere near the pile." Nearly-beardy Alex was adamant.

"Stop being a knob. Take the file for me."

"What's it worth?"

"What do you want?"

Alex considered it for a moment.

"A Kitkat and a coke."

Si's mind seem to search for loopholes. There were always loopholes with Alex. A full minute later he found one.

"Two fingers or four?"

Alex sighed. Rumbled.

"Four."

"Fuck off."

Alex reconsidered his position.

"Ok. A two fingered Kitkat, a coke and a pound."

"No way."

"Well that's my last offer. I guess you're going to have to get up and walk over to the pile yourself."

Alex gestured to the other side of the office, home of the desk that held the Sign Off pile. No more than ten metres away.

"What are you waiting for?" Alex was keen to strike the deal.

"You can't expect me just to roll over and cave at your first offer. But also, I can't be arsed walking this late in the week. That's what you're here for."

Si headed the lobbed paper ball into the imaginary goal, as Alex prepared a couple more for delivery. Letting them glance off his head, he gave it some more thought. He had to retain a bit of respect or else who knows what leverage would be lost the next time. He considered the situation. He showed Alex he was doing this by stroking his chin and looking at the ceiling fan. Alex pretended to be engrossed in the contents of his computer monitor as he waited for the offer. Finally it came.

"A two fingered Kitkat, a coke and a pound but made up from coins in my coppers tin."

Alex gave it a full ten seconds.

"Done."

"Alright then. I'll get counting."

At an adjoining desk was Kyesha. It had only been in the last ten days that the office had started calling her Kyesha. Until then it had been 'the temp', 'the work-experience' or 'the blonde girl'. Finally, after three months of working weekday nine to fives, she'd cracked it. She was still the 'temporary work-experience blonde girl', but she was also Kyesha.

Today was her last day. This made Tilda feel enormously guilty.

"Darling, are we on for later?" Bea bounced over.

"Yes, all sorted. Secretly stashed and ready to go." Tilda replied, indicating under the desk. They shared a secret smile before Bea turned her attentions to Kyesha.

"Sweetie, how's your last day? Will you miss us? Are you bereft at losing Si and Alex from your life?"

Kyesha laughed.

"I will cope somehow. There are only so many times I can listen to a grown man spend thirty minutes begging another to photocopy a document that would have taken him three, before I go mad. How do you stand it?"

As Bea launched into her specific coping mechanisms, Tilda smiled. This office was all she had known of the world of work. Three rows of four desks, each one containing a computer, an in-tray, and depending on the tidiness of the person, an indiscriminate pile of papers and a variety of mugs. To the right of her, the kitchen, a tiny meeting room and Susan's office all shielded with thin, horizontal blinds. Apart from a communal printing and shredding area towards the back, that was it. There was nothing too high-tech, nothing glamorous or overly stimulating. It was bureaucratic and mostly functional. Kyesha should take the summer wage, the use of the placement on her CV, and never look back. She was so young with her whole life ahead of her. In years to come, she wouldn't even remember it.

Tilda saw Susan Donaldson's door open. The department leader emerged from her office with a white envelope in her hand. Everyone knew she hated doing this kind of thing. She considered it one of the drawbacks of being the boss. Now and then it was required of her to take charge in these kinds of tasks and they knew she struggled to find the words necessary. It was quite amusing to watch. Some people rose to the challenge when under pressure, but she floundered. This was not where her skillset lay and yet every few months it had to be done for some reason or other. Give her a disciplinary meeting or straightforward sacking any day. She knew where she was with that.

She stood in front of her department and self-consciously cleared her throat.

"Right everyone, can I have your attention for just one moment. Kelisha, can you come to the front please."

The low titters around the office indicated she had cocked it up already. She cleared her throat again, this time with Kyesha at her side.

"So, Ky...er... so, thank you very much for all your hard work this summer. I am sure the whole department will join me in wishing you well for the future. We would like to give you this, as a token of our appreciation, so you can put it towards books and things you'll need at university." Susan paused, building up to her big finish.

"Just don't go spending it all in the pub on the first night!"

She laughed at her own funny. Seconds later she stopped when she realised no one else had. Kyesha took the envelope with a muttered thanks, and sat down amidst a polite round of applause. Susan missed the opportunity to shake her hand, her usual way of ending a presentation. As it didn't happen, she returned to her office looking slightly anti-climactic. Checking her watch, she picked up her briefcase and coat and walked out of the door to her next meeting, with palpable relief.

"Bore off, love!" A loud voice called out to the departing back of the boss - also known as Tan Tights on account of her 1980s choice of hosiery shade - as the swinging door swung to a close. "Right Alex, give me a hand will you?"

Bea Charleston, a vision in leopard print leggings and daffodil bomber jacket, was clambering up onto one of the empty desks at the top end of the room. She was holding a mug in one hand, which was taking a large amount of effort to keep level. Finally she was on two feet - a splash of colour amidst the drab surroundings of office bland. Swivel chairs swivelled as the awkward frostiness of the previous speech thawed, and Bea's antics spread a much-needed warmth throughout the proceedings. She deliberately cleared her throat, though whether in mockery or homage to Susan Donaldson, it wasn't entirely clear.

"Ladies and gentleman, boys and girls, today is a MOMENTOUS day for the Policy Team. Today is a day that comes but once in a lifetime. Today will be talked about for years to come. Your Grandchildren will ask you with wide eyes about the events of today, and you will answer them nodding, wiping away a tear, and explain that you were privileged to witness such WONDEROUS happenings."

There was laughter of course. Bea hammed it up for all she was worth. Some of the gang could see where this was going, but some still looked puzzled. Si and Alex were confused.

"But finally, finally, it is here. Today has come. For today... today... SOMEONE IS LEAVING THE POLICY TEAM FOR SOMETHING BETTER."

There was a spontaneous and raucous round of applause. Even Tilda laughed along although she'd had a bit more warning than most. Bea, who had shared the plan with her earlier, waited for calm before continuing.

"Kyesha, my darling, you are our great hope for the future. You represent all the failed hopes and dreams contained within these four walls. Today, you take our lost ambition, our battered pride and our lack of self-esteem and you must use them as a warning to HAVE A BLOODY GOOD TIME AND ENJOY YOUR LIFE!" There were more claps and whoops. The Friday afternoon feeling hadn't just arrived. It had moved in and was unpacking its belongings.

"So, as an ACTUAL token of our appreciation, Kyesha, I asked Tilda to wash out all the manky mugs - if Tan Tights had clocked *me* cleaning, our game would've been blown - and share out a few bottles of fizz!"

At her cue, Tilda got up and retrieved a tray of mugs from under her desk. There was an even louder cheer when it became clear there was one for everybody. Smiling at her sudden status of cool, Tilda walked around each desk to wide appreciative smiles until everyone had a mug. Bea waited until she was seated again, and raised her own drink triumphantly in the air.

"So, Kyesha, forget the hours stood at the photocopier, forget how demeaning it is to make tea for a meeting of council tits, and please whatever you do, forget Si and Alex. Only carry the good stuff with you. Carry the fag breaks, carry the free pens and Post Its, carry the unexpected fire alarms! To Kyesha and the wonderful world outside the Policy Planning Department!"

There was a collective raising of mugs, swigging and cheering. Kyesha blushed as she laughed, Bea blew kisses to everyone and the entire Policy Team revelled in the combined beauty of a Friday afternoon, no boss and secret wine

Tilda had enjoyed her part in the fun. Bea was always good value and she hadn't disappointed today. Poor

Kyesha. She hoped she wasn't too embarrassed by all the attention. Tilda would have been mortified at her age. She'd be fairly embarrassed now. Saving her spreadsheet before sitting back with her mug, Tilda enjoyed the change of mood around her. Inside though, there was something stirring. The recent reflections that she kept trying to bat away. Bea had unearthed another slither of the past that was slowly floating to the surface. Now was not the time to ponder but it was definitely there. Tilda acknowledged it for a few more seconds and then put it out of her mind. It was Friday afternoon after all.

A couple of hours later, and the message came through that Susan's meeting was overrunning. She would not be back in the office that afternoon. The message also stated that all members of the Policy Team were to remain at their desks until five o'clock. The snorts of disbelief that accompanied that statement would have occurred regardless of the fizzy contents of the lunchtime mugs. They were just a little louder this time.

"Bloody bitch. If she treats us like kids we might as well act like kids. More wine, Tilda?" Bea surreptitiously removed an unopened bottle from her bag. Tilda smiled.

"Thanks, but no. I'm driving. I'll need to stay 'til five anyway - make sure my last drink is out of my system."

"Boooo. Get the bus like me. There's nothing better than being drunk on the top deck. It makes you feel thirteen again."

Tilda laughed as she continued to read the document in front of her, never entirely sure how much truth came out of Bea's mouth. Focusing on the screen, she attempted to block out the noise around her as she had learnt to do over the years. It seemed she was getting a little rusty these days. Or was she just preoccupied?

There was no doubt about it; she was the only one attempting any work. The next time she looked up, Kyesha had dragged a chair over and was sharing the bottle with Bea, their conversation clearly focused on Kyesha's immediate future. Bea was part mother hen, part bad influence, egging her on to experience untold depravities whilst always remembering to moisturise. A few more minutes of being hunched over the draft Economic Development Policy and Tilda looked up to see Alex sitting with them. The conversation was now focusing on whose university was superior. She gave up. She was getting no work done and it was Friday. *If you can't beat them join them.* She made herself a cup of tea and then sat back at her desk just as Bea shouted across the room.

"Si, you've got a degree. What special needs institution did you graduate from?"

"Yeah, funny. It wasn't for special needs, it was fucking hard and it was Manchester."

Alex piped up.

"You know the problem with Manchester? Full of bloody Mancs."

This incited a mixture of boos and cheers depending on the football allegiances or regional racism of the members of the surrounding desks. Working on the outskirts of the city hadn't diminished Alex's bigotry. Bea ignored them.

"Tell me again, Alex, what university should *your* parents be suing?"

"Funny, Bea. Nottingham. Bloody great 'cos it was full of slappers."

"And yet, you're still a virgin. Bad times. Never mind Kyesha, I'm sure Liverpool will be full of witty, intelligent men with clearly defined pecs."

At the mention of this, Tilda's ears pricked up.

"I went to Liverpool."

Si heard her and shouted across the room.

"I can't imagine you at Uni, Tilda. No offence, like."

Tilda blushed as Bea jumped in, her protective streak further enhanced through drink.

"Well, she can't imagine you having enough brain cells to wipe your own arse. No offence like." She turned back to Tilda.

"I never went myself. I think I spent the whole of sixth form stoned. I emerged from the haze and everyone had left home." She giggled. "What did you study?"

"Geography."

"Oh you're amazing!" Bea slapped the desk.

"Am I?"

"Yes. Absolutely. It always impresses me when people do things that I can't do. I think Geography was one of the lessons I wagged repeatedly. You'd be lured in with promises of exotic holiday talk, but it would only ever amount to a jumpy video about soil. Was it terribly dull?"

Tilda considered the question objectively.

"Sometimes I suppose it could be, but there were lots of field trips that were good fun."

"Oh Christ. *Residentials*?" Bea whispered the word like it might have been decreed a racial slur and she hadn't been informed.

"Yes but they were all right. We'd pile into a mini bus, drive up the M6, stay in a hostel somewhere and spend the weekend looking at soil and lakes and valleys and ..."

"Shit?"

Tilda laughed. There was something about Bea that made it easy to talk about herself. She never shared personal details with anyone else, but Bea was like a really endearing detective. She carried on, thinking back.

"It always seemed better than doing Maths anyway. We'd be outside all day, working on some project, but then every night we'd end up in the pub with everyone else from the youth hostel..."

There was no sudden burst of recognition. It was just there again, reminding her of its existence. Another cause for reflection had arrived as soon as she mentioned residentials. It was a memory that had been resurfacing more and more recently. Popping up when she least expected it. She had kept it at bay for so long, for so many years. Yet now, since her 40th, she was struggling to pack it back inside her. Tilda felt it viscerally. *Of course* it was here again. She breathed hard, her blood running a touch cooler as Bea continued, oblivious to the change that had overcome her colleague.

"The mini bus, youth hostel, outside stuff and shit can do one, but I wholeheartedly approve of the pub bit. Kyesha, you must make sure there're plenty of pubs. Now, let's discuss condoms..."

Glad of the change of subject, Tilda chose that moment to bow out of the intimate girly chat and take stock. The flickers of a spark from Bea's speech and the lightly stoked embers of the long suppressed memories were reignited as brightly as ever. The question was whether to let them fade once more or breathe them back to life by remembering. She'd been avoiding this for a while with no luck. They weren't going away. Perhaps some things shouldn't be remembered when they were over? Maybe some things were best left alone. Was she capable of doing that?

It seemed she was not.

Her mind was thrown into the past. A long time before Si and Alex, before the Policy Team and before the cups of tea for Mike at six. She was back to Tilda Willoughby. To a time when her life spanned out before her and anything was possible. To a time unrecognisable from today. She couldn't do anything about it now. She was at work, and she had things to do. But later on, later on this evening, she might just consider letting her mind do a bit of time travelling and let the memories re-emerge. She just didn't know if she was brave enough.

In spite of her best efforts to delay the tip-toe down Memory Lane, it had been beyond her control. A Drive Time Dave music choice of an old Shamen song sent her straight there as she drove home, taking her back to another journey twenty years before - the rush to make it to the mini bus, the bags thrown in the back, Freya, and Dhanesh, Jonathan and Kenny. She gave up trying to control the flow of the memories, and let her mind wander back to the first time she'd heard that particular song.

CHAPTER SIX

Tilda. Monday 11th March 1996. Liverpool.

The mini bus left the campus car park and made a start on its badly timed journey. It joined the motorway at peak M6 rush hour though no one other than the driver seemed to care. This was a time before jobs, mortgages and expectations. The passengers were happy to listen to music and chat with their friends.

According to the loud assertions coming from the cassette player, Es were good. That's what it kept saying, anyway. Tilda wasn't sure she was hearing it correctly, but that's what it sounded like. *Can they say that on a song*? Dhanesh, who from the front passenger seat had been in charge of all music since leaving the car park, had started to let the power go to his head. This was the fourth time the tape had been rewound and it was starting to grate on even the most ardent of Shamen fans seated in the rows behind.

Oblivious to the potential rising mutiny, Dhanesh continued to rave away. His arms flailed about as Lorna their tutor - whose doctorate thesis had focused on red squirrel habitat mapping and so was therefore out of her depth - did her best to ignore him as she lugged the mini bus up the congested motorway.

Tilda looked around at her fellow students. Dhanesh at the front, and then Jen, Samantha, Roger, Freya and Jonathan, slumped on seats in front and behind her. They were all nice people. She didn't mind spending a week away with them. Then there was Kenny. She involuntarily shuddered at the sight of him. In years to come, his behaviour would be hashtagged as Everyday Sexism but back then, he was 'just being Kenny'. He wasn't being lecherous or inappropriate at this exact moment but only because a packet of Monster Munch was fully occupying his hands. This was the sixth field trip she had been on with this group in the past two years. All focusing on different geographical phenomena, all in varied parts of the country, unique in their own way but still they blurred into each other. The same group of people, a generic youth hostel, a local pub where a different person would be sick each night - there was nothing that differentiated one field trip from another. They all merged into each other.

Tilda sat back and breathed. She was shattered. Freya twisted herself around from her seat in front as she heard her sigh.

"You alright Tilds? You look fucked. All red and sweaty. What's the goss?"

Tilda smiled. She'd have gone for tired, but still.

"No goss, and I'm OK. I had to rush to make it on time. My dad rang as I was leaving."

"No way. It's not his slot?"

"I know. It seems he does listen to some things I say after all. He remembered I was away."

Not quite so helpless as he makes out, Tilda thought, if he can break his routine and respond to new information about when I'm not available.

"What's the deal with him again? Is he just old or is he ill?" Freya was swigging from her bottle of water, as she asked. Tilda tried to work out if she was genuinely interested or just being polite.

"Just old, and likes things the way he likes them. He rings me on Mondays, Wednesdays and Fridays at 6pm on the dot. He likes to keep to the schedule."

"So what's he going to be doing at 6pm instead then? A HOT DATE?"

Freya echoed the voice Billy Crystal had used to say the same three words in *When Harry Met Sally*. It had been on TV the night before and had already been the topic of great debate between Kenny and Dhanesh. Apparently all women were shaggable or not shaggable but friendship was irrelevant. Tilda had sighed then too.

"I can't imagine he'll be doing anything other than watching television. Which is what he'd have been doing at four, if he hadn't rung then."

"Cool. That's ace." Freya seemed to have misjudged the tone, as she turned to root through her bag.

"Here, have this, you look like you've run a marathon." She handed Tilda another water bottle, who gratefully took it. The phone call had been inconvenient, and interrupted her last minute check that she had everything. *Feeling* disorganised was just as bad as *being* disorganised. There was no distinction - both made her tense and unable to relax. She opened the bottle and swigged thirstily, clocking Freya's grin a second too late.

Vodka.

Coughing, she swallowed it down but shook her head in mock indignation.

"Keep it, Tilds. I've got more." Freya patted her bag conspiratorially then settled back into her seat, looking out of the window as the afternoon sun began to pinken, spreading the sky with daubs of colour. Five days of long walks, cave mapping and rock studies. Vodka would more than likely be useful.

They arrived at the hostel amid a flurry of coaches and vans, as lithe and sprightly undergraduates pulled bags from their stowed locations. Kenny immediately scanned the vicinity for females that looked vulnerable enough to be appreciative of his charm. Springing down the mini-bus step, he dragged Dhanesh with him, as he attempted to offer help to a particularly curvaceous redhead struggling with her case. Freya and Tilda looked on, their scorn turning to admiration as the woman made it clear she was not interested. This did not stop the boys and they roamed the unloading area, zeroing in on lone females that could be susceptible to their attention.

Within minutes, the van had cleared as everyone moved inside, intent on discovering how basic and degrading this term's hostel was going to be. Last off, Tilda heaved her rucksack up the steps. She forced her way through a gaggle of students as she neared the top.

"Oi, watch it!"

The words seemed to come from her own mouth. An unprecedented burst of annoyance shot out of her as the cause of it flashed past in a blur of autumnal khaki. The man, who seconds before had barged into her and knocked her bag from her hand, turned briefly, running backwards as he yelped a 'sorry' before continuing on his urgent mission.

Arse.

Freya's head popped around the door, before her body joined her and she found herself dragging a limping Tilda inside. Her bag had bruised her foot. What had she packed that was so heavy? The thought bounced around until she remembered the bath-towel wrapped bottle of Blossom Hill that she'd smuggled. At least she hadn't forgotten that.

"Come on Tilds, hurry up. I've found us a twin room. A TWIN ROOM! Can you believe it? No dormitories for us this week. We have moved up to the next level.

Proper posh! Dump your bag so we can all go for a drink."

Tilda let Freya grab one handle as she took the other, and they entered their home for the next five days. A twin room was a definite bonus, Tilda thought. Maybe this trip might not be so forgettable after all.

CHAPTER SEVEN

Alice. Friday 16th September 2016. York.

As evening fell the black Mondeo that led the mini-convoy, snaked up the hill. With a quarter of an hour before they clocked on, Alice noticed the surroundings for perhaps the first time since her team's recent employment. Row after row of what had once been workers' cottages fanned out on either side of the lane - the only concession to modernity being the occasional satellite dish or brightly illuminated gable. 'Cosy and full of character'. That's how they'd be described by an estate agent. 'Small and impossible to contain a three-piece suite' would be another way to go.

Alice continued her careful incline until she reached the summit. The vehicles following caught up and they paused neatly in a row at the top of the hill, in front of a set of gates. Imposing and iron, they sent a clear message to the outside world regarding the likelihood of a warm welcome beyond. Reaching into the glove box, she found the digital fob that controlled them and aimed it in the right general direction. The metal barriers moved slowly, creaking open, their stilted movements emphasizing the unwanted nature of all visitors that dared to enter. Once inside, she resumed her journey, with her car leading the way as it followed the curve of the driveway. The noise of the gravel crunched under the tyres as she arched around the landscaped lawn and headed for the gothic building ahead.

Alice's team had been in place for nearly a week

now. There was nothing especially novel about this job or about this specific client in terms of his requirements. It was just another day at the office, same as always. They would be employed until the time came and it was all over. It's just that for some reason with all her professionalism and years of experience, Alice couldn't wait for that day to come.

She braked to a stop. A second or two later and another car drew to a halt. A dated Citroen in an indeterminate shade of green parked alongside her. Both cars - now in front of the large window - spilled open. Gregor stumbled out, and assumed his role of 'general dogsbody'. He emptied the Mondeo's boot of supplies and lugged the bags inside just as the third and final car entered the grounds. Flo slowed with clear caution. Checking her hair in her mirror, and smoothing down a few stray wisps, she eventually joined her colleagues outside.

Three professionals, dressed in white, stood in front of the wooden doors. Another shift, another night inside the fortress. The stone walls, locally sourced from a quarry centuries before, stood solid and proud, showing no indication of what lay inside. No lights could be seen from within, no noises or telephones or TVs or laughter. All was still. Alice used the key that had been sent in the post, and let her team into their current employ.

"Take your bets. Do you think he'll be in a better mood tonight?" Gregor whispered as he took off his coat.

"No chance. But he can't get much worse than yesterday can he?" said Flo. "I was fuming when I got home. Fuming. The things that came out of his mouth were disgusting."

She smoothed her hands over the starched uniform

currently being stretched across her considerable frame. They walked past the staircase and continued towards the makeshift bedroom on the ground floor.

Alice looked at her team with some sympathy. It was fair to say this particular client was more challenging than most. Not in terms of medical need but definitely as far as his bigoted views were concerned. Flo had every right to be angry, as indeed they all did, and she was clearly still carrying that anger today. But this was par for the course. This is what happened in their line of work.

Knowing she needed to make it right before they began, she voiced aloud the thoughts that had occurred to her at the start of this job.

"I'm not defending him, because the things he says are horrible, but Flo, look around. This might be a grand house to live in but there are no photographs, no visitors and no evidence that anyone cares. Inside that room is a weak little man. No amount of money can make it easier to die alone."

She let her words carry into Flo and Gregor's consciousness. They nodded. Tonight was a new shift, a fresh page. They had to be professional. He was just scared.

"Right, come on. We'd better change him before bed."

CHAPTER EIGHT

The Solicitor. Friday 16th September 2016. York.

In a street just a few miles from that night shift, a hired taxi was making a similarly winding journey to a destination ahead. With a far more dockland feel than the gothic manor house, the illuminated orbs lining the river made the drive feel almost exotic. It could be romantic Paris. It could be historic Bruges. It could be steamy Buenos Aires. It was in fact, rainy York.

The solicitor stared out of the taxi window with his thoughts elsewhere. He watched individual raindrops land, grow, and burst into mini streams as the rain fell, and the car continued to deliver him home, to the official start of the weekend. From deep inside his briefcase, a device beeped. He began to root.

"Any plans?" The driver broke the silence. His flat vowels swelled over the words as he openly made conversation whilst maintaining as unsmiling a face as possible.

"What?" The man looked up momentarily from his iPad.

"Any plans this weekend?"

"No. None."

The sliver of conversation ended and he returned to his email. It was just a message from Rosie about Monday's staff meeting. It could wait.

They journeyed on with less than half a mile to go, yet the evening traffic kept their pace slower than he'd have liked.

"The missus said there's a fair on tomorrow, down this way."

"Sorry?"

"She wants us to take the grandkiddies. Not if it's raining, I told her."

Still grimly serious, the man paused at the crossing, as some bare-skinned young women ran across, heels castanetting and voices shrieking as sparkly slashes of material barely covered them. Both men appeared unmoved. They let the tableau of goose-pimpled, fake-tanned flesh, flash past and move on. The car started up once more.

"You heard about it?"

"Heard of what?"

"The fair."

"No."

"Right then."

Whether it was coincidence or design, the exchange ended just as the car reached the desired section of road. Pushing a note into the hand of the driver, the solicitor grabbed his briefcase, climbed out of the cab, and walked towards the glass-walled apartment block in front of him.

Home.

He nodded curtly to the man on the door whose name he could never remember then rode the lift until it pinged that he had arrived at the fourteenth floor.

Lower floors boasted two or sometimes even three apartments per level but the fourteenth floor was all his. Wise investments and a strict upbringing in the management of money had enabled him to own a much-desired property slap bang in the riverside area of town. Perfect for the office, court and gym. It also seemed to attract a similar sort of resident. The unencumbered and single-minded focus of the young professional. On second thoughts *young* might be a stretch for some, but there was no danger of hearing a child's wail or encountering a chatty neighbour in the lift. Everyone liked their anonymity and no one had the need to borrow sugar.

He removed his coat and placed his briefcase on the floor, only then noticing the hole in the wall had been filled. About time. He'd reported it days ago. Running his finger over the smooth white plaster, he checked himself in the mirror. He'd have to fit in a wet shave next week to sort out his recurring dry skin, but other than that he was looking good. The greying curls that he kept at bay were still two more weeks from needing to be trimmed and his goatee was as neat as ever. The bags were new, but then it was the end of a busy week and it had been a long day.

The man rubbed his eyes and sighed. The medicinal effects of his lunch had long evaporated so he headed for the drinks cabinet and selected one of the oak-aged malts. His tie loosened, his button undone and his insides slowly warming, he randomly chose a labelled plastic box from the refrigerator. He didn't bother to read what it said. Sue, his current housekeeper knew what she was doing with food, so whatever he picked would be acceptable. The microwave did its work and minutes later he was sitting in the lounge area, eating some sort of gravy covered meat, washed down with a refilled tumbler of booze.

The boats on the river were specks from this height. He looked out at his view, the reflection of himself there as an addition to the vista. Today had been particularly long.

From nowhere, the evicted mother's face flashed in his memory. Staring at the window, he found himself grimacing. A wolfish, gnarled expression that made him look disturbed, like a stranger. Just what he was snarling at, he wasn't sure. At the woman? At the fact she brought her children with her when it was clearly an unsuitable place for babies? At the landlord? He had been irritating but not enough to warrant a second thought. Over-analysing a closed case was not the way he wanted to spend his evening. He physically shook his head in a bid to rid himself of these unwelcome thoughts and then he paced across the polished wooden floors to the drinks cabinet, pouring himself a generous refill. He looked back at the space spread out in front of him. His sanctuary. His haven.

There were no photographs, no visitors and absolutely no evidence that anyone cared.

CHAPTER NINE

Tilda. Friday 16th September 2016. Stockport.

Tilda pressed pause on her memories as she turned left at the junction and into the traffic. She had to. It was becoming too raw to deal with as she drove. Instead she mentally changed the subject. Work had been different today. Kyesha's impromptu drinks party and the high jinx of lunchtime had continued to create a laid back 'early finish' feel to the remaining hours of the working day. In spite of this, she'd followed the diktat of staying till five. The only one who had, it seemed. Most people had made up reasons to go at least an hour before.

Regardless of their lack of line management supervision, her colleagues still played the game for a while. They hadn't just downed tools and left. But there were a remarkable amount of suddenly remembered meetings taking place elsewhere that they simply had to attend, as they grabbed laptops and jackets and made it outside with minimal suspicion. Si and Alex had been working on their excuses since lunchtime although their initial attempts hadn't held up to Bea's scrutiny for a second. She had cornered Alex as he edged towards the door a little after 2pm with Si close behind.

"Where are you going?"

"The toilet."

"In your coat?"

"It's chilly?"

"Where's Si going?"

"The toilet."

"Is he chilly too?"

"I guess."

"Do you think we're stupid?"

The excuses that then poured from their collective mouths over the ensuing hour involved a dodgy stomach, a dental appointment, someone's dog at a vets and the need to meet a locksmith due to an elderly parent's keys left at home. Bea soon tired of being their interrogator. Especially as she had dreams of her own great escape not long after. The upshot was that both men were seen leaving the building at three forty-five with smiles wide at having beaten the system. This only happened after a lengthy negotiation between them that resulted in the promise of Alex shaving off his beard if come Monday, Si could provide photographic evidence that he'd pulled 'a grown woman' over the weekend. Tilda rolled her eyes as she remembered it. They were banal at best, irritating at worst. It wouldn't be long before they were Chief Execs.

It wasn't that she was a jobsworth. She didn't begrudge the entire office leaving early on the rare occasion that they could get away with it. She just got enormous pleasure in completing tasks and ticking boxes. The routine that nine to five gave her was perfect - clear cut and ordered. Besides, what would she do with the extra hour and a half?

She carried on her drive home, experiencing it at the correct time, with no feelings of guilt surrounding her departure. She continued to keep her memories on pause. The radio blared.

"So Debbie, what plans have you got this weekend? Anything interesting?"

"I'm going to see a play tomorrow night actually. The one at the Palace."

"*That's great Debs. I once performed in a stage show. It was all about puns. Really it was just a play on words.*"

"*That's terrible, Dave.*"

"*I know, I know, I guess I'll have to follow the instructions of the next band. Here's No Doubt, with Don't Speak. It's seven minutes past five.*"

The traffic was busier than usual, a fact that was not helped by being stuck behind a coach packed full of primary children. Flailing arms and gurning faces poked between the back seats. A burst bag of wheaty orange shapes littered the back window and every so often one of the more willful characters would stick two fingers up at a peer.

Children always made Tilda feel slightly maudlin. Only slightly, but a pall would be cast when she observed them. Without ever having explicitly discussed it with him, it seemed she and Mike had probably wanted to have a family at some point. It hadn't happened, and - without having discussed it again - they didn't do anything about it. Whist technically not too late, it was definitely the 11th hour to start a conversation. She couldn't pin point whether he would be open to the idea of trying, or gobsmacked that she had even brought it up. So many thoughts unsaid and nothing particularly shared. She only ever experienced a luke-warm maternal feeling these days, but at times like this, when she felt that she could have brought up a child better than to stick the Vs up at a passing motorist, it gave her pause. There was, obviously, the other aspect of her child-related despondency too. The pain from her own youth still existed even if only in a burst of seconds these days. Childhood had been tough, no question. Time healed wounds but the scar tissue could still ache. Another memory to bat away, alongside the thoughts she was determined to keep on hold until she was alone at home.

Today's drive home was becoming emotionally fraught for so many reasons.

The coach indicated right at the cross section at St. Gabriel's. It was a while before a kind oncoming motorist took pity on the driver and flashed him to turn, but once that happened, Tilda was on her way once more. The road finally clearing, she made it home one minute after her usual time, accompanied by the cheesy banter of Drive Time Dave and the long suffering Debbie. Tilda pressed her fob and waited for the garage door to rise so she could stow her Corsa for the night. The weather was supposed to be turning cold this weekend so it would probably end up staying there till Monday morning. She had no plans. It would be a quiet one. Just like normal.

If she kept it up like this, she could put what she *wasn't* thinking about, out of her mind for even longer.

Hundreds of miles away under what had been until recently, clear blue sunny skies, the light was finally fading. It was time to call it a day. The man stretched out his legs and lay back on the grassy cliff top, attempting to correct the hunch that had been his position of choice for the last eight hours. The sky was stunning. Pink streaks from the setting sun ripped through the cobalt. Vivid hues from God's palate. He wasn't a religious man but it was impossible not to feel a spiritual high when looking up at such overwhelming magnificence. Back where he had been sitting, his easel reflected the scene from the start of the day's work. The tide lapping at the rocks below, the gulls hovering above, the light reflecting on the water. It was a good painting. He could be objective about his work and he was happy to admit when it hadn't come together, but this was good. It had been a satisfying day.

He decided he'd give himself a few more minutes of sky

gazing before he packed up. After all his hard work it was only fair he got some relaxation time. Lying back on the cliff with his hands under his head, watching the light fade and the colours change, seemed to be the best thing he could think of to achieve that.

This indeed, was the life.

Not for the first time in recent months, Tilda felt old. Turning forty hadn't been a big deal. Not at first. Bea had decorated the office with banners and made her stand in the middle while they all sang *Happy Birthday*. Blushing as usual, she groaned with the indignity of it, whilst laughing at how invested Bea was in her humiliation. Later that evening, a quiet meal with Mike and her in-laws had been as good a way as any to mark the occasion. Yet since then, possibly since that very meal, she was a little more reflective. Mike, Mike's parents, Mike's sister, Mike's sister's boyfriend, Mike's sister's boyfriend's daughter. Six people all there to share her special day. Six people around a table to celebrate her reaching the big 4-0. It had been the next morning when the thought had first emerged. The thought that she couldn't shake, the one that had started to keep her awake at night.

No one was there for her.

They were there because it was Mike's wife's birthday and they were being supportive of Mike. No one around that table knew Tilda very well. Polite, kind and full of small talk, yes. But very little else. And that was a realisation that Tilda was finding increasingly hard to handle.

As that thought took root, the front door was barged open, and Mike strode into the house.

"Thank God that week's over. I'm shattered."

"Tea?"

"Thanks love."

Tilda moved herself from the chair, and followed Mike into the kitchen, ready for another drink herself.

"How was your day?"

"Fine." She eyed him suspiciously. "You don't usually ask how my day was."

"Don't I? Oh well, I still want to know. I probably just don't make it as far as actually asking most of the time. What's for tea?"

"Pizza. Aren't you going to the Crown tonight?"

"Yeah, but I'll want something for when I get in. My head will be buggered tomorrow if I don't eat something later."

"Well don't drink so much then. And have a pint of water before you go to bed."

"Don't worry, love. I'll be fine."

He smiled. His boyish grin causing her to smile back.

There had been an email doing the rounds at work, a meme that had been seen by millions before she opened it. It had shown a cartoon of a harassed woman, saying something along the lines of 'Your husband will always be your biggest and oldest child that requires the most supervision'. Tilda had deleted it after a rolled-eyed acknowledgement that it was lazy humour and not especially funny. But here she was talking to her perpetually child-like husband as though she were his mother. He was able to hold down a job, drive a car, and enjoy weekly visits to the Crown where he played with sharp-pointed darts. He could look after himself. When it came to his home life, however, he might as well have asked 'What's for tea, Mum?' before downing a pint of milk from the bottle and leaving a sports kit by the washing machine for her to deal with later.

She loved him. She knew she did. She couldn't really

imagine life without him now. She couldn't imagine *her* life anyway - her life of supermarket trolleys, house- work, office drudgery, and nightly TV. It was a good life. She had a roof over her head, food in the kitchen, and enough money at the end of each month to put towards a holiday every now and then. She was very lucky and she knew she needed to remember that. She needed to remember that when she heard Bea's debauched tales of weekend excess, or Alex's wedding plans that seemed to be causing him more pain and stress with every day. She needed to remember it when she dreamt of the sea, the cliffs and the sky, with no Mike in sight.

She was lucky and she must try harder to remember that more.

Mike's state of 'shattered' seemed to disappear mi- raculously as he drained his tea, changed into a pair of jeans, and had 'top bants' via text with the lads that were already a pint down and waiting for him. He left soon after.

Tilda changed into her pyjamas for the evening. The thoughts that had been unearthed that day were still restless. They were still unsettling her and stopping her from fully focusing on much else. She thought it over as she ate her Friday night pizza. She let it distract her as she stared at the News, paying no attention to the words of the reader or the horrors he relayed. If only Bea hadn't made that stupid speech. It had been years since she had allowed herself to dwell on this, so if she'd been able to continue to put it out of her mind, it would have made no difference. On the other hand, since lunchtime, it kept returning, kept needing to be forced back in its place, kept pushing her to remember.

It was no use. She needed to rip this particular memory off like a plaster. It would be one swift, clean movement - an initial shock of pain but minimal damage in the long term? Maybe, maybe not. But she had to do something. She couldn't *not*.

The umming and aahing could have gone on all night but her phone rang. An onslaught of noise burst through the calm. A blaring juke-box and chattering drinkers were being drowned out by a very tipsy, very loud Mike.

"Til-daaa! Til-daaa! If you were Dutch you'd have used Guil-daaa." Mike shouted his nonsense as if he were chanting in a football crowd. "Tilda! Tilda! Are you there, Tilda!"

"Mike. What's up? Are you OK?" She put him on loudspeaker as she washed her plate and baking tray, and topped up her half empty glass of Pinot Grigio.

"I am MORE than OK. Tilda, Tilda! Can you hear me? Tilda?"

"I can, Mike. What's the matter?"

The thought occurred that he might be angling for a lift home in a couple of hours' time. Cosy and warm in her pyjamas, the thought of heading out now did not appeal. He would have to get a taxi. She swigged her wine back so that there would be no reason to lie when she said she was unable.

"There is nothing wrong Tilda. Nothing wrong at all. I bloody love you Tilda. I bloody love you Tilda Rudd!"

"That's great Mike." She refilled her glass. "Was that all? How're the darts? Hitting the board each time?" She barely cared, but felt she should show willing. Being selected for the Crown's darts team had been the highlight of Mike's year.

"Tilda. Tilda? TILDA? Can you hear me?"

"I can, Mike. No need to shout." She turned off the TV and pulled the wall lamp cords. She was finished downstairs for the night.

"The darts are going brilliantly. I am awesome."

"Well that's good to know. Is there anything else? I was just about to head upstairs."

Wedging the bottle's neck between her fingers, and holding the glass and phone in her hands, she took it slowly. The noisy laughter coming down the phone continued as Mike fumbled about at his end. She wasn't sure if he thought he'd hung up, or if he'd just dropped it. She got to the top of the stairs and readjusted her cargo.

"Tilda, Tilda? Are you there? TILDA?"

"I'm here Mike. What do you want?"

There was a loud hiccup.

"Any chance of a lift later?"

With Mike being given short shrift, and the conversation abruptly ending, Tilda stood on her landing and looked up. It was always going to come to this. This was the end game she'd been avoiding all afternoon. If only she'd started a film tonight, she could have kept herself distracted. She might have been able to avoid it if she'd slept on it, but now it was no use.

The long pole that pushed open the loft door was leaning against the spare room wall. She retrieved it, guided it towards the ceiling, and waited for the trapdoor to open and the ladder to fall. Its speed caused her to jump back in surprise, but then it was there. A stairway to an attic of junk, of forgotten bric a brac and, in a dark corner towards the back, the stowed remnants of Tilda Willoughby.

A bare bulb swung from the low ceiling as she crawled her way around Christmas decorations and suitcases. The last few boxes from her Dad's house were here, still awaiting her attention. It wasn't the time for that. Dealing with Dad could be put off indefinitely.

She moved college files and textbooks out of the way, noting a stack of records that she no longer had the technology to hear. Her wedding dress was laid out in a storage bag, and a box labelled 'Mike and Tilda - Wedding '99' was propping it up from beneath. *There's so much junk here* she thought, as she kept pushing crates and storage containers out of the way. The thought crossed her mind that she really needed to spend a long weekend going through all this stuff. It was a fire hazard of disregarded CD players, old papers and wires for machines long since obsolete. She would get round to it one day but not now.

Not a massive loft by any means, she knew the vague area in which she needed to root. The box she was looking for was somewhere along the far wall, behind more of her Dad's belongings. The memory of placing it there when she moved in was as clear as if it had been yesterday. Except it wasn't yesterday. It was seventeen years ago. The time had gone nowhere.

Crawling across a path she had cleared, she made her way over to the other side. The roof was too low for her to stand up, so she settled back cross-legged and used her hands to reach behind the initial wall of cardboard boxes.

It was there.

Kneeling as high as the space allowed, she leaned forward and pulled at the wooden box with both hands. It wasn't heavy, but it was wedged in, so took more effort than a long week at work and two large glasses of wine could initially handle. Persevering, she gave it all she'd got, and eventually shifted it over the top of the cardboard barrier. It landed onto her lap with a thud.

Just as she remembered, the wooden hinged box - bought in a charity shop during her final year at University - sat on her knees. The last time she'd visited Liverpool that same shop had turned into a sun bed salon, but back in her day they hadn't seemed to exist. She ran her hands over the domed lid. The edges were carved with an ornate pattern that invited running fingers, whilst the metal hinges and clasp were rusty. It was all here just as she knew it was.

Dragging the box with one hand and moving on her knees to the trapdoor, Tilda took care to get herself back on to the firm footing of the ladder, one step at a time, one-handed and being as careful as possible with her load. Suddenly, the pale green carpet was underfoot and she was back. She retrieved her wine glass from the bannister and sank down onto the landing floor, leaning on the wall for support. With the box across her legs, she carefully undid the latch, and took a deep breath as she braced herself for a view of the contents for the first time in years. This was not going to be easy but it had suddenly felt very necessary. It would be a couple of hours before Mike's return so she had the mental space to do this.

She had time to remember the person she used to be and the future she had once planned to have.

She opened the lid and let it all came flooding back.

CHAPTER TEN

Tilda. Monday 11th March 1996. The Lake District.

"I'm not being funny, but that takes the piss."

Dhanesh returned to the table, manoeuvring himself around as he settled the precariously balanced tray, and took a seat.

"£1.60 for a pint. I'm not even shitting you. Bloody tourists, driving the prices up. Like the services where they fleeced me for a Mars Bar. Bastards."

Now settled, he grabbed his lager and took a hearty swig.

"What I love about you, Dhanesh..." Jonathan began as he helped himself to a pint from the tray, "...is that two years ago you were teetotal, and yet after just twenty-four months of scholarly life, you feel genuinely aggrieved at inflated beer prices. You've had quite the journey, my friend."

Jonathan's mature student status, coupled with his beard, tended to give him a fatherly tone to his opinions, despite the reality of being only seven years older than the rest of the Geographers. Dhanesh was still riled.

"I'm just saying, it takes the piss when we can get the same drink for a quid in the Union which is just as nice as in here."

He may have been convincing with his earlier point, but this was a step too far. His audience turned on him through shouts of derision or just plain laughter. Sam threw a beer mat at him as she responded.

"Are you serious? Look at this place. A log fire, wooden beams, cosy alcoves - this is in a completely different league to the scabby Union."

"It's still a rip off," Dhanesh said, as he settled into a wing-backed chair. "I'm just saying."

An invisible line seemed to be drawn, as if no more needed saying on the subject. The conversation paused and drinks were sipped before it splintered into the usual friendship factions, becoming as diverse as the group itself. Kenny took the opportunity to scan the pub for potential one-night stands. All this involved was getting up from his seat and checking the parts of the room he couldn't immediately see, but it seemed to make him feel proactive. Dhanesh continued to develop his appreciation for alcohol through a real-ale discussion with Jonathan, who was a self-confessed aficionado of all things bitter. Sam and Jen offered increasingly intimate details of their current relationships, over-sharing a little more with every swig of lager. For Tilda and Freya it was a chance to bend the ear of Lorna about the study that they would be expected to complete when they returned home.

The minutes ticked by, the evening wore on. Lorna had been stifling yawns for some time, so after a final check of her watch, stood up to make her move.

"Right folks, I'm turning in. Don't stay too late, it's an 8am breakfast." She grabbed her coat and scarf and twisted herself out of the space that she'd occupied. She added an afterthought.

"And please, don't do anything stupid. We want to be able to come back next year. Please?"

She looked at Kenny as she said this, who looked back with wide-eyed innocence coupled with a cheeky smile.

"It's as if you don't trust us, Lorna. Come on, you know we'll be good little boys and girls."

He laughed as Lorna sighed.

"Kenny, I was not born yesterday. The fewer fires I have to put out, the better. Now enjoy the rest of your evening and be good."

The group spread out into her vacated space and settled in for the rest of the night. No one was going anywhere. As unpalatable as the higher prices may be to some, this was one of the more picturesque pubs they'd had the chance to frequent. They were going to enjoy it.

Jonathan cleared his throat and attempted to stand up although the low beam above, and tight table in front, impeded his mobility somewhat. It was time for a speech. He delivered it with all the gravitas he could muster.

"As the most senior person here, in years at least, I feel it is my place to take charge. People, colleagues, friends... I think it would be very remiss of us not to support the local economy while we are here. We shall *not* sit here and nurse our dregs all night. We need more drinks and we need then now! I suggest a round of shots in addition to the order."

His idea was given a positive reception, yet no one moved.

He cleared his throat for a second time.

"I'm wedged it seems, so who's going?"

Dhanesh's shout of 'bagsy not' alongside the fact that most people were penned in meant it was down to Freya or Tilda. After a few seconds of them waiting for the other person to offer, Tilda gave in and got up.

"Fine. I'll go. It's probably my turn anyway. Any particular requests?"

"Surprise us," Jonathan called out to her departing back.

For a Monday night the pub was lively. Full of students from the hostel, local villagers and tourists from the pretty B&Bs lining the lanes that meandered away from the high street. The air buzzed with chatter as cigarettes were smoked, the log fire crackled, and warming booze fumes littered the air. Tilda squashed herself into a space at the bar, which was at least three-deep with thirsty bodies waiting for service. If she had been Freya, she would have batted her eyelashes and pushed her chest out, flirting her way to the front in record time. Unfortunately she was wearing a baggy t-shirt and had long since smudged off her morning's mascara. Using her sexuality was an option that was currently closed to her. She was going to have to wait it out.

"Hi."

Tilda looked up and saw a tall man looking down at her. His khaki coat and dark hair seemed familiar.

"Busy, isn't it?" he said.

She looked around and then back at him.

"Are you talking to me?"

"Sure. Why not? We might as well do something to pass the time."

He looked ahead, able to see over the tops of the hair-dos in front. Something Tilda's five foot four stature was unable to attempt.

"They've only got two staff on, that's the problem. They mustn't have realised the hostel would be full tonight. That's where you're staying, isn't it?"

Tilda's penny dropped. *The man in a hurry.* She looked at him properly. The long nose and curls weren't whizzing past and barging into her now, but they belonged to the same person. In the face of her silence, he continued.

"Me too. I mean, that's where I'm staying too. I think we're all here for the Geography thing. That is why you're here isn't it? Caves by day, pub by night?"

He clearly didn't remember her. The blonde woman with the bag that he'd barged into and run off without a word of apology. Well, not an audible one anyway. She felt a wave of irritation rise up.

"You hurt my foot."

"I'm sorry?"

"Yes, well, you should be."

"No, I mean, I'm sorry, what did you say?"

Tilda rolled her eyes.

"You hurt my foot. Outside the hostel earlier. You ran straight past me and knocked my bag out of my hands." He still looked blank. "It landed on my foot."

She could tell the man smothered a laugh, but he looked straight at her, regardless. The way he did it was slightly unnerving. A direct stare, except it didn't feel that way. Rather than trying to bore through to her soul and find all her inner secrets, it was as if he were showing her that he himself was an open book with nothing to hide, and she was welcome to delve as deeply as she wished. She did not wish, and dropped her gaze, feeling the blush rise. He spoke again.

"And how is your foot now? Can I do anything? Will you need surgery?"

Tilda felt stupid. It hadn't really hurt at all. She was just annoyed at his indifference to her presence. She started to wish she could go back in time and never start this conversation.

"It's fine. I'm fine."

The man nodded, happy with this state of affairs, and looked ahead as he considered his next move.

"Let me take this opportunity to say I'm so very sorry for all the pain caused. Honestly, I am. And if I'd realised I'd inflicted such damage to your foot, and ruined your day in quite so disastrous a way, I would have stopped and rung the emergency services myself. I was on my way to the phone box as it was. Did they take *very* long to come?"

"Stop being sarcastic. You're not as funny as you think you are." Tilda looked up at the man, her mouth a resolutely drawn line, but her eyes betrayed her relaxing stance on the matter. His casually intense gaze stayed on her face as he considered how to respond. It took mere seconds.

"Well, look. How's this for a plan? If I get served first, I'll buy you a drink, and if you get served first, then I'll still buy you a drink. What do you think? It's a win-win for you. For me, it's a financial obligation."

She smiled briefly, although her commitment to the economy of the Lake District could not be ignored.

"I'm with my friends. I've got to get our normal round plus shots. There're seven of us."

"Ah. I don't think that would be within my budget, I'm afraid."

"It's fine. I don't want to bankrupt you."

"But I can't have you carrying around all this anger. It's not good for you. I clearly have to make amends for my reckless behaviour or I just won't sleep tonight."

The hint of a smile returned, causing his eyes to twinkle. He didn't try to hide it this time but Tilda was no longer annoyed. She knew she'd been daft. It was time to get over it, and join in with some self-mockery.

"Well if you're desperate, and to be fair, you should be as it's all I can do to stop myself from limping, you can get me a cider and black and I'll sort the rest out."

"A cider and black?"

"Yes. Then you'll be on the way to making it up to

me. It'll do for starters anyway."

The man smiled. He was quite attractive in a Heath-cliff-on-the-moors sort of way. He was also useful. During their conversation he'd been able to spot where gaps had appeared in the queue. He beckoned her to follow him as he shimmied his way past a couple of people propping up the bar. Far quicker than if it had been under her own steam, she had made it to the front. He was now officially forgiven.

"I'm Tilda." She offered her hand, then had second thoughts when she realised she was in a pub and not a board meeting. She wasn't very good at this, she knew that and felt stupid once again. Without noticing her hesitation, or maybe just choosing to ignore it, he took her hand and shook firmly.

"Pleased to meet you, Tilda. I'm Grady."

On the other side of the pub, the Geographers were deep in conversation. Despite their drinks running low and the promise of shots hanging in the air, they continued their chatter, oblivious to the developments at the bar. Had they looked up, they would have seen a very unexpected sight.

"That's a bit of a weird name isn't it? Grady. It sounds like Gravy when you say it fast." Tilda's frostiness had thawed.

"Ah, yes. Thanks for that. Without any clues from me, you have inadvertently chanced upon my primary school nickname. Unbelievable, as it is so nuanced and subtle." He smiled to show he was taking her mock derogation in good spirit. "Actually, Grady is my last name. My first name's John, but I prefer Grady. There are too many Johns in the world."

"So definitely not Gravy, then? Because I quite like that."

"If you *really* feel the need to awaken long-put-to-bed memories then I guess I can't stop you, but Grady would be my preferred choice. It's completely up to you."

"So GRAY-DEE," Tilda continued, "Why the army coat? Are you trying to look all tough and macho? Do you spend your weekends scrambling under nets and auditioning for the Krypton Factor?"

"If I did, would you be impressed?" he replied, quick as a flash.

She considered her views on the subject.

"No. Not at all, I'm afraid. I prefer people who read books and drink tea come Saturday. I think physical activity is for people who need distracting from the boredom of their own thoughts."

As soon as the words came out of her mouth, she blushed. Who did she think she was? This perfectly polite young man might love nothing more than running marathons or playing five-a-side in his spare time. When had she become so *cutting*? She began to apologise but he had already started to reply.

"Then it's just as well we met. Reading books and drinking tea is all I do from Saturday morning to Sunday night. There is quite simply no time for anything else. It can be exhausting turning all those pages, and have you ever noticed how frustrating it is when the kettle takes a full minute to boil. I mean, jeez. What are we, cavemen?"

Tilda, relieved she had not grievously offended him, giggled and nodded in agreement.

"Tell me about it. And it can be *shattering* having so much to fit into such a small space of time. How on earth do we cope along with the nine hours a week of lectures? It's a bloody grind."

They both laughed now, the ice was breaking clean away, leaving the floor open for the next stage of the 'Get To Know Each Other' talks.

Tilda looked straight at him, inhibitions melting. He was a puzzle. One minute, making her uncharacteristically mad, and the next charming her with disarming vulnerability and a twinkly grin. And what was happening? She was in a pub, and she was *flirting* with a stranger. It was as if she had inadvertently become Freya for the evening. She smiled back and returned to the interesting new developments in hand.

"So, Gravy, Grady, whatever - where's that drink I was promised?"

Across the room, it all seemed to happen in slow motion. The first domino to fall was when Freya looked down at her empty glass. This led to her voicing concerns that Tilda had got lost in the crowd, which in turn meant Dhanesh stood up and scanned the bar. Jonathan then followed on with the thought that she might have gone to start to write up her fieldwork before she had actually been in the field and the rest of the table laughed. Even Freya chuckled, though not out of cruelty, more out of recognition that Tilda would if she could. Finally Kenny got up and, using it as pretext for another scouting mission, walked over to the edge of the waiting patrons, trying to get a handle on their potential waiting time. Within seconds he was back.

"I don't believe it."

"I thought we'd agreed on no more Victor Meldrew, Kenny. Not since Lowestoft." Jonathan's voice of authority spoke again.

"Seriously, I don't believe it, and I'm not even doing Victor Meldrew. I just really don't believe it."

"What's happened? Where's Tilda?" Freya was getting thirsty now.

"Oh so suddenly you all want to know what I have to say, do you? It's not 'Piss Off Kenny' now, is it? You've all realised how valuable I am now that I have something to tell you that you are interested in. Well I might tell you I might not. I might wait until..."

Sam threw another beer mat, this time at Kenny's head. It was starting to be her signature move.

"Kenny, stop being a bellend. What's going on?"

He sighed and gave in. His moment was over.

"Timid Tilda ... has pulled! A man, too. A real life, actual man."

"Don't lie. What's really going on?" As Tilda's friend, Freya was the only one who could be honest in her reaction without seeming mean.

"I'm not lying. Look over there. She's with that tall bloke."

Shouts of disbelief were the main response people chose before collectively investigating Kenny's claims. A couple of pints in, the notions of subtlety and finesse were lost on the gang, but still they tried. Standing up at different angles and heights, pretending to look with great interest at a picture above the optics, or just choosing to out and out stare - although this was only Freya who was genuinely intrigued - the Geography group located, observed and then analysed the new situation that was being played out in front of them.

Back at the bar and oblivious to the ruckus they were causing, Tilda and Grady sipped their drinks and continued to chat. Shared university experiences such as annoying flat mates and the lack of disposable money opened up to more weighty topics. Whether Geography as a degree was ever going to get them a career or if they would have a life resigned to graduate schemes in generic offices. They were just moving on to the effect that Charles and Di's imminent divorce may have on the royal family when Tilda spotted something in the background.

Kenny.

It was when he'd walked past for the fourth or fifth time that Tilda's eye had been caught and she looked back at the table. Grady paused what he was saying, caught her glance and looked too. As if triggered by a starting pistol, everyone suddenly changed their position. Jonathan sat down and looked straight ahead, Sam got off the stool she had been kneeling on and turned to the wall. Dhanesh put down the piece of paper that said 'TILDA, ARE YOU OK?' and Freya just waved and smiled.

Tilda sighed audibly, as Grady turned back to look at her.

"I'm so sorry, I've been keeping you here when you've got a table of people waiting for you. Do you want to go back to your friends?"

Tilda looked across at the table. It contained her one friend Freya, who was in no need of her company to have a good time, along with some other people she felt less warmly about. Then she looked up at this fascinating new man with whom she was having the easiest conversation with, ever. Did she want to go back to her friends?

"No thanks. I'm fine where I am."

Tilda. Friday 16th September 2016. Stockport.

The half-empty wine glass had been placed on the bannister to avoid accidental spillages. The wooden box was empty and had been put out of the way on the window sill. Tilda sat with her legs stretched out in front of her, leaning on a pillow against the wall. Her back ached but she didn't notice. She had been in the same position for nearly two hours and had only just scratched the surface.

Across her legs lay a jumble of papers. Photographs that had begun to fade with age, a peeling beer mat with a scrawled signature in the corner, a slim volume of poetry by an American essayist. She had picked through each item with care, as if excavating an important archaeological find. The memory of why she kept it, and the resurrection of the events surrounding its inclusion meant that it had been a long-winded task. She hadn't even got to the letters and there were dozens of those.

Tilda leaned back and took stock. She was holding it together but only just. The lurch of her stomach as she was reminded of a conversation here, or a mutual understanding there, meant that she was swinging wildly between needing a stiff drink and wanting to be sick. At one point she'd tried to stuff all the items back into the box without carrying on, knowing this feeling was going to get worse before it could get better. It hadn't worked though. She knew she had to see this through. Once the evening was over, she would place the box away for another decade or two and everything would return to normal.

For now, however, there was still history to unearth. Moving the bundle of letters to one side, she picked up a small watercolour sketch. It depicted the opening to some caves she had once visited. The sky was bright with a few clouds and there was some greenery around the cave mouth. The impression of a girl sitting on a rock had been lightly added, the whirling watery paint creating an idea of her presence rather than a clear image. Tilda sighed and allowed the latest stab of pain to ease and make way for the less traumatic appearance of recognition and nostalgia. She also got up and retrieved her wine. She didn't think she could handle this level of emotion without it.

The bundle of letters continued to sit where she had placed them. Unassuming white oblongs, each containing a couple of sheets of jagged-edged notebook pages covered in scrawl. She could just leave them. She could wallow in all the peripheral mementoes without the full immersion of his actual words.

Yeah, right.

Knowing it had to be done, she finally picked up the bound pile of correspondence. The same handwriting in the same black fineliner. It was as if they had been sent yesterday. The self-pity bubbled up from within as she unwound the rubber band and selected the first envelope. As she removed the letter, the first tears fell. She couldn't help it. She was amazed she had held on for this long.

She sobbed as she read and remembered him. She heard his voice as she read his words. So long ago yet still so raw. The life she now had was far removed from the one she'd planned, all those years earlier. What had happened to her? What had gone wrong? She had been fun and flirty, relaxed and witty. Now she viewed the world through dead eyes and pursed lips. She was no fun and she hated it. She missed her past and she missed who she had nearly become.

The tears continued to fall as she leant back on the wall and mourned her lost potential.

What happened, Tilda? Where did you go?

CHAPTER TWELVE

Tilda. Tuesday 12th March 1996. The Lake District.

Tilda lay in the single bed, straight backed and rigid. The hostel curtains had long given up the responsibility of shielding light from the room, so the emergence of dawn through the threadbare fabric had been clear. Her arm was dead - dead numb from having her entire body weight lie atop it, sideways on. It didn't register for a while, mainly because she'd been in a truly deep sleep, but as the rest of her senses and body parts sniffed at the new day and individually made decisions about how ready they were to partake in its events, the comatose nature of her arm became more pressing. Not fully ready to admit she was gradually waking, she did her best to roll her body off its limb-plinth and free up the blood supply from the internal bottleneck in her shoulder. As she did this, a couple of realisations made themselves known. Firstly, her head felt as if it had been hit repeatedly with a frying pan or mallet, à la Tom and Jerry. It was as if her brain were being squeezed in a vice. She was fairly sure that neither of those things had happened in the hours preceding this thought, so the cause of the horrendous pain remained a mystery.

The second piece of information that became apparent as she moved her body across the narrow bed, was that she was not alone.

Eyes suddenly wide, she scanned the room from her paralysed state, not daring to do anything to alert the person currently spooning her from behind that she was no longer at peace. It didn't take long for a clue. Hanging on the back of the door was an all too familiar khaki coat.

This was a new experience for Tilda. Having lived in a small town for the first eighteen years of her life, with a slightly over-bearing, worrier of a Dad, in a community where everybody knew each other and most people's sense of discretion and privacy only applied to themselves, waking up in bed with a stranger had never happened. Nowadays, in her student house, she often chanced upon boys coming out of the bathroom - ones she vaguely recognised from lectures - before Freya would stagger along and usher them out of the door. Never anything to do with Tilda, she marvelled at the confidence her friend must have. To be so relaxed in such a mortifying situation. Prickly legs and a dry mouth, there was nothing worse. Tilda had only ever slept alone.

And now, as soon as she acknowledged her situation, in this tiny dolls' house of a bed, a million and one new thoughts swarmed into her consciousness. *This* was one hell of an alarm call all right. My God, was she awake.

Tilda trawled her mind for any details, any at all that could help her plot how she found herself in this situation. The pub. The bar. *The flirting.* Within the space of about thirty seconds of chatter to a random stranger, her personality had changed into someone unrecognisable. She had been interesting. She had been funny. She had been someone that an attractive man chose to talk to all evening. She felt as if she were in a parallel universe. This type of experience did not happen to her. Not even a little bit.

The euphoria that did its best to course through her alcohol-sodden veins was short lived. A feeling of doom quickly followed, spreading throughout her gut. Of course... how could she have been so stupid? There was no mystery about it. She hadn't sparkled or radiated. There was no alluring spell cast that had caused the seemingly lovely man to want to listen to her jokes. It was nothing to do with her dazzling wit or her illuminating smile. He'd been looking for a shag. As simple as that. She could have been anyone, he just happened to have seen her first.

Now she understood the situation, her stomach lurched about as she tried to recall anything that could shed light on the events leading up to this rude awakening. At what point had she given into wild abandon and brought him back to her room? Her face burned as her mind darted into new areas of morning-after shame. Had the twinkly man with the scruffy coat got her drunk and seduced her...*in front of Freya? And oh God, let there be a condom. Let there be a condom, times a zillion.*

With a concerted effort, Tilda raised her head so that she could see her roommate's face currently being obscured by the melamine table separating them. Her eyes glanced over her files and journal, taking some minutes to confirm Freya was still fast asleep, as she moved by stealth, battling a mix of blinding headache and inescapable shame with an increasingly bitter feeling of disappointment thrown in for good measure. She had been duped into thinking she had what it took. That it wasn't just Freya who could charm and sparkle on a night out, but that she, Tilda Willoughby could enjoy a man's company, make him laugh and be warmed by feeling desirable and vivacious. Except, he didn't seem very lovely now. Not now she'd sussed out his game plan and caught him in the act. He was just like Kenny or Dhanesh or any of the other hundreds of students she met on a daily basis. It hadn't been special at all. She just happened to be the one that went to the bar. It could have been Jen. It could have been Freya. It could have been anyone. That feeling of disappointment that had been nudging through the headache and shock of the morning's revelations now imploded into deeply suppressed heartbreak.

It hadn't been special at all.

CHAPTER THIRTEEN

Grady. Tuesday 12th March 1996. The Lake District.

He could tell she was awake. A few moments ago, her body has stiffened under his arm, the arm that he had carefully placed across her waist in the night when he had woken. She had been asleep but seemed to indicate consent by settling back into him, her body pressed against his as they snuggled up in the smallest bed known to man.

He had never felt so content.

He didn't know why - he couldn't put his finger on the reason - but from the moment in the pub, when she'd been momentarily cross about his earlier clumsiness, he knew he needed to get to know her better. She looked so serious, it was as if she were issuing a direct but unspoken challenge to make her laugh. A challenge he readily accepted. There hadn't been many women in his life - something sadly truer than its initial implication - but he wanted to know a little more about this particular one before the field trip was over.

His head throbbed. Admittedly, the lock-in had seemed a better idea at the time than it did now. Silently groaning, he moved his free arm in an attempt to get a glimpse of his watch. It was 7.06. That'd be a full four hours of sleep then. *Oh great.*

Ordinarily, no rest and a hangover would cause Grady to be less than his usual cheery self. He'd mope around his room, playing Dylan until night fell once more. Today, however, he was lying in bed with a fascinating and funny woman. He had a day outdoors lying ahead and the sun was shining brightly through the patchiest of curtains.

He felt invigorated and alive.

Now he just wished Tilda would acknowledge she was awake so they could start the day.

CHAPTER FOURTEEN

Tilda. Tuesday 12th March 1996. The Lake District.

It was no use. She was going to have to move. Without turning around, she slowly slid herself to the edge of the bed, lowering her legs to the floor and sitting up in what she hoped was one fluid movement. Tiptoeing towards the door, she rubbed feeling back into her arm before pulling down her oversized t-shirt, desperate to preserve some sense of modesty for as long as possible.

"Morning."

She stopped still as her heart jumped. She thought she'd been so quiet.

"Hello. Grady."

"How are you feeling?"

"Headachy. And I need the loo. Give me a minute?"

He nodded and smiled, his eyes still displaying a raw kindness that warmed his whole face.

"I'll be here," he said softly.

She nodded in return but struggled to respond with a smile. Kind face or not, he'd still taken advantage. She wished she could remember the exact sequence of events leading up to it. She wished she could be sure there had been a condom, and Freya hadn't witnessed anything too shameful. Her thoughts troubled her as she left the room and escaped to the welcome embrace of the bleached communal bathroom. She reckoned she had ten minutes to work out what to say.

As it turned out, her carefully rehearsed brush off, composed whilst staring into the sink mirror, was a waste of time. Her earnest admonishment of, 'I thought you really liked me,' had been quickly discarded when it sounded too desperate spoken aloud. Instead she leant towards, 'I knew you were too good to be true, you're just like everyone else,' which was preferable because it conveyed disappointment alongside the implication that he was one of many.

This suggestion could not be further from the truth. Aside from a few teenage snogs on the local playing fields, her entire sexual history was confined to Freshers' Week, two years before. With the giddy freedom of finally being away from home, she had lost her virginity to Tom from Kent. He was the recent recipient of two As and a B and he wanted a career in marketing. It lasted for as long as it took the queue outside the disabled toilet to start knocking. The earth hadn't moved but at least she was no longer a virgin - a piece of information that she no longer cared quite so much about.

Since then there had been little else in the way of male attention. This was not something she was keen to share with anyone, let alone the annoyingly attractive man with whom she had been so let down. She had to make sure she regained control of the situation. Ultimately the 'thanks, it was fun, see you around,' line was what she settled on, in order to convey she couldn't be bothered less by his antics.

When she finally plucked up the courage to return to the room, she heard their voices before she opened the door. When she did, she saw Freya - sporting the most spectacular bedhead she had ever seen - sitting up against her pillow, regaling Grady with the exact nature of the vomit she had excreted somewhere between the pub and the youth hostel, only hours before. For someone whose stomach had been somewhat delicate recently, she was putting on an incredibly brave face.

And was far too loud.

"Morning, Tilds. How're you feeling today?"

There was little point in giving her speech now, flooding Tilda with some relief but a little concern that she was even further away from regaining the control she so desperately wanted.

"I'm fine, thanks. I've got a banging head but I'll be OK after a couple of tablets. Have you still got some?"

Freya nodded eagerly, demonstrating her head was nowhere near as tender as the rest of the room's. She leant down to get her bag from the floor and rooted around until she found the foil strip.

"There you are, matey. I feel sooooo much better for spewing. I was just telling... what was your name again... Graham?... No? Well, anyway, I was just telling your friend that after we left the pub, I knew today was going to be a total write off if I didn't take action, so I made myself sick round the back of the cheese shop."

Tilda listened, partly out of politeness but also because it dawned on her that she had no memory of leaving the pub. She began to process some thoughts but was interrupted by her euphemistically termed 'friend'.

"I think it's time I made a move. I'd better go and find wherever it was I was supposed to sleep. I'll have a shower and then see you at breakfast, yeah?"

He left this hanging in the air but Tilda didn't really feel like responding to his specific enquiry.

"Bye then. Nice to have met you. See you around." It was almost what she'd planned to say so she could live with that. Stepping backwards, she unhooked his coat and opened the door for him. His smile faded a little at her coldness but she didn't care. She felt used and stupid.

Facing her, he attempted a hug but she stayed firm so

it ended up being more of an arm rub. Without another word, he walked away, the door closing behind him. His confusion was obvious as he left, clearly unsure as to what had just happened.

Back inside the room, Tilda slumped on to her bed, lying face down on the pillow, a pillow that smelt re-markably masculine and - she was loath to admit - a little bit intoxicating. Freya eventually broke the silence.

"What the frig is wrong with you?"

Freya rarely chose to mince her words and with the volume higher than her current state could withstand, Tilda selected the only option open to her. She pulled the pillow over her head.

"Tilda Willoughby. I am in shock. First of all, you pull. I mean, you actually PULL. That's the first shock. Second, the guy in question is fit. No offence but he's a hottie! A properly good-looking manly man. Thirdly, I woke up this morning to find you lying in his arms. Yes LYING IN HIS ARMS! Like it's a sodding rom-com. I mean, Christ, it's like you're Meg Ryan for fuck's sake. And now, just as I'm getting my head around this crazy new world order, you come back from your wee, look really weird and ignore the guy you've just had a bril-liant night with. Then you go all psycho-bitch on his ass. Tilds! Are you mental?"

Tilda gave it another half minute and then removed the pillow. Freya shrieked.

"Christ, you look terrible. What happened? Did he say something nasty? Did he do something bad? I don't understand what happened. Tell me, what did he do?"

Tilda sighed, recognising she was going to have to discuss this, even in the briefest of terms with Freya. It wasn't the worst plan. She was her pal and she had a ton of life experience so would know how best to handle it. Was the full cold shoulder treatment worth it or should polite indifference be her tactic? How should she be-have when dealing with a man she fell a little bit in love with, just because he spoke to her like she was *something*? How should she behave when he used her and wormed his way into her affections, just for a drunken bunk up? How should she behave when she had to face a week of bumping into him, completing an inter-university field study with him and watching his friends laugh at her every time they saw her?

Freya would know what to do. This was right up her street.

CHAPTER FIFTEEN

Flo. Friday 16ᵗʰ September 2016. York.

She cleared her throat and projected her words across the room.

> *"There was no earthly sound, no sound at all,*
> *From the top of the attic to the bottom of the hall.*
> *It was the dead of night all through the house,*
> *Not a creature was stirring, not even a mouse…"*

"Err…Flo? WTF?"

Gregor's hipster beard appeared from around the doorway. He said those three letters a lot, especially to Flo. It amused her that he thought she didn't know what they stood for. Of course she knew. She was an avid fan of Big Brother on the sly so knew all the latest terminology.

"Were you reciting *The Night Before Christmas* but really wrongly?"

Flo threw her hands up as if to say 'you got me,' and smiled.

"I thought making up another of my poems would help make the time pass. Wait… had I merged into something else? Lord, that's what a week of nightshifts does to you."

"Whevs, Flo. I'm making a brew. You in?"

"Ooh yes please, good for you, Gregor. One of my herbals, thanks. You can surprise me."

Flo settled back in the chair. One minute you're taking a temperature or checking a pulse and the next, you're coming up with some shockingly mediocre poetry before plagiarising a half-remembered seasonal verse. In September. Sweet Jesus!

A few ankle rotations and buttock clenches later, and the DVTs with which she regularly battled were kept at bay a while longer. Heaving herself out of the chair, she paced around a bit and let her eyes wander. The high ceilings and intricate coving could have been something out of a stately home. The kind that ageing historians would point out to bored school children, who were only interested in the treasures to be found in the gift shop. She sighed. Such luxury. It was gratifying to see that money couldn't stop the inevitable. No matter what riches you accumulated in life, it all counted for nothing when you were dependent on others for your basic care. Perhaps there was a poem in that. Her mind started to wander again as she ran through a list of rhyming words for 'health and wealth'. She could only think of stealth. Perhaps she could get away with 'shelf' or 'self', even though they weren't strictly correct.

Flo's mind often wandered during these moments. Sitting next to the heavily sedated with their regulated breath created a kind of mental vacuum whereby ideas and images popped into her head. She had often thought she should write the poems down, but the one time she did, reading them back in the cold light of day had made her cringe with their awfulness. It was all right for Alice. She had all the paper work to keep her busy. Currently seated in the room next door, her supervisor was hauled up with a packet of biscuits and a file of papers, keeping the medical notes up to date. Gregor seemed to cope with the long hours of boredom, too. Although prohibited by their firm, she was pretty sure she'd seen him playing on his phone when it was his turn to do the bedside shift. She wouldn't tell anyone about it, of course, but it was enormously useful to have a hold over him for when there was a task needing to be done that she didn't fancy.

Having completed a couple of circuits on the luxurious carpet, she returned to the chair by the bed. The breathing was still steady and a glance at the machine told her nothing had changed. He had been unconscious since their arrival and didn't look to be bursting forth with a surge of energy any time soon. *Thank the Lord for that.*

Gregor slunk around the door, a mug in each hand.

"Here you *go,* Flo! Ha ha ha. Now who's the poet?" He handed her the drink. "I think its elderflower or blueberry, or some other such nonsense."

"Leave my herbals alone. They're calming."

"Well I'll take my caffeine fix over your calming flowery water any day. It's all about staying awake." Gregor wandered over to the chair at the desk and sat in it, looking as if he was masterminding a space mission, it gave him such gravitas.

"Maybe." Flo sipped her tea.

"You think this was his office?"

Flo looked at the desk, computer, and filing cabinets, surrounding the window. Gregor could be really stupid sometimes.

"I'd say so, wouldn't you?"

"Well, duh! I know that. I was just wondering why they made his bedroom in *here*. Why set him up in the office when there are plenty of other rooms that they could use. And another thing. Why do you need to relax? Are you still wound up because of yesterday?"

Flo sighed and considered the question. As much of a professional as she was, she was struggling to feel anything positive for this particular client. Yesterday certainly hadn't helped.

"I'm not sure. I don't think it can be the 'black bitch' incident. Besides he wasn't very clear."

No, he defo only said 'blaaa bish'. Far less threatening and offensive." Gregor smiled encouragingly as he swigged back his coffee.

"It wasn't that. Not on its own. I worked in the NHS for fifteen years. I heard far worse than that on a daily basis."

"And that was just the staff? - boom boom."

"Hilarious as always, Gregor." Flo deadpanned, before continuing in earnest.

"His bigotry is no worse than any other comments I've heard before. Even if it still felt like vinegar in a paper cut, yesterday."

"Vinegar in a paper cut?"

"Yeah, you know... there is always an initial smarting feeling. Then the sting subsides quickly and just leaves a feeling of being marked. It's a little moment in the day that has been spoilt. If it's only one moment in isolation, then it can be brushed off and I'm left to enjoy all the other normal, kind moments until I eventually forget about it. But when it happens again and again, then it is much more painful."

"I totally get that, Flo. It was the same with me and hashtag fag-gate." Gregor crossed two sets of fingers to mime the symbol without pausing for breath. "I was tense that night, I can tell you. Luckily, I went out and pulled the fittest guy I've had in years. Not so tense by 6am the next day. This old bugger was more than forgotten about. You should try it!"

Flo smiled at his positivity whilst wincing at the implication of casual, gay sex. She hadn't been the only one that had borne the brunt of this client's hatred of people. Gregor had put up with a lot too. As she continued to ponder, she knew the vitriol from yesterday wasn't even bothering her anymore. What with people being generally polite most of the time, those odd moments had reduced over the years and were now usually consigned to the status of 'one off incident'. Flo could still remember how it was when she was a girl, but that was a long time ago and she was happy to forget. These days, the spoilt moments of her day were rare and that was why she was struggling to understand why she disliked the dying man so much. He was dying. She should pity him.

During his conscious moments, he looked at her like she was scum - again, not a new occurrence – but since being unconscious, he'd been the model patient. Lying in the over-sized bed, his shrunken frame and sunken eyes, weighing the same as a weaker variety of twelve-year old girl, he should have evoked immediate empathy. Flo looked at his hand, with protruding veins and sagging skin, and tried to hold it, like she had on so many other occasions with so many other clients. There was just something about him that meant she preferred not. She moved her hand away, knowing that if he woke, he'd tell her to get off anyway.

Usually in this situation, there'd be friends and family visiting throughout the days leading up to the end. They'd regale the nursing team with stories and anecdotes about the client in their younger days so that a picture of a vibrant and youthful person would be imprinted in the minds of those tasked with tending to their final hours. The fact that there had been no one to provide such a picture was perhaps the root of her lack of empathy. She simply didn't care enough.

At that moment, Alice popped her head in.

"Any change?"

"None whatsoever."

"Right, well I think it's time. The office have sent the NOK details over and it seems to be a local number. They've been getting invoiced so they must be significant. I'll try and get hold of then now. Someone should be here for him."

Alice's face disappeared from the doorframe and Flo relaxed back in the chair once more. She looked around the lavishly papered walls, at the wooden shelves that housed thick volumes of leather bound books, at the bedside table that was empty save for pill bottles. If there *were* a relative, the impact on the man's life was negligible to say the least. Surely there'd be photos. Just the one at least, tucked away somewhere. Surely they would have visited. It made no sense.

CHAPTER SIXTEEN

Tilda. Friday 16th September 2016. Stockport.

Meanwhile, in a quiet suburb on the outskirts of Manchester, Mike returned from the Crown. It was half past eleven when the sound of the key in the lock caused a sudden flurry of activity on the landing. Eyes were wiped, wine was gulped and letters, papers, cards and photos were shoved back into their box. A voice from downstairs rang out.

"Alright love....did you miss me? Where are you? I need that pint of water. I was awesome tonight. What've you been up to? Any food on the go?"

He climbed the stairs as Tilda stowed the loft ladder away, her face stained with tears.

"There's some pizza left on the side in the kitchen. You should have that. If not, put it in the fridge." She sniffed, and wound her hair up with a bobble on her wrist. Time to regain composure.

She knew he wasn't totally insensitive. It was clear that she was upset, but she knew he wouldn't comment on it. He didn't handle these sorts of situations very well so he simply chose to opt out of them. He would assume it was a particularly emotional episode of Corrie or that she was in the middle of her period. Actually upon reflection, Tilda had a better idea of what her husband would think. He had heard her put away the loft ladder so he would guess it was do with her Dad. He would never ask. He would presume that she'd tell him or deal with it herself. He knew she was very capable of dealing with sensitive issues alone, because that is exactly the way Tilda acted around him. But there had been times, especially regarding her Dad, that she would have really appreciated an actual show of love and support, rather than just the implication it was there if she requested it.

She cleared her throat, swallowed the lump that had accompanied her evening and slapped on her poker face.

"Did you have a nice evening?"

"I had the very best evening in the world. I loved it. I absolutely rock. How about you?"

"It's been fine."

He attempted to ruffle her newly fixed hair, although the lager swirling round his stomach caused a brief stumble that propelled him towards her with a speed that surprised them both.

"Careful!"

"Sorry, love. Come here." He steadied himself, achieved the hair ruffle and added a robotic back pat. His face made it clear he knew she'd be fine.

"Ask me why I had such a brilliant night."

Tilda sighed.

"Why did you have such a brilliant night?"

"Because I thought it was all over at first, but I kept throwing, and kept trying and Ginger Dave was on fire, and I just couldn't make any mark, but then when the second half kicked off, I started throwing the darts I knew I had inside me, and Ginger Dave's bottle went and..."

Tilda's eyes continued to look forward just as her face continued to smile bravely. As Mike's tales of sporting triumph gathered momentum, she found herself drifting miles away from the bannister she was leaning against, and the mint green carpet she was standing on, wondering what *he* was doing at the exact same moment.

The small torch doubled as a lantern with the flick of a switch. From the light it emitted, he was just able to see the page he was writing as well as the location of his hip flask towards the wall of the tent. The satisfaction of the day was still palpable and he attempted to convey this through his words. He never thought too hard about what he wrote. He'd learnt from someone, a long time ago, that to record your thoughts before sleep was a sensible way to order your mind. It stopped any disturbing dreams where your unfettered subconscious did the job for you. It was also a useful winding down activity. When his friend had told him this, all those years ago, he'd laughed. He liked having an unfettered subconscious and had never felt the need to wind down before bed. But she had been earnest and he wanted to please her. Twenty years on, this was a habit that had stuck. It also reminded him of her on a nightly basis, not that he needed a prompt to do that.

Reading back what he'd recorded, he smiled as he thought back to the light of the day's sky. If he had been able to capture a fraction of its impact on canvas, he would sleep well. A final swig of his flask and the click of the pen meant he was ready to turn in. To allow his rampant inner thoughts all the opportunity they wanted to disturb him, in spite of his journaling efforts at order. Retrieving his well-worn bookmark from the back of the notebook, he looked at it intently. An old photo. The shy blonde caught by surprise. Every night he allowed himself this luxury. To look at her once again before shutting his eyes. If he died in his sleep, she would be the last person on his mind. He didn't see this as a morbid thought, more like the most comforting way to end each day. Smiling at her and at the memories they

shared together, he slipped her in place before stowing the
book down the side of his sleeping bag and switching off the
torch.

Subconscious! Do your worst.

Tilda recognised she was supposed to be impressed. With what felt like a super human effort, she smiled.

"That's great, Mike. Really. Will you be selected for the tournament now?" He continued to focus on standing up straight.

"Mike?"

"Hmmm...what's that? Oh, yeah maybe, love."

Now his monologue had come to an end, he wasn't listening to her. She could tell that. In his head he was Phil 'The Power' Taylor, and was reliving every throw. He wandered towards the bathroom, taking slightly longer than usual with the basic task of loading his toothbrush with toothpaste. It was difficult to imagine him gliding the delicate metal darts through the air with finesse and skill, whilst watching him botch up the bedtime task of cleaning his teeth. Resisting the urge to do it for him, Tilda brushed her own teeth next to him. The practical nature of the night-time routine forced her emotions back on track after the whirlwind of earlier. Mike sloped into the bedroom, stripping down to boxers in record time and became submerged under the duvet just as Tilda followed. It would only be a minute or two. She knew that. It would be no time at all, especially with the light off. Flicking the switch next to her bed, she settled back into the pillows and waited.

No more than two minutes later, the first of the night's beer-fuelled snores were heard from the other side of the bed. He was asleep. It was time to continue remembering.

CHAPTER SEVENTEEN

Tilda and Grady. Tuesday 12th March 1996. The Lake District.

It had taken four mugs of tea, several rounds of toast, two doses of paracetamol and now, five hours later, the first chance to sit down before Tilda had started to feel human again. The out-of-time percussion section in her head had finally abated and she was now returning to her more usual state of ordered calm. Across her legs was a pad of scribbled notes as she stretched out on the rocky surface she'd found. Caves and a hangover were not natural bedfellows, which, if she could pass on nothing else but that information, future generations of Geographers would be all the wiser for it. They could all learn from her mistakes. No one, in years to come, would enter an enclosed and underground area of limited capacity whilst experiencing a combination of nausea, dry-mouth and gurgling stomach. It would become the folklore of the course.

Letting the Spring sun warm her face, Tilda allowed this whimsical train of thought to fade as she considered the day so far. The feelings of nausea tended to intensify every time she thought back to the morning's events. Waking up with a stranger! How very un-Tilda-like that was. She had struggled to get beyond that thought all morning - how very un-Tilda-like she had been. It had lodged itself in her brain, like a trapped grain of sand - tiny in size to anyone else, but causing untold discomfort every time it grazed her memory. During her luke-warm shower and five-minute bathroom slot, she had pondered what being un-Tilda-like actually meant. What would be written next to 'Un-Tilda-like' in the dictionary? Not thinking through the consequences of one's behaviour? Reckless and potentially dangerous actions overtaking common sense and a clear head? As she'd sat on her bed, pulling on walking socks and lacing up boots, the inverse characteristics dawned on her. Being un-Tilda-like meant not living in the moment, not being spontaneous and not having fun. Regardless of the epic fear of the morning-after, she had to admit, she'd never enjoyed herself so much as the parts of the previous night that she could remember. Standing at the bar, chatting, smiling, someone listening to her with no pre-conceptions about how dull she could be. Last night had been pretty wonderful.

So much for playing it cool.

"Excellent, I found my way back. Tea?"

She gratefully accepted the Styrofoam cup, with its weak contents, that he handed to her. Any liquid was welcome today. The sun continued to beam as she gulped a mouthful. It had been a long time since breakfast.

Once Freya had returned from the bathroom that morning, Tilda had managed to find the words or perhaps just the courage, to ask about the exact nature of the previous evening's sleeping arrangements. It was mortifying but essential. Sitting up on her bed, fully dressed for the day ahead, Tilda spoke carefully and deliberately as she delivered the second rehearsed speech of the day. She was getting to be quite the actress.

"So, what time did you come back last night?"

"Tilds, I have absolutely no idea. I was still in the pub at two, 'cause I remember looking up at the clock and saying, 'Shit, it's two'. Why?"

"Just wondering. The end of the evening is a bit... erm... hazy."

"That's probably all the Sambuca. Except it wasn't proper Sambuca was it? It was some local brand. It was possibly the rankest thing I've ever tasted. I just wish I'd realised that when I was on my seventh." Freya rifled through the clothes on the floor, giving an armpit a sniff before grimacing and discarding it immediately.

"So..." Tilda tried to steer it back to her script. She needed to get this straight in her head. Had she and ...Grady... - it was a struggle even to think his name - behaved *completely* inappropriately in front of Freya? And her fingers were still crossed about the condom situation.

"So... did you happen to notice what time I, I mean we, or ...maybe just I... got back? I don't remember looking at my watch at any point."

The combination of inner shame and embarrassment reached its peak as Freya stared at her friend's increasingly uncontrollable blushes.

"Jesus, Tilda! You can't remember anything can you? Not a thing. Blimey. And you're always the one who tells me who I snogged and where I fell over. This is hilarious! This is UNPRECEDENTED."

"Please... I just need to know."

"Oh matey, where to begin!"

With the empty cups resting neatly by her side on the grass, she flicked through the pages she had completed that morning. They had been encouraged to spend as much time as possible exploring the area, using the information pack and workbook as a guide. In a post-breakfast speech, Lorna had implored them to take advantage of the full day, reminding them that once they returned to the village they would have no opportunity to gather any missing details. The coach back to the hostel was leaving at 4pm and they needed to be on it, complete with a full set of data, diagrams and notes.

Those were the words Lorna had used. What the students heard however, was 'Spend no more than an hour at the cave today - just enough to blag your way through the workbook. Then use the rest of the day to sunbathe or find a beer garden. Or both.' And now here she was. Tilda, behaving un-Tilda-like. Again. She had raced through the questions and tasks, even making up some of the answers and was now sitting in an idyllic suntrap feeling, although not completely tip top, the best she'd felt so far today, drinking tea and wondering what she was going to do for the next three hours. Three hours with her new friend.

"You definitely did not do it."
"Definitely not?"
Freya was firm.
"Definitely not."
"How can you be so sure?"
"Because, Tilds, my little stud-muffin, you just didn't have the opportunity. I left you in the pub, but with my vom-diversion, we arrived back here together. Then - and I didn't understand this last night, and I still don't - you proceeded to talk. Talk, talk, talk, all frigging night. I zoned in and out of sleep but every time I woke up, you were still chatting. I've known you for over two years and I have never heard you say that much in your life. You remained fully clothed at all times, only taking your jeans off when you got into bed. I was awake at that

point. In fact, I think I actually asked you to keep the noise down. I mean, how funny is that! Ha ha. We had one hell of a role reversal, matey. I even had to go and get the drinks you forgot to buy, like it was ME who was the sensible one making sure everyone was OK. What happened to us last night? Ha ha."

These revelations had provided immediate relief. Freya had continued to laugh as Tilda mentally un-crossed her fingers and breathed out loudly. She had been worrying about where she would find a Morning After Pill in the middle of the Lake District and now she didn't need to. Thank God for that. But now a new ave-nue of worry forced its way in. If she hadn't been having sex, what the hell had she been doing? She couldn't im-agine anything she could have done that would have filled hours and that someone else would have wanted to share.

"Freya, did you see what was going on? What was I talking about? Oh, God, was I really embarrassing? What was Grady doing? Was he bored?"

Freya snorted.

"Bored? Yeah right. He was listening intently and then giving you a load of chat back. It was like you both told each other everything you think about everything - IN ONE NIGHT. It was mental."

"But not embarrassing?"

Freya considered her response for a moment whilst pulling on a jumper from her rucksack.

"I think YOU might think you'd embarrassed your-self, because you were so *unlike* you, if you know what I mean."

Did she ever.

"But - and this is the most important bit - you were just like a friendly, chatty, normal person. No offence, Tilds, but you know what I mean. You never talk about yourself, which is totally cool, and I'm not saying you should. But most people do. So last night, you were like most other people."

"I was like a normal person? I can cope with that, I think."

"No, on second thoughts, you were more than that. Normal people are boring and talk shit every so often. You didn't. Everything you said was interesting and the Graham bloke was really listening. Like, properly listening. And you sort of... sparkled. It was like there was a light shining on your face. You didn't look like yourself, but you looked better than normal."

"Oh. Right. Thank you, I think."

Freya was now fully dressed and ready to hit breakfast. She sensed it was time to move things on. Picking up her bag, she lightened the mood.

"So, Tilda, my chatty chum, worry no more. Rest assured your worst fears are unfounded. You did not ride Graham's bone in my face whilst being off your tits on dodgy Sambuca!" She burst into a cackle of laughter at Tilda's admonishing face.

"Freya! You're disgusting and his name is Grady. Let's go and get some food to shut you up."

Tilda, well used to Freya's turn of phrase was still shocked now and then. Freya chuckled, as she always did when grossing out Timid-Tilda. Not so Timid last night though. Not so timid at all.

"How are you feeling?"

He nudged up to her as he moved his bag and file out of the way.

"Much better I think. Thanks for the tea. That definitely helped."

"I knew I'd seen a kiosk on the way in. Not great but

better than nothing. How have we done with the pack? Do you think we can cobble together the write-up with what we've got?"

"I think so. I made some more notes while you were away. There should be enough there. If not, someone from your course will help, I'm sure."

Grady took his fleece from his backpack and rolled it up. Placing it under his head, he settled back on the rocks, and looked up at the sky. Such a beautiful day. Such a *strange* day. It had started out so wonderfully, then gone terribly wrong, but with the misunderstanding cleared up at breakfast it was now back on track. It amused him to realise she had no recollection of most of their conversation. It had been intense and illuminating. It had been euphoric. It was the best night he'd had in a long time. The fact she was unable to recall much of what had been said after about 11pm caused him a big sigh of relief. He had probably bored her senseless, banging on and on the way he did when he was pissed. As it was, he felt like he'd been given a second chance at impressing her. A second chance to get to know her. He didn't want to cock it up again. Not now they had a few hours to spare and a sunny afternoon just waiting for them.

"Do you think the powers that be will be *very* cross that we worked together? You know, blurring the University lines." Tilda had worried about this all morning. They had been clearly told to partner up with fellow colleagues. It had been Freya that had pushed her towards Grady.

"I'm sure they won't care as long as we get the work done. Anyway, we've finished it for the day. Now we can do whatever we like."

"I want to sit here and never move." Tilda said, emphasising her point by leaning back on her arms, content like a cat in the sun.

"That's a perfect plan. Do you mind if I continue to join you? He sat up momentarily in case she had suddenly changed her mind and bade him leave. He didn't want to presume how she felt, again. She giggled in response.

"Of course you can join me. I explained about this morning - I was just embarrassed. And annoyed my memory was being such a let down."

He lay back down, one hand behind his head, looking up at the sky.

"The good news about your lack of memory, is I can treat last night as a rehearsal for the edited, wittier, more polished conversation we are about to have. If an anecdote bombed last night, it can get cut today. If I tried to make you laugh yesterday and you looked at me weirdly, then I know to avoid that joke now."

"That's great for you," Tilda replied, "but what about me? I'm going to end up repeating myself over and over, and sending you to sleep."

He flashed a smile for a second before seeming to take her seriously again.

"Tilda Willoughby, you proved last night that you are not going to send me to sleep. I wish you had so that I wouldn't feel so knackered today. Now, let's see if you give the same answers sober as you do when you are shit-faced. What's your favourite type of music?"

"Oh God, I hate this question. I never know what to say."

"Brilliant, that's exactly what you said last night."

"Did I? Well it must be the truth." Tilda laughed. "I suppose whenever I buy a tape it's always a compilation - I've got the Greatest Hits of 91, 92, 93, and 94."

"What happened last year?"

"I think my Dad forgot. Those ones are usually a Christmas present from him. I listen to them all but not enough to feel the need to keep the set up-to-date. What's your favourite music? You'll have told me this already, won't you?"

"I did mention it, but it's fine. The fact you are kind enough to ask again means so much more." He smiled and Tilda laughed. She was getting used to recognising when he was being serious and when he was teasing her. It seemed about a fifty-fifty split.

"Like I said last night, anything vaguely folky and from the sixties or early seventies. Principally, Bob Dylan but there are others. I like Joan Baez, Donovan, some of the Beatles…"

"That's unusual, for someone our age, isn't it? I know 2 Unlimited aren't everybody's cup of tea, but you can't knock their musical contribution to the world."

He paused for a split-second too long, indicating she had him, before laughing in relief.

"Wow, I really thought you were serious then. I need to pay better attention. Yes, it's unusual I suppose, but they were my Mum's favourite music and I guess I just inherited her taste. Now then, what about books? Do you read, and if so, who?"

"I *do* read, but not as often as I should."

"How often do you think you *should* read?"

"Well you know how some people always have a book on the go? You see them on the bus and they're engrossed. They miss their stop because they're paying no attention to anything else. I wish I was like that but I'm not. I can't imagine being so reckless as to lose all sense of time, just because something is distracting me."

Grady sat up again and gave Tilda an accusing look.

"Oh really?"

She blushed.

"I thought I'd explained. Last night was completely out of character for me. And you didn't distract me, you got me drunk. That's different."

Of course! How could I forget?" Grady lay back down, smiling. "It was *me* that repeatedly forced shots down your neck. How remiss of me to forget."

"You're not funny so stop trying to be," she said, struggling to hide her grin.

"OK, OK, I'm sorry. But you still haven't told me what books you like."

She considered her answer. It was another question that made her appear dull and unadventurous.

"I suppose anything with a good story. I like thrillers and mysteries. Stories where the last chapter has a couple of unexpected twists."

"Are you in the middle of anything at the moment?"

"An Inspector Morse novel, you know?"

"Yes, I know. Any good?"

"It's all right, but I've seen the TV episode so I know what's going to happen. That's probably why I only read a couple of chapters every few weeks. Twists aren't so gripping when you know they're coming."

"I guess they're not."

"So, what are you reading at the moment? Anything you want to recommend?"

Delighted by her interest, Grady reached out and grabbed his rucksack from the side of the rocks. Fishing around inside, he eventually pulled out what looked like a battered volume of poetry. Slim, grey and clearly well read.

"I've recently discovered Ralph Waldo-Emerson."

"He must be so pleased."

He smiled at her joke, but continued in earnest.

"You know when you meet a new person or you read

someone's writing and they have exactly the same thoughts and feelings as you do, and yet they put them across in a far more eloquent way, so you're in awe of them but also feel like they share your soul as well?"

Grady's eyes were dancing with excitement. He looked child-like.

"I don't think I've found that in Colin Dexter but go on."

"I know I sound like an arse, but seriously, I love this guy. He's a more intelligent, more experienced, wittier, more enlightened version of me. He's brilliant."

"Then that begs the question, why on earth am I wasting my time listening to you whitter on, when I could be getting the undiluted original version some- where else?"

"I imagine his death over a hundred years ago has levelled the playing field a bit. I might even have the edge on him now." Grady returned the book to his bag, before continuing.

"Last night was the first night in months that I ha- ven't read a few pages before I went to sleep."

"I can only offer my humblest apologies," Tilda said.

She looked up, checking he knew she was being sar- castic. It seemed he did. With his bag zipped up once more, Grady returned to his spot in the sun.

"So, you don't read much, according to your protes- tations this morning you don't take random men home, and you're not really into music either. What do you *do* before you go to bed? My mind is boggling."

"Get your filthy mind out of the sewer. I brush my teeth, write my journal and turn out the light."

"Your journal?" Grady was alert once more.

"Yes, journal. I know it sounds daft, but I like to rec- ord my thoughts from the day, before going to sleep. I'd rather my conscious mind took charge instead of my subconscious having to sort it out in the night. I'm not a fan of bad dreams."

"Does it work?"

"I'm not sure, to be honest. It's just a habit now. I do like to try and make sense of the day, though. Forget *your* reading, last night was the first time in *years* I didn't record something... anything."

"What would you have written if you had?"

He immediately wished he hadn't asked the question. He didn't want to hear anything approaching regret or worse... dismissal in her voice. If she had noticed his panic, she didn't acknowledge it and he was grateful.

"If I'd written yesterday, I would've mentioned the journey which was long and annoying, added some details about the Youth Hostel, described the country pub and the fire that made it all so cosy..."

Tilda paused as she considered her next words. It would be wrong to imply he had made no impact on her, but she still clung to some notion that playing it cool was a good idea, for a little while longer at least.

"Anything else?" Grady fished.

Tilda breathed in. So far, playing it cool hadn't worked that well today. Maybe she should just be honest.

"I *might* have added that I met a lovely boy in the pub and we put the world to rights whilst consuming copious amounts of alcohol. Even though I wouldn't have remembered any of that if I'd written it before I went to bed."

Grady felt a sense of relief. For an awful moment he thought she was going to pretend they hadn't had a connection. If *he* had written a journal last night it would have filled pages. Time to lighten the mood again.

"Boy? Is that how you see me? I'm six foot four, you know."

"I know, you're massive."

"Why, thank you very much."

Tilda blushed. Every sentence was a potential minefield.

"Stop it. I didn't mean it like that. Anyway, 'man' feels too grown up. We're not ready for titles like that yet. I'm certainly no lady."

Grady laughed loudly at her chosen words, as she blushed even harder with the realisation of what she'd said. How he loved winding her up.

"That is excellent news! You must be very popular with the other *boys*."

"Shut up. You know what I meant."

"Yeah, I know. So, you write your diary..."

"Journal! Diary sounds teenagery."

"OK, so you write your journal in order to control your subconscious when you sleep?"

"Yes. Something like that."

"Blimey, Freud would have a field day with you."

"He'd just tell me I had penis-envy and that my personality was the result of botched potty training." Tilda thought for a second. "Actually you're right, Freud would have a lot to say."

"Why?"

Tilda thought it over for a few seconds. Had they reached *that* point? The point where she would over share and everything would change. Up to now, the afternoon had been full of lighthearted repartee, mutual teasing and genuine interest in each other's thoughts. If she took a step back from where she'd started to head, she could steer Grady away from the reality of her, the reality of Tilda. Away from the thoughts that made her less fun than she had managed to seem so far.

Silently, Tilda continued her whistle stop tour of the darker spaces in her head, to find the opposing argument. All she could come up with was the fact he'd asked her a question and so far, she'd liked answering everything he'd asked. '*Why would Freud have a field day with her?*' Looking at him waiting patiently for her response, she was reassured. He didn't look, or act, like any other boy - or man - she had ever met. Maybe it would be good to continue to trust him with herself.

She took a deep breath, and said it quickly.

"I think Freud would have a field day with me because my Mum died when I was a child. I remember her, and I remember her dying. I'm sure it will have affected me in some way. I'm not sure in what way yet, other than obvious bereavement stuff, but that would be Freud's problem to figure out, not mine."

Grady looked at her, her clear eyes looking back with an air of resignation. She seemed full of acceptance, like it had happened to someone else, and she was just retelling the story. He must have sensed it, on some level at least. This must be why he was drawn to her.

"When did she die?"

"March 6th 1983. I was seven."

"I'm really sorry."

"Thank you, but don't be. It was a long time ago and she'd been ill for most of my life."

"She loved you for seven years. That's got to mean something." His voice caught in his throat, causing him to cough. Reaching out, he took Tilda's hand. She was touched by the gesture and the comment. He seemed far more affected than he was allowing himself to appear. She, on the other hand, was calm and distant from the pain. It was just fact-sharing. Or at least it had been so far.

"I'm fine about it, seriously."

He was quiet for a moment. He wanted to know everything about her but he didn't want to pry or make her upset. This was one area of conversation that had not been rehearsed last night. Finally he spoke.

"Do you have brothers and sisters?"

Tilda sighed. She still focused on the facts but feelings were beginning to surface. The dull ache was starting. Soon it would feel distinctly stabby.

"No, none. I think it would have been much easier if I had. There'd be others I could talk to, you know, relive memories or laugh at funny things she used to say. Instead, there's just me and my Dad, and almost overnight, he sank into old age."

Tilda's voice dropped as she cast her mind back to that time. So long ago, but now she was dwelling on it, surprisingly raw.

"He was only forty, but when you look at the photos in the album from one Christmas to the next, he looks terrible. Grey, slumped, forcing a smile for the camera. It must have been awful for him."

"It must have been awful for you too," Grady said, softly.

"Yes, I suppose it was. People were very nice."

Tilda continued to let Grady hold her hand. It felt good, in spite of the stomach-churning memories that were being unearthed. The sleepless nights when all she could hear were her Dad's sobs. The sympathetic yet inappropriate stares from anyone she walked past on the street, or Mrs. Wilson the kindly next-door neighbour that plied her dad with casseroles and her - when the time came - with a hand-me-down trainer bra and packets of sanitary towels. These were memories she rarely visited and so that when she did - for this brief moment - it felt reassuring to have someone with her. Grady squeezed her hand before letting go. She looked up and breathed deeply. The lid needed to be closed on the box. Time to move on.

Tilda cleared her throat.

"Enough about me. What about you? Tell me about your parents. What was your childhood like?"

At this, Grady shuffled himself upright and sat cross-legged in front of her. She wasn't sure if she was being overly sensitive but it seemed his body-language was now far nearer the brace position than when he'd been contentedly outstretched earlier. Maybe she shouldn't have asked.

"It seems, Tilda Willoughby, that we have more in common that we first realised."

Tilda guessed before he said it. *Oh dear. How tragic their lives were.*

"I, too, was raised by my father after the untimely death of my mother. It happened when I was a baby. I have no memory of her whatsoever."

"Grady, I'm so sorry. Look at the pair of us. Not a mother between us." She took his hand, not consciously realising she was mirroring his gesture from moments ago.

"You said you'd inherited her taste in music? How did you?"

"I was rooting in a cupboard one day and I found a box. I must have been about ten years old. It was full of records. People I'd never heard of. I asked my dad and he said I could have them. Turns out they had belonged to my Mum. The only music we had on at home was the radio and then it would be something classical. Not that it happened very often. I'd spend hours listening to those records, with my headphones on, shutting out everyone else and trying to imagine what she was like.

I've only ever seen a couple of old photos. The music makes me feel like I know her."

He forced a smile towards her, that when she reflected back at him, made him smile for real. Like Tilda, he didn't tend to share this much detail within hours of meeting someone. It didn't feel wrong or uncomfortable, though, so he continued.

"I was the only kid at school without a Mum. And there was always some event that made that crystal clear. A sports day, an end of year play, an awards evening - I was always the kid without anyone there. It was pretty shit really."

"What about your Dad?" Tilda asked gently.

"He'd be busy with work. We had a series of au pairs move in but they were usually only there for a few months, until they got homesick or got a proper job. One was there for longer - Anna. She spent eight years with us. I remember her as a little boy and how fun she made things. She still keeps in touch. It was her birthday yesterday actually. She was the reason I was in such a rush to get to the phone box when I ran into you. I wanted to be there for six."

Something inside Tilda slotted into place. She had assumed it was a girlfriend he was calling. The thought hadn't quite made itself known until she knew the real reason for his call. And now, her inner caution had released her and she could relax. She continued the chat, free to listen and free to hear everything he said. In spite of the subject matter, she felt lighter inside.

"Au pairs? You must have been well off."

"Yes, it seems we were. It's only when I left home and met other people that I realised how comfortable we must be. I never wanted for anything that could be bought, and it seems I'm the only student I know without the full complement of loans to my name. But still, money can only buy you so much."

Tilda looked at his face, the cloud now seeming to pass as he smiled down at her. He had been lost in thought but was now back. She returned the smile and his shoulders visibly relaxed as she laced her fingers between his as he settled back on the rocks.

"Well that all got a bit heavy, didn't it, especially with your hangover. We'd better change the subject before we all start weeping in unison. Tilda, tell me, what on earth do you plan to do in approximately six months time when you are the lucky recipient of a first class Geography degree?"

Tilda burst out laughing. The atmosphere was comical once more. She met his sarcasm head on.

"For the record, I think they'll have to create a *Super-Duper A Star First* category because my final grades will be *that* impressive. Not. And secondly, I have no idea, other than the fact I can't bear the thought of having studied a subject like Geography and having only seen a fraction of the world. Not even that, a fraction of the country."

"Haven't you had lots of residentials like we have?"

"Yes, but to all the same kinds of places. Caves, rocks and lakes. I've stayed in some really stunning areas but I've spent so much time with my head in a notebook, constantly thinking about what I need to record for the assignment, that I've not noticed anything about the place I'm in. They've all merged together in my mind, and other than the specific natural phenomenon we've been studying, I couldn't tell you anything about each trip. The beauty hasn't stuck with me. It's been lost in all the boring detail. Isn't that sad?"

Grady nodded, solemnly.

"Very sad. It reminds me of something I read the

other day. Wait a second, let me find it."

Once again, Grady rooted in his bag for his book, and then flicked through the pages until he found the place he wanted.

"Ready for this? It's classic Emerson."

"Ooh, classic Emerson," she teased. "I'm ready."

He cleared his throat.

"*Though we travel the world over to find the beautiful, we must carry it with us or we find it not.* Pretty good, isn't it?"

"I suppose so. What does it mean?"

"I think it means that all the fantastically exotic travel experiences in the world don't mean shit if we are blind to the wonders that the more mundane of details provide, and keep them inside us forever."

"OK, I see that, I suppose."

"And so, as you have already admitted, one week in the English countryside has begun to merge into every other week you've spent in the English countryside. Am I right?"

"That's what I said, yes." Tilda was amused with how seriously he was taking this. He continued.

"And you also admitted that you felt that was a sad state of affairs to be in, yes?"

"Yes I suppose I did."

"So in that case, we must do something about it."

"Oh yeah? And what do you suggest we do?"

"We are going to lie here..." he spread out his fleece and beckoned her to lie back on it, as he did the same, supporting himself with one hand behind his head, "... and take in every detail of today. We are going to remember the sky, the rocks, the cave entrance, the smell of the wild flowers, the buzz of the insects, the..."

"OK, OK, I've got the gist. You're telling me to pay attention to the details. I need to find the beauty in the smallest of... *things*. I get it."

Tilda shimmied herself into position, and lay her head on the fabric. Grady's earnest enthusiasm for this task was so endearing she felt duty bound to take it seriously. She breathed in and out, filling her lungs with fresh air. Her closed eyes heightened her other senses, enabling her to hear the echoing muffles of visitors currently in the cave. She opened them to see the clouds, still and expansive, filling the sky like marshmallows. Turning her head, she noticed the myriad of colours on the outcrop of stone to her left. Greys, chocolates and fawns were enlivened by a shimmer of greens here, and a silvery splash there. It was almost dazzling in the sun. Texture and tone creating movement and light before her very eyes. Just a moment ago, she'd have described the rock as 'brown'.

Grady shifted his position, draping an arm casually across her waist - the second time in less than twelve hours. She was conscious this time and she snuggled herself back into his body just as before, as she continued to notice, continued to really *see* the world around her. He looked at her face as she took in her surroundings. God, how he'd love to paint her. To capture the life that was pouring out of her as she noticed each new petal or clump of moss. How he hoped this trip would not be forgotten as easily as the others had. She turned to him, breathlessly, her skin radiant with the fresh air, and her eyes shining brightly.

"It's beautiful," she said.

Despite having thought of little else since meeting her, he hadn't planned this. He had no idea what to do, or how to proceed when his brain was screaming at him, 'kiss her'. This was truly organic - a meeting of lost souls, of fellow adventurers in life. He hadn't tried to force the issue, or convince her of his credentials. He'd been more open and honest with her than with anyone else he could remember. She'd had plenty of time to run for the hills and yet had remained where she was. But still, the doubts lingered. Maybe she was just a kind person that chatted to anyone. Perhaps she had fallen out with her friends and had no one else to pair up with today. He lay there in limbo, his arms around her, her face so close yet he was paralysed with fear. *For God's sake Grady, act!*

Luckily for him, she took charge. Before the moment was lost forever, she lifted her face towards his and kissed him. The echoes from the cave, the fragrance of the flowers and the shades of rock all faded into the background, as another beautiful detail in a world crammed full, firmly took its place.

Part Two

CHAPTER EIGHTEEN

Alice. Friday 23rd September 2016. York.

The big house was silent. Only the beep of machines and the quiet footsteps of her staff punctuated the peace. Alice held the phone to her ear and repeated what in the past week, had fast become the most irritating aspect of this employment.

"Still no luck?" Flo popped her head around the door as she passed.

"No, nothing."

"Almost like they're avoiding us, don't you think?"

Alice ignored her and continued to listen to the ringing tone. This had never happened before. Someone always answered eventually.

"Anything I can do?" Flo was still leaning on the doorframe. Alice knew her sudden spurt of helpfulness was because she was avoiding having to go and sit with the man. Now that he was sleeping most of the time, there was little to do and the long hours had suddenly become much longer. She should tell her to get back to her post but she was feeling the shift drag just as much.

"Maybe you could put the kettle on? I think a strong coffee is exactly what I need. Would that be ok?"

"No problem, coming right up."

With a sanctioned skive under her belt, Flo swept away. Her energy levels appeared to rise over the course of the conversation and there was a hint of bounce in her step as she left Gregor alone for a little

longer. Alice ignored it and kept on with her increasingly fruitless task.

The phone continued to ring out. There wasn't even
an answer-phone that took charge after twenty rings.
Alice knew this because she had waited until twenty-
one. Then the next time, just in case, she'd waited until
thirty. Now she was pretty sure it had rung over fifty
times. She didn't have time for this.

Neither did the man. Neither did William.

It had been a conscious effort on her part to encour-
age the team to call 'the man', William. It was a standard
professional courtesy to engage with a client by the repeated use of their name. It happened in similar
situations on a daily basis in hospital wards the world
over. It came naturally almost all of the time. The trouble with *William* was that it had been very difficult to
establish a rapport, a sense of a relationship, or to see
him as fully human. He was either deeply asleep, or
thoroughly unpleasant. Alice was getting tired of trying
to defend him because he was on his last legs. In his
most recent moments of consciousness, twenty hours
ago, he had continued his racist diatribe against Flo,
done his best to physically assault Gregor as he was trying to give him some water and, albeit with slurred
speech, made grotesquely lascivious remarks about her
own body, to the point where she would have feared for
her physical safety if her abuser had not been at death's
door and attached to a machine.

...fifty-nine, sixty, sixty-one...

She hung up again. The Next of Kin had clearly had
enough of the man - of *William* - as they had. She
checked the details once more. A York address. Reasonably local. No reason why he'd be unable to come and
visit if he wanted. Alice had seen relatives fly in from

Australia to witness their family members drift off into the great unknown. This particular Next of Kin was definitely making a choice.

A quick knock and the door opened again. It was Gregor.

"You said to let you know if anything changed, well, he's awake again but only just. Not saying much but looking like he hates me. So, you know... he's properly conscious, not just looking like it. I think he'll go back to sleep in a bit, but if you wanted to tap him up for details, now's your chance."

Alice nodded. Gregor was a good nurse but not the best communicator. 'Tapping him up for details' meant gently venturing towards the subject of who, if anyone, he was related to and why they weren't there. She knew this was a pointless exercise but it had to be attempted nonetheless. Alice put down the phone and followed Gregor into the makeshift bedroom.

"Good afternoon, William, how are you feeling today?"

"Fff off." His meaning was clear even when his speech was less so.

"I will fuck off in a minute, William, but before I do, I just wanted to see if there was anyone you wanted me to ring. Any family or friends I could contact for you? It'd be nice to have people you like here instead of people you dislike."

His dark eyes danced with anger as he flashed them up at Alice, who in spite of her gut feelings was smiling calmly at the end of the bed.

"Noown, gawaay." He closed his eyes, hoping that would make her 'gawaay' without any more effort.

"I have a name here, William. A Mr. Grady? Is that your brother? Your son? A nephew? I don't have any more information so you need to help me. He's been making sure we've been taking care of you. I'm sure he'd like to know how you are. Who is he? He shares your last name."

William Grady's eyes remained closed. It seemed as if he'd drifted back into the sleep that was taking up the majority of his time. Alice stood there for a while longer, casting her eye over the wires and tubes, checking no one had cut any corners. Everything appeared as it should. A quick pulse check - it was weak but steady - and she turned to leave the room. She had notes to finish and she should probably try the elusive Mr. Grady again before calling it a day. She opened the door.

"Snnns."

She turned back in surprise. The eyes were still closed, but he'd managed to speak.

"What was that, William? What did you say?"

A cloud of anger passed over his face, as he had to summon the energy to repeat himself because the *bitch* hadn't heard.

"Snnns. Ife... snns."

Alice stepped nearer, delighted to have made progress however minuscule. This was indeed a breakthrough.

"You have sons? Thank you for telling me, William. Is this Mr. Grady one of your sons? I'd like to chat to him if I can.

The inconvenience of having to say everything twice, suddenly seemed to intensify. William's face, already ravaged with age and disease plummeted further into the depths of anger. Like a cartoon baddie, with laser beams for eyes, he directed his glare at Alice who was quite taken aback with its power.

"I'm sorry, I didn't mean to..."

He interrupted her, although not easily. His breath

was on borrowed time.

"Not snns. Snnn. Ife wn sn."

And at that, William Grady, with one son, sank back into the pillow, closed his eyes and returned to the vegetative state that he'd occupied for the majority of the previous week.

CHAPTER NINETEEN

Tilda and Bea. Friday 23rd September 2016. Stockport.

It had been a week since her trip to the loft.

A week of the nine-to-five routine at the council, a week of quiet meals whilst sitting in front the new season of Autumn Watch, and a week of remembering the person she used to be and the plans she once made. The plans that, for reasons she did not know, had never amounted to anything. How different her life would have been if only...

No Tilda!

She commanded herself to stop thinking about all that. No good could ever come of it. To the outside world she was the same old Tilda. Quietly spoken, meticulous with detail, always reliable and steady. Inside, however, she was on fire. The gut-wrenching pain of lost dreams tinged with the rose-tinted glow of nostalgia meant her mind was highly disordered. Anchoring herself to the monotony of spell-checking a document or making tea for the office forced her to keep it together when she had to be with other people. When she was alone, however, she was a mess. She had unlocked deeply suppressed emotions. She tended to daydream whenever she had the chance. One minute she'd be getting on with her day but then she'd suddenly find herself laughing as she remembered a specific exchange they'd had. Outside the caves, on the phone, through the post - she remembered them all, and they invigorated her. She felt *alive*. But then she would be overwhelmed again, and have to force her mind to focus on the mundane; a shopping list, a colleague's maternity collection, the steam clean for the hall carpet. Her inner world swung between intentional boredom and unrestrained memories. Somewhere in the middle of all that was Tilda, hanging on and waiting for it to calm down to something more manageable. She had coped for a week so far, and would continue to do so until that time came. Or until something else happened that changed everything all over again. She hoped so, anyway.

"Psst... Tilda, come here."

Tilda looked around at the midpoint in her journey from the photocopier to her desk. It was Bea. She had cupped her hands around her mouth, drawing more attention to herself than the almost-shouted 'Psst' had presumably intended to cause.

"Psssssst ... TILDA ... over here."

Tilda sighed and changed direction. Gripping the back of a chair from an adjacent desk, she wheeled it over and sat herself down.

"What can I do for you, Bea. I've only just made a cuppa, if that's what you're angling for."

"Shh, Tilda. Be quiet, it's nothing to do with tea, and I'll do the next one anyway. No, it's something much more exciting."

Tilda smiled. Bea was a useful distraction.

"What is it, then? I'm all agog." To illustrate the point, Tilda did her best impression of what she considered *agog* might look. It turned out more petrified than inquisitive, which resulted in both women bursting into laughter and getting an across-the-office stare from Susan Donaldson.

'Shit. Look, take this policy and pretend we are knee-deep in its every word. I need to talk to you and I can't do it with Tan Tights looking at me."

Tilda took the bundle of papers and gave a reasonable impersonation of someone fascinated by their contents. Seconds later, Susan Donaldson returned to whatever task was taking up this portion of her day so Bea could resume the matter in hand.

"Now, Tilda, Tilda my darling, I don't want you to take this the wrong way."

"That sounds ominous."

"No, it's not. Just listen. I wanted to tell you that I'm not sure what you've done - whether it's a new haircut, or a different body lotion, or you've lost weight - not that you need to, I'm just saying - but you've done something different..."

"Alright then..." Tilda was unsure so let Bea carry on.

"...and whatever you've done, it's making you look *fabulous*."

For Bea, to be described as fabulous was the highest compliment one could possibly receive. Bea lived for fabulous. On the days Bea felt anything less than fabulous, she rang in sick or used her precious flexi-time. Fabulous was a pre-requisite of getting out of bed. However, she knew that not everyone shared her standards. Particularly Tilda.

Tilda Rudd was a wonderful colleague. Always there, always reliable, happy to put up with Bea being Bea, and never one to moan about doing a tea run. But there was no doubt that Tilda was, in the nicest possible way, a complete Plain Jane. Not unattractive, just plain. Several years younger than Bea, she was thinner, had less wrinkles around her eyes, had much clearer skin with very little make up and, as far as Bea could make out, an absolutely perfect arse for someone who sat down for the majority of the day. Bea could see that Tilda screamed potential but that frustratingly, she didn't care about any of that. It had frustrated Bea. It had crossed her mind that as an office bonding activity, when Tilda had first joined the team, she should suggest giving her a make-over. In hindsight, she was very glad she had decided against this. Tilda would have hated it, been offended or just plain uncomfortable and Bea would have lost out on what had become a pretty good friendship. She had learned to accept the situation and rarely thought about it. Until this week. She sat back as her friend responded, genuinely curious as to what Tilda would say.

"I've not changed anything. I promise. If I'm being honest, I've not been sleeping well the last few nights so I'd have thought I look a bit rougher than normal. But thank you very much for the compliment. I appreciate it."

Tilda made to get up, but Bea's firm hand pulled her back down.

"Not so fast Missy, I've not finished. I've given you the chance to explain, which you haven't, so I'm going to have to drag it out of you. For the record, I know exactly what's different."

"Really? Because a minute ago you thought I'd changed my body lotion. I don't even have an original body lotion to move on from."

Tilda smiled but Bea ignored her.

"I'm not stupid. You're wearing eyeliner. It looks great and you should do it more, but I wonder why that's started now? Also, you must think I'm blind but after almost two decades of your hair being pulled back in a black bobble, did you think I wouldn't notice that it's suddenly loose. I mean LOOSE - flowing over your shoulders with a bit of a wave to it. I mean, what the fuck Tilda? It looks gorgeous, but why? Why now? Plus, I think, although I can't be sure, that you are wearing a new cardy. Whether you've bought it this week or if it is something you usually wear at weekends, I don't know. But it is fine knit. Fine knit! Christ, Tilda, I have seen your chunky, comfy, woolly cardies on the back of your chair since you started here. Suddenly you are wearing a sexy, fine knit, figure-hugging piece of knitwear. I can barely recognize you. What the *actual* fuck?"

Tilda continued to laugh off the seriousness of Bea's accusations. It hadn't occurred to her that she'd look any different even if she felt it on the inside. The eye-liner was part distraction from any potential puffiness after a secret emotional episode, and the loose hair was because back in the day, that's how she did it. Grady had only seen her with loose hair and through some sublim-inal thought process she must have decided to revert to her student look. Spending so much mental energy rec-reating those days in her head, it made sense to recreate her physical self that way too. She didn't think anyone else would have paid the slightest bit of attention. And as for the cardy, well it was just a cardy. One she had worn on a Christmas do a couple of years earlier and had been hardly worn since. She had just felt like giving it an airing this week.

"Thanks Bea. I'm glad you like my new look. I just wanted to try something different, that's all. I'll be sure to tell Mike you approve." She stood up. Once again, Bea had other ideas.

"Bullshit, Tilda. Sit down."

Something about her tone made Tilda sit down im-mediately.

"Now, I'm only going to ask you this once and for the record, I will in no way be judging or disapproving of whatever the answer might be. You know that is not my vibe in the slightest. Just tell me."

"OK?"

"Are you shagging someone else?"

With an involuntary hand to her chest, Tilda gasped in surprise.

"No, I am not...*shagging,*" she mouthed, "...someone else. As if I have the time! Or as if I want to," she added hastily.

"Well if you say you're not, then you're not. I believe you."

"Thanks. Good to know."

"But seriously, Tilda. If you were, and you wanted to talk about it, I would be here if you needed me. I'm open-minded and a good listener. Plus, I've done EVERYTHING. I might be just what you need."

"Thanks, I'll bear that in mind. I'm going to go now."

Tilda got up and walked away. She felt sick. The outward control she thought she had on the situation, was clearly not fooling anyone. Or maybe it was just Bea. Either way, something different needed to be done. She couldn't cope with this for much longer.

Across the office, Alex viewed the furtive chat between the women with great suspicion.

"What do you think they're talking about?" He turned to Si, who looked up momentarily.

"God knows. Bras? Waxing?" He shuddered at the next thought. "Tampons?"

"Nah. Bea talks about all that openly. She sent me out on my lunch last week to buy..." - his voice lowered as the painful memory returned - "...feminine wipes."

"Oh mate. I'm sorry." Si felt his pain. He'd not long got over being hit in the side of the face by her playfully thrown Moon Cup. He hadn't known what it was until he'd searched for it later. The trauma was still with him.

"They've defo got a secret. Tilda has never looked so guilty."

Alex considered it for a few seconds.

"Or hot. Tilda has never looked so hot."

"Agreed."

And with the matter sorted, both men got back to the business of the day, which at that moment was finding out which Game of Thrones character they most resembled. It was a busy morning.

It took about an hour. Tilda made another cup of tea and forced herself to type up a draft response to the latest White Paper before she decided to take Bea up on her offer. Bringing a different bundle of decoy documents with her, she returned to the empty chair next to the desk and tried to decide what to say. Bea was in the middle of scouring Facebook so Tilda made conversation.

"What're you looking for this time?"

"Apparently there's a group whose sole focus is the pulling apart of our housing policy sentence by sentence. Tan Tights told me to make sure it's all hot air. I mean, we had it checked by legal, so we're fine. They're just a bunch of grammar pedants. Anyway, ignore me. I've also used the time to update my status. Look."

She turned the monitor towards Tilda who read aloud the mini paragraph being highlighted by a grinning Bea.

"I've just said to a colleague, I'm open-minded, a good listener, and I've done EVERYTHING. That should be my personal ad! LOL."

Bea sat grinning away, as Tilda smiled encouragingly at her.

"That's good. Very funny."

"I know, I amuse myself, anyway. I could never work in a department that didn't have Facebook access. What on earth would I do for the majority of the day? Now, what is it I can do you for?"

Tilda took a breath and launched into her rehearsed monologue.

"I was thinking about what you said earlier. And, no, don't get excited I'm not having an affair..."

Bea made no attempt to hide her disappointment at this admission of fidelity.

"... but, I am a bit distracted this week, and I thought it might help if I talked to someone, you know, to clear my head. Are you game?"

"Am I game? AM I GAME? Tilda, I am all ears. Spill the beans, share the load. Let me help!"

Bea felt genuinely touched that Tilda had come to her, largely forgetting it had been her forcing of the issue that had prompted it. She sat back with pretend papers in her hand, and listened. She hadn't lied, she was a good listener, and she was definitely non-judgmental. She was all ears and ready to help.

It hadn't taken long. There had been a few questions here and there, the odd moment of emotion where Tilda's eyes had watered and, a quite frankly incredulous Bea, who in spite of her proud non-judgmental status, was struggling with several aspects of the story. Then it was over. Tilda sat back taking a few deep breaths whilst Bea considered how best to frame the questions that were somersaulting in her mind. There was no point procrastinating, there'd been too much of that already.

"I'll be honest with you Tilds, I'm struggling with this one. I can't get my head around the way you're behaving."

Tilda stopped surreptitiously wiping her eyes and looked up, the shame of having over-shared plastered across her face.

"I'm so sorry Bea. Please don't tell anyone. I'm so ashamed that I'm even thinking about him. I just needed to get it off my chest, I've not done anything wrong really. I've been happily married for such a long time, I just don't want Mike to..."

Bea cut her off.

"Stop. Please stop. You've got it all wrong. I have no idea about the state of your marriage, or about how wonderful Mike is, which I'm sure is *very*. But all that aside, I cannot for the life of me understand why you haven't found out what happened to this Grady bloke. Is he on Facebook, is he on Twitter, does he post Vines or Insta his meals before blogging about them? In this day and age he MUST be mentioned somewhere on the Internet. I don't get why you haven't done a healthy bit of online stalking and answered some of your questions."

Tilda listened with some confusion. The last week had been such a blur of reminiscence, she hadn't stopped to think about anything she could actively *do*. All her unanswered questions had remained. She hadn't considered she could *do* anything about finding out what had happened. She'd been a passive traveller on this particular rollercoaster, sitting meekly as it twisted and turned but here Bea was implying she'd had the chance to put her arms in the air and scream along with everyone else.

"What can I do? I don't want to be a stalker but I want to do something. I have no knowledge of him after 1997."

"Yeah, you didn't tell me *how* you lost touch."

"Can we save that for another time. I want to think about something positive rather than dwell. Is that OK?"

"Darling, positive is my middle name. Except it's not, it's Angela, but still."

Bea tapped at her keyboard as she opened up new windows and closed down work-related pages.

"Ok, let's start off with a simple one. What's his full name?

"John Grady. I'm pretty sure there was no middle name."

"And have you seriously never searched for him before?" Bea couldn't even begin to understand how this could be.

"No. The Internet came along years after we last saw each other. Or at least, it came along into *my* life years after that anyway. Even now, I don't really use it except for work and online shopping."

"My God Tilda. We'll talk about all the porn you are missing, later."

"No need, Bea. Just this will be fine." Tilda smiled through her apprehension as Bea logged on to a series of websites.

"Right then. Let's start with Facebook."

Seconds later, a list of John Gradys appeared on the screen. She turned the monitor to face Tilda.

"Do any of these look likely?"

Tilda swallowed and moved her chair nearer. She could feel her heart beating in her throat. After all this time, would she even recognise him?

"I don't know. It's been so many years. They're all too small." She blinked and tried to focus. One by one she scanned the thumbnails and let her gut decide.

"Definitely not the first one, he's too old. Not the next, wrong face. Not him, he's too young. Not him, he's got a middle name. Not him, he wasn't black. Not him, he's too short. Not him, he's just... not *him*. Next page please."

"That's the lot, I'm afraid. Not as common a name as you'd think."

Instantly, Tilda felt relief. She sat back as the adrenaline drained and she gathered herself together.

"Well fair enough. He's not on Facebook. Thanks for looking but I guess it's not to be." She got up but Bea stopped her.

"You can sit right back down. We've only just begun. Now, I need to know every factual detail you have about him. Age, job, hometown, family, anything. Somewhere, in a deep dark corner of the Internet, he exists. I accept your challenge..."

"...I haven't set you a challenge..."

"...of spending the rest of the afternoon on this most exciting of missions. Give me an hour and then meet me back here with a cup of tea. I will debrief you on all I have discovered."

Tilda was amused and concerned in equal measure. She sat down once again. Bea's furrowed brow and intense typing were causing her misgivings.

"Look Bea, it's lovely of you to help me, but after all this time, maybe it's best to leave everything in the past. Yes? I'm not sure I can cope with finding out he's married with six kids, or that he finally realised he was gay after meeting me. Maybe what's in my head is enough. Yeah?"

At this, Bea stopped typing and turned around to face her friend. Her friend that she knew so little about, yet who had spent the hour before enlarging with some detail, the man that she had repeatedly described as the love of her life and the most wonderful person she had ever met. And the most illuminating point of all, the reason she had a postcard of some caves on her desk. For all the innuendo and office banter that Bea thrived upon, she was also sensitive to the needs of others. It had taken far too long, but Tilda had reached out. She owed her the same respect back. She owed her the gift of closure.

"One hour, a cup of tea and Tilda, I will find him for you."

CHAPTER TWENTY

The Solicitor. Friday 23rd September 2016. York.

Another day, another hearing, another round of facts, lies and loopholes. The solicitor was in his lucky chambers. He had never been on the losing side in 6A yet he wasn't feeling quite so lucky this morning. The air was stifling. He could feel beads of perspiration form across his forehead and from somewhere outside his body, he could hear his own breath battling raspily for attention alongside his pounding heart and drying throat. He had felt chilly twenty minutes ago but now he was burning up.

Barely hearing the last remarks of the district judge, he held on, waiting until it was officially over before making an escape. He needed to get out of there, into air in which he could breath. Brushing off an outstretched hand to the right of him and ignoring acknowledging nods from colleagues in the corridor, he walked out of the court buildings and slumped panting against the stone wall. His frantic hands loosened his collar as he concentrated on inhaling the required oxygen. In, out. Cool and calm. In, out. In, out. He was going to beat this. He was *not* going to ask for help. He was going to force himself back to normality.

As a plan, it was surprisingly effective. Eventually his breathing became less laboured and he started to be aware of his surroundings. He was just another solicitor having a break outside before hurrying into the latest hearing. *Nothing to see here.* The thought that he'd been noticed sent his pulse rate soaring once again. *Had* anyone seen him? Perhaps it had appeared he'd taken an urgent call, or maybe people thought there was a pressing matter back in the office that needed his attention. Looking around it seemed that anybody nearby was walking straight past him. The realisation that no one had spotted his mini-breakdown created a calming effect, and he was able to focus once again, taking one long breath after another. A rummage in his pockets located an old tissue so after a quick dab of the forehead, he hauled himself to his feet and slunk back inside. He had a briefcase to retrieve.

It didn't take long before he was back outside again. He continued to focus on a steady intake of breath as he fished his phone from his pocket. For the want of anyone more useful, he found himself calling his PA and sharing the basic details.

"Yeah, that's a panic attack. Definitely. Google agrees with me, but I knew it as soon as you described it. My sister has them all the time."

"What does your sister do?"

"It wouldn't hurt to go to your doctor…"

"Not an option. Too busy."

"… or think of your happy place. A place where you can…"

"Rosie, if I wanted you to take the piss, I'd have said so."

"I'm not taking the piss. It's about visualising a calm image so that when it happens again, you can keep breathing and…"

"Just go to Boots and ask them for something. I haven't got time for this."

He hung up, a little dejected, and fully able to imagine the thought processes back in the office, Rosie contemplating, what she considered the futile task on which she was being sent. She'd be sighing audibly like she did when she was annoyed with him and cursing him under her breath. All he had asked her to do was get him something calming. She'd see it differently of course. Her sarcasm would erupt onto the pharmacist with a 'Hello, do you have drugs to solve a psychosomatic problem within my boss, with no prescription and no option of a consultation with him? If you could hurry please, he is such a demanding bastard.' He should never have rung her.

With his phone returned to his pocket, he pushed the familiar door open as the welcome aroma of hops and yeast cloaked him in reassurance. The Lion and Lamb. His second home. A barman he vaguely recognised came over to serve him.

"What can I get you?"

"Double scotch. No ice."

"Right you are, Sir."

From inside his pocket, his phone rang. He almost answered it, assuming it would be Rosie, but saw the number just before he hit 'accept'. This was definitely not the time. Surely they'd have got the message by now? Surely they'd have stopped pestering him and just *got on with it.* As now was an even more inconvenient time than usual, he continued to ignore it as had become his habit.

The Lamb and Lion was quiet for a lunchtime. He usually recognised some of the regular lushes lining the bar but today he was alone. This suited his current state of mind, which was veering from embarrassment at his delicate constitution, to fear that he was seriously ill. Hopefully Rosie would find something suitably effective and then he'd be cured. That thought, whilst welcome, did nothing to stop his hand from shaking. All the more evident as he raised the glass to his lips and gulped hungrily. Was this what a stroke did to you? How was his face? The solicitor attempted to check himself out in the mirror behind the bar but couldn't make out anything beyond his general outline. Failing eyesight another stark reminder of encroaching mortality. Jesus, is this how it was going to be from now on? Stroke and heart attack symptoms interspersed with increasingly erratic memory loss whilst blindness systematically developed. *Sign me up, Dignitas, I'm on my way.*

The whisky, and his insistence at forcing his fears to take root elsewhere, finally had the desired effect. He began to feel normal again. A text from Rosie, alerting him to the difficulty she was having locating pharmaceutical supplies for his condition, relaxed him further. He remembered her sister and the calm manner in which his PA had diagnosed his symptoms. He would be fine. It was just an extreme reaction to a busy week.

"Are you feeling all right, Sir? You look very pale."

The solicitor turned to the barman. He came in here most lunchtimes and this was the most chat he'd ever had. He must look terrible.

"I'm fine thanks. I..."

He faltered. Should he divulge his medical concerns to the man he was relying on for providing his alcohol? What if, because of some obscure European health and safety law, he refused to serve him without a doctor's note? Brexit hadn't happened yet so it wasn't beyond the realms of possibility. Then again, it might help to get a man's perspective on all of this. Rosie, like most women in the office, seemed to spend an inordinate amount of time visiting the doctor. He wasn't accusing all women of being hypochondriacs, but certainly the ones he saw on a daily basis could be fitted into that category.

Men, on the other hand, got on with it. They took a paracetamol here and there and were happy to use a plaster for a bleeding finger, but they didn't feel the need to drop everything and make an appointment across town the second they got a cold. The barman could be the reassuring voice of calm and just what he needed.

"I'm OK. I think I had a bit of a funny turn a few minutes ago. My assistant thinks I had a panic attack, but you know women..."

He tailed off. Despite his reasonably notched bedpost, he didn't really know women at all. Not in any way it mattered.

"A panic attack?"

"Yes. That's what she said."

Already he felt better. The burly barman took the information in his stride, continuing the conversation without pausing in his mission to restock the wineglass shelf above him. This man was exactly what he needed right now.

"Then you've come to the right place, Sir. There's nothing to cause panic in here."

"Good. Thanks. I'm fine now."

The glasses continued to be shelved, the delicate clinking providing the only background noise to the conversation.

"What were you doing at the time?"

"I'm sorry?"

"What were you doing? When the attack happened?"

"Oh, I see. Well nothing out of the ordinary really. I'd just finished prosecuting. In the courts, you know..."

The solicitor gestured behind him, towards the general direction of the Magistrates' Court. He didn't have to explain further. The barman must see the effects of the judicial process every day.

"I see."

The solicitor drained his drink. Perhaps it was time to move to a comfier seat. He was done with chatting. One more drink, just to make sure.

"Same again, thanks."

"Of course Sir." The man busied himself with the optic. "If you don't mind me asking, was this your first day in court?"

"No, of course not. I've been in and out of that building for twenty-three years. I'm always in here, you saw me on Wednesday."

"Yes, Sir. I know, Sir. My point, although rather clumsily made..." he passed the fresh drink across the bar, where the solicitor knocked it back in one "... is that if today is no different from any other, there must have been something out of the ordinary to trigger your panic. Do you see what I mean?"

"I suppose so. But there was nothing out of the ordinary. It was a routine bankruptcy case. They happen all the time."

"I'm sure you're right, Sir." The barman was starting to look a little miffed at the notion that his wise words were becoming an irritant to this short-tempered tall man in a suit. There was a pause as neither of them spoke. The solicitor didn't know what to add, and the barman felt as if he was only going to intrude further. The opening of the pub door finally broke the tension and gave the solicitor the chance to ask for one final drink before the barman's attention was taken with the latest customer. A customer the solicitor knew.

"Hello pal, thought I'd find you in here. Liquid lunch again, eh?"

The solicitor put on his game face and returned fire at this colleague and most recent sparring partner. A face and name he'd known for as long as he'd attended hearings across the road, and yet beyond those most basic of identifying features, knew nothing. Nor did he have any interest in finding out more.

"Bainbridge, you old lush. I knew you'd want to buy me a congratulatory drink, so I came on ahead. Another worthy battle contested."

The solicitor held his hand out which Bainbridge shook with mock resignation.

"Fair enough, pal. What can I get you? Of course this just makes me all the more determined to wallop you next time we're against each other. Scotch?"

"Sure. It's the least I can do."

Bainbridge smiled as he beckoned the barman over and requested a scotch and a mineral water.

"To be totally serious for a second..."

"All right, but only for a second or I'll not believe you're sincere..."

"Ha, yes, well I'm glad I bumped into you actually. I got a bit worried towards the end."

"Why, what happened?"

"What happened? Don't be ridiculous. You turned as white as the proverbial sheet, started to pant heavily and then staggered out whilst the judgment had barely left Goebbels' mouth. I thought I was going to find you lying in a ditch somewhere between there and here. Is everything all right?"

The solicitor inwardly froze. Clearly he'd not been as discreet as he'd hoped. He continued to smile widely, as a professional lifetime of spinning a tale gave him the skills he needed to get through the conversation.

"I'm fine, Bainbridge. I think I'm coming down with a bit of a cold. I needed some air but I'm feeling a lot better now."

"Well that's a relief. I thought it was because of the sob story I'd peddled to delay the bankruptcy order. All to no avail obviously, but I laid it on a bit thick, and that's when you seemed to struggle. I'd started to feel guilty. Thought I'd sent you over the edge."

Bainbridge laughed as he sipped his water. The notion of his feeling guilt towards this colleague seemed ludicrous in the cold light of the dingy pub.

"Not at all, not at all. I just need an early night and a hot toddy. But until then, I'll make do with this." He raised his drink in appreciation before raising it to his lips once more. "Just out of interest, the sob story you told - about Tolliver's Hardware - was it complete bollocks then?"

He shouldn't have asked the question. He should have walked out of the pub assuming Colin Bainbridge had manufactured every detail of the case. If he left now, he could assume the elderly Mr. Tolliver had *not* just witnessed his third generation family business being wound up. If he left now he could imagine the elderly Mr. Tolliver's tears were fake and merely springing from a suggestion offered by Bainbridge at garnering the sympathy vote. If he left now, he could assume that he had not witnessed the elderly Mr. Tolliver's equally elderly wife grasp his weathered hand, as the judge indicated that he, the solicitor had won his case.

As his temperature started to rise and his breathing became shallow once more, he made his excuses and left before he endured a repeat performance of what he was becoming to think of as his middle-aged descent into madness. *One foot in front of the other, out of the door, breath in, breath out, step and step and step and step.* He walked past the court, past the Opera House and headed towards the river. *Breathe in, breathe out, breathe in, breathe out.* Finally, *thank God,* a bench.

He stumbled towards it, sank down on its splintered slats and continued his mission of staying alive. What had Rosie banged on about earlier - his happy place? Jesus Christ, what was that? Desperately, he scoured his mind to think back to a time he had been happy. The very notion seemed so ridiculously hippie-esque that he grimaced as he searched his mind for something suitable. Images of nights in the apartment poring over files, sessions in the gym and meetings in his office were quickly dismissed. But what else did he have? Unremarkable sex with unremarkable women. Not really a memory to focus on, as they all blurred into one. A holiday in Dubai five years ago, but it was too hot and he'd been working through part of it. Christ, this was hard. What made him fucking happy?

He closed his eyes and tried to think. A fleeting image of a garden drifted into view. A curly haired boy with a luminous water pistol, running around in the sun. A bedroom with bunk beds. A blanket draped from the top bunk creating a secret compartment below. Giggles, laughter. The leather-bound atlas, open on a double page. Childish thumb marks where secret journeys were once planned.

The solicitor opened his eyes. His breathing was under control. He had stopped shaking. He was no longer sweating uncontrollably.

Now all he had to do was stop sobbing.

CHAPTER TWENTY-ONE

Tilda and Grady. Thursday 14th March 1996. The Lake District.

The rain had eased. Through the steamed up windows Tilda could see umbrellas being shaken as people toyed with the gamble of assuming the drizzly weather had been issued a reprieve. Inside, in the warmth of the café it couldn't matter to her less. She sank back into the sofa and felt truly content.

Content and a little sad.

"What's up with your face?" Smiling as he teased her, he placed the steaming mugs of tea down, along with a large pebble that had been marked with a number seven.

"Nothing is up with my face. What's that?" Tilda was confused at the rock in his hand.

"I took control and behaved like a man. I have hunted and gathered for you. I am Tarzan. Argharghagh." He beat his chest as Tilda giggled.

"Really. You're Tarzan. Well thank you for sharing."

"OK, maybe not Tarzan but I ordered us toast. Someone will wander over soon, spot our pebble and feed us." Grady grinned as he sat down, and sipped his tea.

"God I needed that. Now come here." He wrapped his outstretched arm around her and pulled her close. She snuggled into his chest willingly. It was a place she had come to know well. She took her own drink in her free hand, as Grady gulped his down thirstily. Although perilously close to spilling both, there was no way they weren't going to cuddle.

"You weren't lying when you said you drink tea all the time. I think it is the most consistent of all your behaviours I have witnessed since meeting you."

"Really?" Grady smiled. "The most consistent of my behaviours is drinking tea? I'd have thought you could come up with a few more exciting things than that. If you think hard enough."

Tilda's face flushed pink. They had certainly kissed a hell of a lot since Tuesday morning on the rocks, when everything had changed and she had begun to float through every moment. She reminisced as she sipped her own drink. A welcome break from the vending machine brews she had suffered. This was exactly what she needed.

"Don't be rude. You know what I mean."

"Tilda Willoughby, I was not being rude. But we can always come back to that topic at a later date."

"Really? *That* topic? I can't imagine what you are talking about." Her flush developed but she could handle it. Here she was, on day three of her special friendship with Grady, engaging in sexually charged repartee. She had started to enjoy not recognising herself.

Grady shifted himself into a sideways position on the sofa and faced his new friend.

"So..."

"So?" she replied.

"You were you looking sad when I came over. Is everything all right? What can I do?"

Tilda smiled. How very lovely he was.

"You are sweet you know. There's nothing you can do and I'm mostly happy. It had just occurred to me how rubbish tomorrow is going to be."

"Ah, yes, tomorrow. It's not going be fun, I agree."

"I hate goodbyes."

"Me too."

They were both quiet for a moment. The wrench that the following day would bring only really dawned on them as they sat together, looking out of the window. Grady kissed her forehead before finally breaking the silence.

"Right, I have made a decision."

"Oh yeah? Are you being manly again?" Tilda found her smile.

"Yes, absolutely. I am taking charge. This is our last full day together and we are going to make it count. Now, we could sit here and eat toast, drink tea, and natter away about not much. And that would be perfect. I could do that for hours. But it might also be a bit of a waste. As our time together is a little precious right now, I suggest we make an agenda."

"An agenda? You mean like we're having a meeting? Should I find Freya so she can take minutes?" Tilda laughed.

"Now don't mock me, Matilda Willoughby. I think this is a good idea. It feels like I've known you forever, but there is still so much to find out. And I know there's loads I want to tell you about me. So, I think we should make a list of topics to cover."

"OK then, you've convinced me. I love a good list." Tilda pulled her notepad from her bag and unclipped the pen from the spiral binding. "What's first?"

"In no particular order...."

"Go for it..."

"Right, number one - where we live, who we live with, what it's like - that kind of thing." Tilda dutifully wrote down 'Homes'.

"Number two - our favourite films."

Tilda kept writing.

"Number three - life goals. Number four - the chat we started yesterday before we were interrupted..."

Tilda's scribbling paused. She smiled to herself, raising an eyebrow before carrying on.

"...And that's about it." Grady sat back and smiled. There was a deliberate look of innocence on his face. Tilda couldn't help but laugh.

"Grady, it's not that I doubt your motives, but could it be that you *only* want to continue the conversation we started yesterday but are trying to cushion it around more innocuous subject matter?"

"I don't know what you are talking about. Unless you find your favourite films to be a very difficult topic to discuss, I really don't have a clue."

He laughed as he spoke. There had been a brief awkwardness the day before. Clumsy thoughts had tumbled out, and both of them had been relieved when Jonathan had knocked on the door.

Grady reached out and held her hand.

"Tilda, honestly, we have loads to talk about. I want to learn everything about you. I want to know it all. So, tell me where you live."

She decided to humour him. There were definitely things to say, even if they built up to them with other topics. And it wasn't so scary. Grady made even the most mortifying of topics seem safe.

"All right then. Let's start. I live about ten minutes from the centre of Liverpool. It's slap bang in the middle of Studentville, it's a bus ride into Uni, and I live in a terraced house with Freya."

"Is it just the two of you?"

"We've had a bit of a revolving door for the third

bedroom but at the moment it is being rented by a guy called Nick. We'll see how long he lasts. Everyone else has dropped out or found somewhere better."

Tilda paused. Her student digs felt a million miles away right now. She would be back there soon enough.

"What about you?"

"I am a similar distance from the centre of York. I answered an ad on the notice board and now I find myself living with Bong Head."

"Bong Head? Ha, brilliant. And how's it going, living with Bong Head?"

"Bong Head is the model flat mate. I hardly see him and he spends a lot of time in his bedroom getting stoned. Last time I clapped eyes on him, I opened my bedroom door to leave for a lecture, only to find him lying flat out on the carpet using a kitchen knife to push the phone bill and a highlighter under my door. He doesn't say much. It works very well."

Tilda smiled as she made a show of checking her notebook.

"Right Grady, item two on the agenda. Favourite films. What's yours?"

"Easy. *War Games*. I could watch it a million times. In fact I probably have. Do you know it?"

"Yes, I know the one you mean. It's always on BBC1 on a Bank Holiday. Computer stuff?"

"Tilda, I imagine our last full day together is not the time to berate you for your casual ignorance of what is THE GREATEST FILM EVER." He smiled through his fake indignation. "Computer stuff, my foot."

She laughed.

"You know what, it is definitely *not* the time for that. Get over it." She returned his laugh. She enjoyed their mock teasing. It was what other people did. People who were funny and relaxed. She was being other people again. Or was this just the new her? New and improved Tilda Willoughby? It was all so confusing. It was as if she had stepped through a portal where everything she knew about herself had become unreliable. Yet rather than be worried and scared about what she might do, she felt as though a world of possibilities had opened up to her. Her smile widened as she continued.

"And so moving on from what is clearly a very touchy subject for you, I will tell you that my favourite film is *Pretty in Pink*. Now it is your turn to tell me you have never seen it."

Grady's eyes lit up.

"No, you see, that is where you're wrong. I have definitely seen *Pretty in Pink*, as I've been a long time admirer of Molly Ringwald. Admittedly the whole 'will she make a nice dress in time for the prom' plot passed me by, but she did look very pretty. In pink."

"If you had seen it, you'd know full well that the film is a social commentary about class, cliques, and 1980s high school angst. It is *so* much more than a dress. But as I reduced *War Games* to 'computer stuff' then you are allowed to get away with that. Just this once."

"How very kind you are." Grady laced his fingers between hers and looked at her. "Do you think we are ready for topic number four yet?"

Tilda consulted the list.

"You mean skip life goals completely? Is that allowed? Maybe I should ask the committee?"

"I am more than happy to chat about life goals first. But I think the two topics may have a bit of a cross over. What do you think?"

Tilda looked at him. He had the most beautiful eyes. Open, wide, honest, childlike. She had never trusted anyone as deeply as she did him. There was something adorable about him. She reached out and stroked his face. He instinctively kissed the palm of her hand as it brushed passed his mouth. Of course she wanted to talk about topic number four. There was no better time. She took a deep breath and found her most confident voice.

"OK then Grady, I'm ready. Let's start yesterday's conversation again. If I remember rightly it boiled down to one simple question. Are we going to have sex together before we go home?"

"Toast?" The waitress had been hovering for a couple of seconds with the plate yet still chose that moment to interrupt.

Tilda's face turned scarlet. Grady laughed loudly and thanked the flustered woman, taking the plate from her hands as he did. She bustled away, muttering to herself as she strode back to the kitchen.

"That was absolutely perfect timing. Are you all right? I am concerned your face is going to explode."

Tilda groaned and hid her head in her hands.

"I cannot *believe* that happened. I have never been so forward in all my life and now I won't be able to speak about it ever again."

Grady laughed as he gently took her hands away from her eyes and guided them to look at him. Even when she was embarrassed she oozed beauty. Perhaps more so in moments like this when she was her most unglued.

He could look at her face forever. The first thing he would be doing when he returned home was taking his films to Boots. Aside from the cave and pub photos, he had taken one picture that he couldn't stop thinking about. The morning on the rocks, when everything had clicked into place, Tilda had turned her head to look at him just as he snapped the shot. He could remember it clearly. Her face was innocent and unguarded, filling the frame. It was the split second before she had started to smile. Her eyes were already there. As soon as he got his photos back, that would be the one he would put in a frame. That was the image he was going to look at as he read her letters and wrote her replies. It was the image he couldn't get out of his head. The image that he returned to again and again.

He held her hands to his mouth and kissed them before speaking, taking the attention off her as she continued to groan to herself in embarrassment.

"If you want, I will start then. While you get yourself together. Is that all right? I don't want to take over."

Tilda nodded, relieved.

"OK, here goes. Yesterday, nothing came out right. We had a quiet five minutes alone, and it all poured out in a big rush. I didn't feel like we got our points of view across, at least I didn't anyway. But I *did* hear what you said. You don't want us to have sex and I totally get that. No, let me finish, I get it."

Tilda had opened her mouth to protest but closed it as he clearly had more to say.

"I agree that it is far too soon. If I'd met you at Uni then I wouldn't have suggested it three days after talking to each other. It just felt like our time here together was running out. I'm so sorry it looked like I was trying to force the issue. I didn't mean it to be like that at all. I want you to be happy and I want to be the one to make you happy, so me pushing for something you aren't sure about is definitely not what I want to do."

Tilda nodded encouragingly. She knew all that. He hadn't said anything bad the day before. She just hadn't expected it.

"That being said, whilst I am happy to go back home tomorrow just as we are, I don't want you to think for one minute that I don't want to go to bed with you."

Tilda's breath quickened. Something changed inside. An ache, like a second heartbeat throbbed deep within. Could this be what Freya called 'The Horns'?

"Yeah, you heard me. I think you are the most gorgeous woman in the world and I would love nothing more than to undress you, and have you undress me. I want to have scx with you, Tilda. I want to make love to you, or shag you, or have you shag me, or… do people still say bonk?… I don't think they do, but whatever they say…"

Tilda laughed as Grady continued in earnest.

"…whatever you want to call it, I want to do it with you. But I agree that a youth hostel bedroom with a flimsy lock is not the most romantic place to share something so lovely. And it would be lovely. It would be better than lovely. It would be euphoric and intense and…. all the other perfectly brilliant adjectives I can't think of now. So with that in mind, I'd prefer to wait too. As long as you want. I want to wait for it to be all those things and more. I guess what I am saying is that I agree with you. I think. At least I agree with the 'should we do it?' question. I think not doing it is the best thing for now. I don't know if your reasons are the same, but if they are not, maybe you…"

"Grady. Stop talking now. I get it."

Grady took a breath and did as he was told. His initially coherent points had long since descended into a ramble. Tilda had listened to his nervous speech without saying a word but it was time to clear up her own thoughts from the day before. She held his hand.

"When I said I didn't think we should do it, that was because you brought it up out of the blue. I was surprised. I hadn't really thought about it…"

Tilda stopped and realised she didn't want to lie.

"Actually, that's rubbish. Of course I'd thought about it." She cast her mind back over the lifetime she had lived since meeting him.

"I thought about it when you pulled your fleece off and I saw the top of your boxers sticking out above your jeans. I thought about it when you kissed me, on the rocks, and I could feel you hard against my leg."

Now it was Grady's turn to blush.

"Sorry." He smiled sheepishly.

"Don't be. I liked it. But I especially thought about it yesterday in my room, just before you started to talk. When we were kissing, and your hand was under my top on my back, it was all I could think about. If we hadn't stopped to discuss it, I think we'd have ended up doing it right there."

"Damn, me and my manners." Grady smiled. He knew exactly what she meant. It was precisely why he had stopped to talk. He didn't want her to do anything without thinking and then regret it afterwards. That would have been too much to bear.

"So, yes I agree with you. I'm not sure where that leaves us, but yeah, we shouldn't force it to happen here, but I want to, regardless."

She took a piece of toast and began to eat. This kind of honest, sensitive talk needed regular pauses to refuel her confidence.

"So what we're saying is, we have a sort of plan then. A plan for after tomorrow?" Grady hedged around the subject tentatively.

Tilda laughed loudly.

"You mean we don't do it here, but we meet in a hotel room next week? Somewhere central like Leeds, just to get it done?" She was deliberately misunderstanding to be funny except she wasn't sure what plan he had in mind.

He laughed too.

"Oh Tilda, I don't really know what I mean, except I can't bear the thought of tomorrow being *it*. If it's not too forward, I really want us to see each other again. What do you think?"

As he said the words, Grady was nervous of the answer. Maybe, as good as it had been, she didn't want to have the hassle of keeping in touch. He'd pictured them writing long letters to each other and making plans to meet again, but maybe it was all in his head.

She saw his panic and answered quickly.

"I really want that too, definitely. Of course we'll see each other again."

She pulled his face to her mouth and kissed him. This wasn't something that happened to her every weekend. She wasn't Freya with a rolling conveyor belt of men that lasted ten minutes each. This was something beyond explanation. With the certainty of that realisation came an unfamiliar confidence about sharing her next words.

"Four days ago I didn't know you existed, and now I can't imagine not seeing you every day. You have become part of me. There is no doubt in my mind we will make plans to meet up as soon as we're free. And then the future is ours to play with."

Grady exhaled a sigh of relief. He hadn't misread the signals and he hadn't gone too far. He wrapped his arms around her and pulled her close. She resumed her favourite position, of leaning her head against his heart, a little shocked at how candid she had been. As she felt the rhythmic thumps against her ear, she regulated her own breathing to be in time with his. She'd have said both of their heartbeats were quicker than usual, if she had to make a guess. She breathed deeply, in and out, savouring the moment of peace and contentment. Grady sat back, his arm around her, as he nuzzled the top of her head.

"There are many things I am unsure of at the moment regarding the future, but I am so certain about you and me. You are the calm in the middle of the storm."

She tilted her head to look up at him.

"That is a lovely, if not cheesy, thing to say."

"Yeah, I realised that as I said it, but I don't think I care. Will you put up with my corny compliments and overwhelmingly positive feelings for you?"

"I will happily welcome them all, you div." She laughed and resumed her position. Everything felt so right. She could have snuggled there all day but there was still so much to chat about.

"So speaking of the uncertain future, do you think you'll move back home after you finish? My Dad thinks I will be, but I just can't see it, myself. I've enjoyed my own space too much."

"I will be doing everything in my power to avoid it ever coming to that." Grady said. "It just wouldn't work now I've been gone so long. Maybe just a month or so until I have a plan." His face clouded for a few seconds before he turned his attention back to Tilda.

"What about you? Are things really so bad with your Dad?"

Tilda sighed, and sat up properly. After hearing about the coldness Grady had grown up with, it felt very different to her own experiences.

"Things aren't bad really. I know he loves me. He tries to smile when he asks me about college. He makes an effort to joke with Freya when she rings. But the truth is, he is sad and lonely. And that means that I feel sad and lonely when I live there. Then I feel guilty, because it isn't his fault my Mum died, and l feel like I should try harder."

"From what you've said, you do a lot to make it easier for him. Didn't you say you go home every weekend?"

"Yes. It's just been that way since the first year. Like we made an unspoken compromise when I moved out, and now it's just habit."

"So what will you do? Go home and suck it up or do you have a plan?"

Tilda emitted another sigh. She had been thinking this over for a while now but hadn't shared it with anybody. Now seemed as good a time as any.

"First of all, I am planning NOT to move back after graduation, not permanently anyway. I have a few months before then, so I was thinking of missing out every other weekend visit. That way he gets practice at me not being there on a Saturday and Sunday."

"Sounds like a good idea." Grady held her hand as she continued to speak.

"He'll struggle at first, but he'll get used to it. It's not like I actually do anything when I'm at home. He goes to Asda and I watch telly. That is pretty much all that happens."

"For the whole weekend?" Grady laughed as he asked.

"It feels like that anyway. I actually have no idea what we do every weekend. Nothing significant. We are just *there*."

"So you are going to train him to get used to your absence, and then what?"

"Well that's the bit that is a little more vague. I've been looking at what's out there and nothing is tempting me. I know I don't want to work in an office." Tilda was emphatic. "I can't imagine anything worse than being stuck behind a desk all day when there's a whole world beyond the window. All the graduate schemes I keep seeing advertised, don't appeal for a second."

"I know exactly what you mean. It feels like a waste of a life."

"Yes, I agree. But that doesn't help me work out what to do. I really envy people who have a planned career in mind, but so far I haven't got a clue. Do you know what you want to do as a job?"

Grady shook his head in silence. Like Tilda, he knew what he *didn't* want to do, despite the expectations of his father. That was as far as he had got. She continued.

"I know I want to travel and see new places, but backpacking around Tibet isn't really my thing. So what I've been thinking recently is I'd like to travel around the UK, around the coast. Stay a few weeks or even just a few days in each place, maybe camping or hostelling. It would all depend on how pretty it was. If I ran out of money, I could try and get work behind a bar or something but would be on the move over the course of a year or so. I like the idea of being nomadic for once. What do you think?"

Now that she said it out loud, Tilda felt silly. *She could get work behind a bar or something?* It sounded ill thought out and juvenile. She didn't have much left of her student loan, and the basic problem of how she would travel from each coastal location was something she still hadn't considered. Clearly she was clutching at any straw that meant she didn't have to move back in with her Dad.

Grady, who had been listening intently to all she had said, cleared his throat.

"Tilda, that is a *beyond awesome* idea."

Tilda paused her critical train of thought.

"You think so?"

"Yes, definitely. You could do a complete circuit. You could go all around the top of Scotland, and down to the bottom of Cornwall. Think of all the beautiful places you would see. Tilda, I love that plan."

"You do? I was afraid it sounded a bit daft when I said it. I haven't given it any practical thought, though. I just like the idea of doing that and not living in Stockport for the rest of my life."

"Is it that bad?" Grady smiled at how adamant she was.

She sighed and gave his question a considered answer.

"It's not bad at all, if you have known other places, and lived in other towns. There are some parts that are even quite scenic. I just find it depressing when people never move from the town in which they were born. It's just rude."

"Rude?"

"Yes. There is so much to see, and to ignore it, feels like a massive snub to the rest of the world." Tilda paused. "I'm not making sense now, am I?"

"You're making perfect sense." Grady took a swig of tea, and a bite of toast. He was fascinated by her plans and wanted to work out the logistics.

"Would you do your coastal travelling on your own?"

"I've no idea. I don't think it's really Freya's cup of tea."

The thought of Freya camping in a tent, or tolerating another year of Youth Hostels amused Tilda. There was no way she'd be interested.

"Well if it's not too forward, I'd be happy to apply for the role of travel companion." Grady said it aloud as soon as the idea occurred to him. His filter really was taking a break today. "That is, of course, if you hadn't planned to do it alone. Or with anyone else. Or you might just think you don't want me to..."

"Grady, you're rambling again." Tilda laughed. "Let me get a word in edgeways."

"Sorry. I just asked without even considering you might have something else in mind. However, if you want a friend to accompany you - or even a boyfriend? - then I'd love to come. We could plan our route together and work out the most interesting places to visit. Nowhere would be too remote or obscure. I'd spend the days painting, you could write your journal and we'd lie in our tent - or tents if you prefer - and listen to the wind and the birds and the tide and all the sounds that other people are too busy to hear. Tilda, it would be the perfect way to spend our time. But now as I'm saying all this I realise how presumptuous I have been. You might have this all planned out differently and be hoping to get Jonathan or Sam, or someone like that involved. So I still offer myself as a travel buddy, but it is totally fine if you don't want me to..."

"Grady. Stop."

Grady stopped. He held up his hands in surrender before miming a zip across his mouth, grinning as he gave her a chance to speak.

"I have no idea of how or when or where yet. But the thought of you and me planning this together is very tempting. I think I'd quite like that actually, if being with me twenty four-seven isn't too scary a thought. It might be a crazy idea but it feels far less so now I've shared it with you. So, yeah, why not? Let's do it."

Grady let out a cry of excitement.

"Woohoo! We have plans! We have something to look forward to. Tomorrow won't be a 'goodbye'. It'll just be a 'see you soon'."

The reality of what had just happened dawned on her. Since arriving in the Lakes on Monday she had got herself a boyfriend, a plan for future sex and the next year of her life devoted to exploring the UK with him. Was she mad? She shared her question.

"Do you think it's a bit mad how quick all this has happened?"

She looked at Grady. She wasn't worried. She wasn't concerned she was being too reckless. She just wondered how others would perceive it.

He returned her smile, shrugged and answered honestly.

"The way I see it is, you know when you know. It's like Emerson. I was reading him the other day and he said, 'Once you make a decision, the universe conspires to make it happen'. That's us. We decide what we want, and then nothing can stop us. None of this feels wrong to me. I love you. Did you know that? You probably should. And the fact that we get to plan an adventure together after we go home tomorrow feels like the most exciting thing ever. I know I sound a bit giddy now, but the idea of there being an 'us' after today has made me so happy."

Tilda had tuned out most of his words. Except for the three that were racing around her head.

"You love me?"

"Yes. Is that OK? You don't have to say it back. I just wanted to put it out there."

"I love you too."

"You do? Really?" Grady's smile could have lit the room.

"Yeah. I do. Is that all right with you?" Tilda smiled as she looked at him. He was beaming.

She snuggled back into her well-worn spot on his

chest, as their heartbeats raced, the rain fell, and the waitress rattled plates in the kitchen.

CHAPTER TWENTY-TWO

Tilda. Friday 23rd September 2016. Stockport.

Despite Bea's clear instructions, Tilda had struggled *not* to clock-watch obsessively. Aware of the metaphorical boiling pot, she had attempted to busy herself with work until she saw signs of Bea starting to boil, but it had been difficult. Across the desk, her colleague had been tapping away since she'd left her. Her only break being when she retrieved pages from the printer.

Tilda had given up on the policy rewrite in her in-tray so filled in time by tidying her desk. As she was not in the habit of enduring a messy working area, this took seconds. Next, she shredded the contents of her paper bin. With that pointless task ticked off, she photocopied every one of the nine documents she was currently working on so there would be a paper backup if the network were hacked, or armed bandits stormed the offices and stole the technology. She knew she was ridiculous but her mind needed occupation. After a ruthless clear-out of her email folders she finally admitted defeat, made two cups of tea, and slunk over to the opposing desk with ten minutes to spare. She felt sick.

Without looking up from the screen, Bea motioned to her to sit down.

"Lovely stuff, Tilds. Thanks for the brew. I'll be one minute. Just finishing up."

Tilda's eyes darted about the room, taking in her surrounding colleagues, the wider corners of the office and eventually settling on the notice board on the back wall.

Her stare found a curling Swine Flu poster semi-covered by more pressing issues of recent years. She focused on it, mentally reminded herself how to sneeze into her elbow and the correct procedure for hand washing, before summoning up the courage to glance at the screen. She wasn't sure what she was expecting, but knew it was making her stomach flip. When she craned her head enough to see, the nerves soon stopped.

"Oh. Those're the housing stats. I just photocopied them for myself."

"But we got them this morning," Bea said, still tapping away.

"I know. I did a backup. Have you been doing housing data for the past hour?"

Tilda's nausea ebbed a little, but was rooted more in annoyance than in nervous tension. Had she really been fobbed off so Bea could get on with some work? *That would be the last time I ever reach out to my so-called friend Bea Charleston. Next time she needs..."*

"Right, done. Let's talk John Grady." Bea sat back in her chair and swivelled to face Tilda.

"Tilds, are you alright? You look terrible." Concern filled Bea's face as she looked at her friend.

"I'm fine. Sorry, I just thought you were... I couldn't see anything to do with him, with Grady, on your desk, that's all."

"Don't fret mon amie, I have made a special folder for you, look."

Bea opened her drawer and retrieved a plain brown file from the top of strewn paper and empty chocolate wrappers. It might as well have had TOP SECRET stamped on it in red letters such was the furtive nature in which she produced it. Stowing it back in its hiding place, she turned her computer screen to face them both, and brought several minimised pages into view. Tilda's apprehension levels were making it difficult to swallow. She sipped her tea with a shaking hand.

"Now, first of all, it took me mere minutes to get some info, so I do have knowledge to share. I cannot believe you have never done this before by the way...."

Tilda gestured a hand, to imply she agreed with her on some level, before letting her continue.

"...I've printed off everything I found, and I'll give you the copies after I've gone through it now. Nothing on there is incriminating towards you in any way, so feel free to take the file home."

"Thanks but I've still done nothing wrong in theory."

"Perhaps, but we'll talk about that in a minute. Now, have a look at this."

Tilda strained her head towards the screen and looked at what appeared to be a website. She could see the name screaming from the top but still asked the question. Now would not be the time to make assumptions.

"What am I looking at?"

"You are looking at the website of Grady and Son Solicitors. Based in York for all of your soliciting needs, specialising in debt recovery and insolvency."

Tilda let the information sink in.

"He has a son?"

"That's what I thought at first but I don't think so. The son would only just be an adult and only if he had him straight after you lost touch. This firm's been around for over fifty years so I don't think Grady has a son."

"I don't understand." Tilda sat back and looked up at Bea expectantly. Her head was fuzzy and it hurt to think. Bea looked at her straight in the eyes waiting to prise open the worm-filled can. The expression on her friend's face was calm and gave no hint that she had anything bad to share. She just needed to say something.

"What have you found, Bea?"

Bea sat back, crossed her legs and picked up her mug. A brief sip later and she spoke.

"Tilda, I think *he's* the son."

A few junctions up the M6 and one windy A-road away, the last rays of the afternoon sun were still bright. Pouring through the window, they illuminated the gallery with no need for artificial intervention. This was the way he'd always intended it to be. This was his dream being realised. The years when he had worked three jobs at once, budgeting and living frugally, scrimping and saving every penny - the possibility of owning his own gallery and studio seemed the stuff of fiction. And yet here he was, bathed in sunshine, seeing his life's work surround him, still excited about getting up in the morning and experiencing what the day had to offer. Settling down had taken him longer than most but now that he had, he was content.

Mostly content.

A large glass window covered the front of the shop, allowing those inside to people-watch as blatantly as they liked. Pictures hung at every level on every wall, depicting landscapes of all shapes and sizes. In the street outside, tourists mixed with locals throughout the year - the 'out of season' months still filled with day-trippers and dog walkers from neighbouring villages. The gallery owner replaced a recently sold piece with one completed on his latest camping adventure. He stepped back to assess the angle. It was perfect. The picture, the simple white frame, the spacing of it alongside the other work, and the memories of the trip itself. He had enjoyed painting that particular landscape. The Scottish weather had been glorious, the sea had shim-

mered, and he'd finished the Dylan biography that he'd found in the charity shop. Not only that, but he'd come away with not one, not two but three brand new paintings to sell in his shop. His little shop in the pretty market town in the Lakes, that he was now lucky enough to call home.

From the outside looking in, his life was certainly enviable. And although he was aware of that, there were times when he didn't feel it quite so keenly. The feeling of loss and sadness came upon him as suddenly as it always did. A fleeting memory, a second or two of visceral ache, and then it would pass. He recognised the feeling, and at times it gave him a twisted comfort. It was reliable, reassuring, always there. He'd had to live with his decision for a long time. A decision made when he was too young to understand the implications. A decision made when he thought he knew everything about the world, and yet in reality knew nothing.

Before being lost forever to the ghosts of the past - one shy, blonde ghost in particular - he was jolted out of his daze by a knock on the window and a cheery wave from Pete the butcher, two doors down.

Grady smiled and waved back.

"Was his dad a solicitor, or not?" Bea was becoming impatient with Tilda's vague responses to her questions. She needed to know that her mission had been successful and she'd tracked down the right guy.

"I think that was it, yes. He definitely owned a business. There was a family firm, I remember that part."

"This is him then. Or at least the firm is his. Right name, right location, so it must be. Now, I've searched every part of this website. It is basic to say the least."

Tilda's nausea returned.

"Are there any staff photos? Is there a 'Meet the Team' section? Is he on there?"

"Easy Tiger. All in good time. There *is* a section on staff, but no pictures and an incredibly non-specific mission statement that could be about anything. It also appears to be out of date because when I rang to speak to Nazima Babu who, according to the website information, could tell me everything I need to know about small claims tribunals, she left the firm two years ago to do charity work in South America. Seriously. Two years ago. Someone in their IT department should be shot. That is if they even have an IT department. Honest to God, that's a basic Comms fail if ever I heard..."

Tilda's patience started to wear thin. She couldn't care less about the quality of a website at which she had only glanced.

"Bea, please. Can we move on? I'm in bits here. I feel sick, I can't stop remembering, I don't know what to do. Put me out my misery, please!"

Bea paused, and looked at her friend. No more build up, no more dramatic pauses. It was time to share her plan.

"Fair enough, let's crack on. I searched every corner of the Internet and this is the nearest I've found to being your Grady. I *know* it is his firm, even if I can't prove it. It's a stone's throw from where he lived, for one thing."

Tilda took the mouse and clicked on a few areas. It was plausible but unconfirmed.

"Then after Ms. Babu turned out to be living it up in the Brazilian slums, I asked if there was anyone else I could speak to, regarding a small claims matter."

Bea had begun to look decidedly shifty which did nothing to calm Tilda's increasing panic.

"What have you done, Bea?"

"The kind lady told me that I *could* speak to Mr. Grady himself if I wanted, but I would have to make an appointment."

"At which point, you said 'thank you kindly' and hung up, I presume."

Tilda clung on to this hope in spite of the screaming in her head telling her it was otherwise.

"At which point I asked if it was Mr. Grady, or Son, and she said Son, so..."

Bea's voice had sped up far beyond her control.

"... I made an appointment for you for two weeks to-day, in York and booked you a room in a Travel Inn and there are the details in this file. Here."

Bea finished her bout of verbal diarrhoea by passing the file from the drawer back towards Tilda, who had turned an alarming shade of scarlet.

"What else is in here?" Tilda whispered.

"Just the basics. The hotel information, a couple of Google Map printouts, a list of J Gradys in the York area. That kind of thing. You can tell Mike we are having a girls' weekend. You can tell him you're accompanying *me* as I track down an ex-lover. You know he'd buy that."

Tilda opened the file and looked at each page, silently turning them, reading the odd word here and there, but taking nothing in. What on earth had she got herself into? What had Bea got her into, more to the point? This had got out of control. Well, no more. It had to stop before it went any further. Her legs shook beneath her as she stood up and somehow found the strength to return to her desk. As of now, this was over. No more wondering, no more fantasising. It was just Tilda and Mike, and their simple, uneventful, everyday life together.

Tilda sat back at her desk and tried not to think. She tried not to remember that once upon a time, she had wanted so much more.

CHAPTER TWENTY-THREE

Tilda. Friday 10th May 1996. Liverpool.

The digital display on the VCR seemed to be stuck. It had been 17.57 for much longer than a minute. Tilda held her breath in the hope that by suggesting she wouldn't exhale until it changed, the laws of time might get a move on.

There was a knock on the door before being pushed ajar.

"Tilds, are you *absolutely* sure you won't come out tonight? I feel bad about you staying in on your own."

"There is nothing to feel bad about, Freya. I stay in most weeks."

"I know, but Tilds, come on."

"Come on, nothing. I've had a great day but it's Friday night and you should go out. I prefer staying in, anyway."

"Christ, Willoughby, if you were anyone else, I wouldn't give up so easily but I actually believe you when you say that. Are you sure you'll be all right?"

"I'll be fine. Now go."

Freya flashed a smile that gave away a hint of relief as she removed herself from the gap in the door and darted upstairs to finish glittering her eyelids. As she did, the phone rang.

"I've got it." Tilda sprinted to the bottom of the stairs. *Finally.*

She used the most adorable tone she could muster.

"Hey you."

There was a brief silence.

"Hello? Hello? Is Tilda there please?"

Tilda jumped as she recognised the voice.

"Dad? Dad, what are you ringing me for? I spoke to you earlier. We said you'd leave it tonight."

"Did we? Oh dear. I must have just slipped into the normal routine. How are you, anyway? Have you had a lovely day?"

"I'm fine, Dad. Like I was before."

She realised she sounded grumpy, which was exactly how she felt inside. Her Dad meant well but of all the wrong times to ring, this was the most wrong. She tried to be nicer.

"After we chatted, I had lunch with Freya - in the Wetherspoons by the station? Then we looked around the shops for a bit, and I bought a new top in the Etam sale and then we came back here. Nothing else to report."

"Well as long as you've had fun. That's all that matters. I'll leave you to it now. I am sure you've got much more exciting things to be doing than chatting to your old Dad."

Tilda felt a surge of guilt.

"No, it's fine, really. I just wasn't expecting you to call again, that's all. How's your day been?"

"Oh you know, same as usual. The bins came this morning but they've started to refuse to take garden waste, so I had to drive to the tip with the boot full of leaves. I had a ham sandwich for lunch and I think I'm going to heat up the rest of the shepherd's pie in a bit. You make a very good shepherd's pie, Tilda. I defrosted this one on Tuesday and it's done me three meals this week."

"That's great Dad. Anything else?"

"No, I think that's my news. Anything else from

you?"

"Not that I can think of." She cringed inside at her impatience to end the conversation. She was a terrible daughter.

"Right then. Well have a good evening. Say hello to that Freya. I'll call on Monday."

"Ok Dad. Thanks again for the vouchers. Bye."

Tilda replaced the handset, feeling horrible and yet relieved all at once. Within five seconds it rang again. *Please let it be Grady. Please let it be Grady.*

"Hello, hello?"

"Hi. Tilda, is that you? Are you OK, you sound a bit stressed?"

"Oh thank God. I was worried it was my Dad again."

"Ah, *that's* what happened. I wondered if he'd forgotten. I got the engaged tone a couple of times. Is he all right?"

Tilda sighed.

"Yes, he's the same as usual. I could have killed him for ringing at our time though. I'd told him this morning I was going to be busy."

After only a few seconds of telephone connection between them, Tilda could feel the guilt and stress melt away. She sighed with contentment as her breathing calmed and she settled as comfortably as she could on the bottom stair.

"It's so good to hear your voice. I've been looking forward to this all day."

"Me too. But before we begin, there is something very important I have to do."

"OK?"

"Tilda, are you ready?"

"I think so. What is it?"

Grady cleared his throat.

"*Happy birthday to you, happy birthday to you, happy birthday dear Tilda, happy birthday to you.*"

Slightly taken aback by this musical interlude, Tilda laughed loudly. It was the first time she had ever heard him sing.

"Why thank you Grady, now my day is definitely complete. I am deeply touched by your musical stylings."

Grady laughed back.

"Yeah yeah, I know I can't hold a tune. But still, it's not every day the love of my life turns twenty-one. Have you had a lovely day?"

Tilda paused before answering. It was the second time she had been asked that in the last five minutes but it was a much harder question to answer when it came from Grady. She always preferred to be honest with him.

"It has been all right, thanks. Lunch with Freya was nice. We had a good natter about Rob, her latest potential boyfriend. Other than that, it's been fairly quiet. The truth is, I've been looking forward to this phone call all day. Nothing else has mattered. Are you sure we can chat for so long?"

"Definitely. I told Bong Head I'd be on the phone for at least two hours tonight and that he should get any important calls out of the way first. He's been in his room for the past hour so I don't think I'll see him again this evening. How about your house?"

"Freya is getting ready to go out and I haven't seen Nick all week. I think he's been at his parents' since the weekend, so all quiet here."

At that moment, Freya - a lycra-clad spectacle in turquoise - clonked down the stairs in shoes that would undoubtedly be the cause of a broken ankle one day.

"When I say all quiet, obviously I mean when Freya

has actually LEFT THE BUILDING." Tilda emphasised the last part for her flat mate's benefit, whilst a teetering Freya stuck two good-natured fingers up at her. Seconds later the door had closed behind her and Tilda had the place to herself.

"Right, Ms. Willoughby, back to more serious business. Did a parcel arrive today?"

"Yes!" Tilda jumped up. Stretching the cord of the phone as far as it would go, she managed to reach the package that had been propped against the hall table since the morning. "I didn't open it. I followed your instructions, don't worry."

"Glad to hear it. Now the time has come, you are finally allowed to look. Happy birthday, Tilda. I really hope you like it."

Tilda put him on speakerphone as she placed the receiver on the stairs and peeled back the parcel tape. She had spent some time that morning shaking it, and wondering what it could be. Its generic box shape didn't give much away.

"How's it going? Have you unwrapped it yet?"

"I'm getting there. Just getting the tape off. Give me a clue!"

"As if!" Grady laughed. "You need to get quicker at unwrapping."

Tilda pulled the last strip of tape off and pulled the brown paper away from the box. Underneath was a plain, white cardboard box. She placed it on her knees, carefully pulling the lid away.

"Where are you up to?" Grady was getting impatient.

"I've got a box and the lid is off. I can see white tissue paper."

"Blimey, you are dragging this out. Look what's inside the tissue paper." Grady laughed, doing his best to hide the nerves that were setting in.

Tilda peeled back the delicate paper and looked.

There was silence on the phone. Grady was holding his breath, hoping the gift he had spent so long looking for, was up to scratch. As for Tilda, she was feeling something new. Something she had never experienced before.

"What do you think? Is that OK?" I thought of you as soon as I saw it."

Tilda reached into the box and pulled out a journal. A tan-coloured, leather-bound journal. She opened it and flicked through the thick cream pages. Large, blank pages just waiting to be filled with her thoughts. Her hand automatically stroked it, so soft was the padded leather. As she closed it shut, she gasped, and had to stifle a sob. In the centre of the front cover were two small initials in gold, decorative type - TW.

"Grady, I don't know what to say."

He could hear the crack in her voice as she got the words out. There was every chance this had been a really crap idea.

"Well say *something*. I mean, is it all right? Could you use it? I thought you could save it for when we begin our next chapter together. It could be a record of all your feelings when we are travelling. Except you might end up hating me, and it would be filled with rants about how I sing out of tune, and I don't care if I wear odd socks, or I..."

"Grady, stop! I'm trying to work out what to say and you keep talking. Let me just look at it for a minute."

Grady smiled ruefully to himself.

"I've got it, Tilda. *Back off Grady, stop talking shit for five seconds.*"

Grady stopped talking and waited as Tilda opened the book once again, feeling it's tactile irresistibility.

This really was quite something. Her current journal was an A5 exercise book, the kind found in schools. It had been the cheapest option last time she needed one. Other than that, she had only ever had basic diaries from WH Smiths. This journal however, was a world away from that. It was a work of art in itself. She had never received a gift so personal. She cleared her throat and swallowed a couple of times.

"Right, I think I can speak now."

"Are you OK? I am worried you hate it. I can easily swap it for something else. I didn't mean to make you cry."

Tilda sniffed into a tissue and composed herself.

"I'm not crying. Not properly crying anyway. I just can't believe you've given me something so beautiful. It's without doubt, the best present I have ever had."

Grady beamed, with relief as much as at her hyperbole.

"Oh don't be daft. I'm sure you got other great presents today. Let alone in the past. What did your dad get you?"

"Boots vouchers."

"Oh, well what about Freya?"

"I told you. She took me out to lunch. It was lovely. I had jacket potato and chilli, and a glass of wine."

"What else did you get?"

Tilda smiled at how awkward this conversation was getting. She was used to her pitiful existence. It just sounded worse when she had to explain it to others.

"There is no one else, Grady. My Dad, Freya, and now you. And I'm not exaggerating when I tell you that this has been one of the best birthdays I can ever remember."

With gift formalities out of the way and a ten-minute tea and toilet break incorporated, Tilda and Grady were still chatting an hour later. She'd had the sense to grab a pillow and blanket from her bed before settling back down with her drink, so was feeling quite snug as she leaned back on the stairs.

Tilda was aware she had shocked Grady earlier. His initial silence, and then his attempts at pretending she *hadn't* just told him the saddest piece of information he'd ever heard, had been very sweet. This was not news to her. She knew she was alone in the world. Other than a couple of school friends that she might bump into in the holidays, there was no one else. Obviously she knew her Dad was always there should she need him. It was just the idea of actually turning to him for emotional support was laughable. It had always been the other way round, as long as she could remember. Since moving to Liverpool, she had found Freya. Freya, who at times was slightly self-involved, albeit good fun. Silly, warm, over-the-top Freya. Freya, who would probably lose touch the minute the graduation ceremony was over. Tilda hoped that wouldn't be the case but she wasn't getting her hopes up.

Because of the hand dealt to her, she had learned over the years to be self-sufficient in all aspects of her life. What Grady still didn't fully realise was how much he had influenced her to open up emotionally and share herself with him. It was a new feeling to want to be vulnerable in front of another person, and at the start, it had been equally unnerving as it was exhilarating. But now, a couple of months into their relationship, whilst it was still a surprise when she found herself sharing personal details about her feelings, she found herself doing it more and more. Grady had released her and in doing so had made her a whole person. She would never be able to repay that debt as long as she lived.

As it so often had in recent months, Tilda and Grady's conversation turned to thoughts of life after University. Grady was always keen to make plans.

"So we do our travelling... yeah?"

"Yeah?"

"We spend at least a year together, living in tents and bunk beds and anywhere we can find..."

"You are making it sound so romantic, Grady."

"I know, but what I'm getting to, is..."

"Go on..."

"What do you think you want to do *after* that?"

Tilda thought for a moment, before clarifying her confusion.

"Do you mean, what do you want *us* to do after that? Or do you mean my basic life plans?"

"Ah, Ms. Willoughby, once again, who says they can't be the same thing?" Grady's wise old professor voice belied the fact he had no idea if her long-term life plans would feature him.

Tilda could always hear it in his voice. She loved his vulnerability, even though he was often at pains to hide it.

"I suppose the sensible thing to say at this point would be, let's see how the next year goes. We might end up having a great time but then decide we should just be friends."

"Do you think that will happen?"

"No. Course not." She laughed at his panic. "I'm just being cautious and saying that we have no idea how it will go."

"Tilda Willoughby, stop being so sensible. Let's make crazy plans and then only worry about them not happening, if that's what happens at the time. Am I making any sense? I know I tend to lose my natural eloquence when I'm talking to you. Stop giggling."

Tilda tried to, but found Grady's earnestness so adorable, she struggled to take it seriously. She didn't mind talking about the future at all. It was just that she hadn't given it much thought before."

"OK Grady, what kind of goals are you talking about? What areas of life should we discuss?"

"Hmmm...let's see. How about, do you think you'll ever get married?"

"Is that a proposal?" She couldn't help but tease him.

"No. Not yet anyway. Let's see how the whole camping-for-a-year-together goes first. This is purely hypothetical."

"Good thinking. I suppose I have never considered it before. I am not against marriage. I think it is probably a good thing in general but beyond that, I don't really have an opinion. Do you?"

Grady laughed.

"Of course I do, Tilda. You know me. If there is soppy sentimentality to be had, then I will have it. I would love to get married one day. To know you are with somebody else forever must be an amazing feeling."

"Until one of them dies, anyway."

Grady gasped.

"Woah, Tilda! Way to kill the romantic mood I'm doing my best to create."

Tilda laughed at her own cynicism. Where had that come from? It must have been the glass of wine at lunchtime.

"I'm sorry Grady. I guess I have never really imagined the long-term future *with* anybody. Everybody ends up alone, so I guess I just assumed that's how it would be for me too. Although I must reiterate, I have never given it conscious thought until today."

Tilda was aware she was sounding like a cold-hearted cow. And Grady's next question did nothing to change that.

"Do you want to have children? Do you imagine yourself as a mum in the future? I do realise we are talking years off for this stuff, by the way. I'm not trying to rush you into any ill-thought out quick decisions. Honest."

Grady laughed nervously, not having a clue of the answer. Tilda, he had had come to learn, kept her feelings close to her chest on everything.

She sighed as she thought about it. She knew her honest answers would only disappoint him and yet there was no other way to respond to him. She could never hide her true feelings when it came to Grady.

"I suppose my answer is, I just don't know. It feels a million years away, so I am well aware I have lots of time to think about it. There is just something missing in me that feels a desperation to have a child. I remember a few years ago, our neighbour, Mrs. Wilson, telling my Dad how her daughter was having IVF treatment. I didn't understand what it was and so he had to explain it to me." Tilda smiled at the memory of how mortified they had both been at the time. "He glossed over the technical details, but I do remember thinking why would anyone go to that much trouble to have a baby. I didn't understand it. I guess I still don't."

Grady had been quiet as she had spoken. He had asked her these questions, so he had to accept her answers. In spite of that, he felt a little dejected. He saw the future differently.

"Are you alright, Grady? Have I killed the mood with my short-sighted vision of the years ahead?"

Tilda took a swig of her now-cold tea as she waited

for his response. He couldn't seriously be upset that she had said she wasn't sure about having kids, or that marriage might not be all she had ever wanted. Tilda had experienced fourteen years of being an only child to a single father. There were no aunts and uncles, no cousins, and the future loomed ahead with no nieces or nephews, brothers or sisters in law. Bringing a baby into that situation might be the most selfish thing in the world. *You were only conceived so I'd have someone to talk to, darling.* It was definitely not something to rush into without lots of thought.

"Grady, talk to me. What do *you* think?"

Grady cleared his throat again.

"I know I asked you hypothetically and so I appreciate your answers are clear, and logical, and thought out. My thoughts on the subject aren't so theoretical, though."

Tilda shifted her pillow under her back as she waited for Grady to share his thoughts. She could sense there was another perfectly rambling outpouring on the way.

"I've been thinking about this for a few weeks now. You remember I went home for the Easter weekend?"

"Yes, course I do. You stayed in your room and got on with your dissertation in the warm."

"That's right. Anyway, it was fine because my father was in work all day and night. But on Easter Sunday, I'd been typing for hours, and my back was achy and I just needed a break. The house was empty, so I got the nicest bottle of red wine I could find, opened it, and sat in my Dad's study."

"Why your Dad's study?"

"As much as I despise him, that room has one of the best views in the house. I kept the lights off and sat at his big desk chair, and turned it so I was facing the bay window. It's on top of a hill, and it looks down at lots of cottages and side roads leading into the valley."

"Sounds pretty."

"It is, although most of the neighbours are really overlooked by us. They must hate it. I never go in there usually, but that evening I was in a reflective mood. I just wanted to feel a bit of space. So I drank my wine, and looked out of the window for a couple of hours."

Tilda wondered where this was going. Grady's voice had taken on a wistful tone, as though he were back in that room now. She didn't interrupt. He'd get there if she let him.

"It was like a fly on the wall documentary. Little nuggets of real life kept popping up as I sat there. In the nearest house on the right, there was a man reading a story to his toddler. I could see right into the living room. The little lad was curled up on his knee, whilst his dad held a big picture book, utterly engrossing the little boy. Every so often the man's face would be animated, and the child would look up and laugh. I reckoned that was when he was doing a funny voice."

"That sounds cute."

"Yeah, it was. Just watching them made me feel peaceful. Some time after that, a car pulled up a little further down the road. A middle aged guy - probably about forty - got out, and grabbed the biggest bunch of flowers I have ever seen from the back seat. He ran up to the door of the house, and knocked. When it opened, he presented them to the woman that lived there, and her face was transformed into something so beautiful. It was only flowers yet this woman went from being, kind of plain, in my humble opinion, to being radiant and dazzling because of a gesture. It was wonderful to see."

"You must have sat there for a long time."

"I did a bit. My mind had been focused on work all

day so it was like a release to let life happen around me for a while. And I'm glad I did, because then I saw my favourite part of the evening."

"Go on." Tilda loved hearing his gentle enthusiasm simmering through his words.

"The next house down from mine is an old cottage. It was revamped a couple of years ago when new people moved in, and now there are lots of floor to ceiling windows. I could see they were having some sort of gathering. There had been a few cars and taxis arriving as I'd been there. By the time the other neighbour had read his story and the girlfriend down the hill had been given flowers, the party was in full swing."

"What could you see?"

"There was a big table with about ten people sitting around it. There were large dishes of food in the middle, and I watched them sharing a meal, and eating together. It wasn't anything wild or crazy. It was just a lovely scene. They were passing plates to each other and topping up wine. All of them seemed a similar age so I decided it must be a group of friends rather than a family. Everyone knew each other. Their faces were alive with laughter and conversation. No one was left out or quiet. I watched them for ages. A close-knit circle of friends, having a ball in each other's company. It was beautiful."

"It sounds it."

"I sat there for ages as these real, warm and loving life experiences happened all around me. And that's when it hit me."

"What hit you?"

"That's what I want. All of it. Each snapshot was like a picture of the future I want, the one I want with you. I'd love to surprise you with flowers when I got home from work, even if we'd been married for years and years. We would have brilliant evenings of food and drink with our mates. Music in the background, everyone laughing as you roll your eyes as I get too enthusiastic about whatever it is I'm talking about. Can you picture it Tilda, because I can. And finally, the image of us taking turns to read a bedtime story to our child - including silly voices - is about as perfect an idea as I can think of right now. I know I have overthought it but it all made perfect sense as I sat there and watched other people being happy. I want all that happiness, and I want it with you."

"You do? I don't know what to say." Tilda gasped, and yet felt strangely calm. He certainly painted an attractive picture.

"I *know* this is all years away. Don't panic, of course I know that. But it felt like I'd glimpsed into the future, and you were well and truly it."

"I'm your future?" Tilda's eyes were welling up.

"I think I guessed it the first night in the pub but I know it for sure now. And now I'm hearing myself share all this with you, I'm worrying if I've gone too far. I wonder if I'll know when I've shared too much. It doesn't feel like it just yet. It feels like everything I've said is exactly right to say. I want you to know everything - all my thoughts, feelings and passions. I want you to know them all. I hope that is OK. Please tell me if I should shut up."

Tilda found her screwed-up tissue from earlier and wiped her eyes. He always managed to do this. She would have established logical feelings about a topic, and know what her stance was. Then he would share his own feelings, with a confidence that caused him to be able to utter them in the first place, mixed with a vulnerability about their raw nature. And she would listen and she would melt. This had become their dynamic.

Of course she wanted those things too. To continue living as isolated as she had been brought up would never do. She wanted people, she wanted family, she wanted life. She wanted to grow old with Grady.

She told him this and then it was *his* turn to cry.

CHAPTER TWENTY-FOUR

Tilda. Friday 23rd September 2016. Stockport.

After a decidedly blurry afternoon, a text from Mike to say he would be in late and a non-descript mince-based evening meal, Tilda found herself lying in the bath. The capful of Radox had provided scant coverage, though to add more would have been frivolous. It wasn't Christmas. She used her hand to waft a cluster of bubbles towards her torso. It was never going to relax her today so even the little she had used was a waste. On the side table stood a glass of wine, her mobile phone and an unopened book. She wasn't in the mood for drinking or reading and her phone was only there out of habit. All she could do was simply lie there and breathe. Numb apathy and a twisting pain were fighting it out inside her body and so far numb apathy was winning. The pain was there but dulled by the frozen layers. The bath was doing nothing to thaw her. She should have added a second capful after all. Or the bottle.

A text alert pinged next to her. Bea.

CAN YOU TALK?
CAN I RING YOU?
ARE YOU ALONE?

Tilda rolled her eyes at the three questions. Questions that would certainly arouse suspicion if Mike were in the habit of reading her messages. The movement of picking up her phone stirred some life back into her limbs. She sat up and scrolled to Bea's number. She had to put an end to this.

"Hi Bea. It's me."

"Darling, are you alright?"

"I'm fine."

"I was so worried. I didn't know if I'd upset you or freaked you out, or made you happy or completely offended you?"

Tilda sighed.

"Why are you worried Bea? What do you think you have done?"

"I've been umming and ahhing about calling all night. Is it safe? Are we being overheard? Are you free to discuss our 'situation'?"

Tilda sighed again. This time she made it audible so that Bea might take the hint. She didn't.

"So darling, have I done wrong? Are you *very* cross with me?"

"Why do you think I would be cross?"

"So you're not. Phew, that's a relief."

"No, I meant that as a question. Why do you think I'd be cross? What have you done that I might be cross about?"

Bea sensed a steely tone in Tilda she rarely heard. A tone of voice she had only witnessed on Tilda's later phone calls with her Dad. When she was cooking his meals every week and he was refusing to eat them. She'd watch her hang up the phone, frustrated and sad because she'd had to be assertive. Bea had crossed a line.

"I'm so sorry Tilds. I've gone too far haven't I? You just wanted to chat, and there I went pushing you towards a secret rendezvous, with hotels and lies and God knows what else. I have been a truly terrible friend to you. I promise I will cancel everything and pretend it never happened. You can bin the secret folder and noth-ing more will be said."

Tilda found herself wanting to sigh for a third time but felt it was a step too far. Instead she had questions.

"Bea, I'm not cross. Not really, I just..."

"Oh thank you, darling, because you know I would never..."

"Stop. It's my turn now, let me speak."

Bea stopped. It seemed Assertive Tilda was still talk-ing. The tone could not be ignored.

"I'm not cross. All right, maybe a little, but it's more that I wasn't expecting you to plan anything for real. I just thought you were going to tell me you'd found where he lives, or that you'd spotted an artists' forum he had posted on. I didn't expect a dirty weekend away, all planned out with cover stories for Mike and false meet-ings about legal matters with a real solicitor. You took me by surprise. And what I am wondering now is why you thought I would be interested in any of that? Did you think I would lie to Mike just like that? Did you think I would get a perverse kick out of the deception? Or did you forget to think about me at all? Was this just an easy way of giving you a bit of a thrill on an other-wise boring afternoon?"

Tilda took a breath, feeling slightly shocked at her-self for having said so much. She didn't want to upset Bea but all the unsaid feelings from the day had come tumbling out. God, she could be rude sometimes.

"Look, Bea... I'm sorry. I didn't mean to..."

"No Tilda. Don't. You have absolutely nothing to apologise for. Nothing at all. You came to me to share feelings and worries that had been playing on your mind, and I took it upon myself to make decisions for you that were not mine to make."

"It's fine, Bea, honestly. I shouldn't have said all that. I know you were only thinking of me."

"Tilda, you should definitely have said all that. It was how you feel and you should share more."

Tilda laughed.

"Now I know you're being funny. Sharing my feelings isn't really my style, you know."

"I'm being serious, darling. Twice today, you have let me in a little, and shown me what you are thinking. You told me about the lovely Grady who, I have to say, sounds adorable, and now you've just told me that you've judged my motives and you're annoyed with me."

"No, Bea. I didn't mean it like that."

"Stop Tilda. My turn. Now, as far as I can see, in twenty years of having worked with you, those are the only times I have ever seen you unravel. You are usually professional and controlled. Professional on nights out and staff meals too. I mean, seriously? I hear you on the phone with Mike and it's like you are talking to someone you share a house with but not a life. I used to hear you talk to your Dad when you had to make sure he'd taken his tablets. You talk to me like you're my slightly disapproving older sister, even though - and this is classified - I have almost ten years on you. Do not breathe a word. But anyway, do you see what I am saying?"

Tilda was still sitting up in the bath, the water rapidly cooling as she grappled with Bea's words. Did she see what she was saying?

"I'm sorry Bea. I have no idea what you are getting at."

It was Bea's turn to sigh.

"OK, let me put it like this. Since you have been thinking about Grady again - just thinking about him, nothing more - you have changed your hair style, your make up, you smile more, you are more relaxed, you are more emotional, you have reached out to me and you are spending every spare minute wondering how he is and what he has done with his life."

"Fine, so I haven't tied my hair back for a couple of weeks and I've been feeling relaxed about Autumn coming and the television being better at night. It doesn't mean I want to run away for the weekend amidst a web of lies."

"Oh Tilda. I have watched you for years. I love you to bits but you have never changed. Everything is the same - your work ethic, your stoicism, your clothes, your eye rolls at my weekend shenanigans. Everything has remained the same in all that time. Until now. Did you know you'd sent the bedroom tax stats to Si this morning?"

"No. Of course I didn't. They were for you. Why would I send them to someone else?"

"Because you are unravelling."

Tilda was silent for a moment. A mis-sent email. That never happened to her.

Her voice wavered as she carried on.

"I don't want to unravel. I want to be back in control. What can I do?"

Bea wished she were there face to face. To give her a big hug and tell her everything was going to be all right. She knew it would be but she also knew the unravelling was an essential part of it.

"Darling, you need to give yourself some time. You are currently dealing with events from your past that you never dealt with back then. They have been shut up tight, but now that they're not, they are flooding you. Grady is too big a part of your life to cram back into the mental compartment, darling."

"I don't want to unravel. I have to keep it together, at work *and* at home."

Bea bit her lip. Now was not the time to share her thoughts on Mundane Mike. She ignored Tilda's implication of her happy home life.

"I suppose that's why I thought the weekend in York might be a good idea. If you could find out what had happened to Grady, that he's a successful solicitor, happy with his wife and kids, then that would bring you some sort of closure. It might hurt, especially if he is happy with someone else but at least you'd know. At least you could stop wondering and move on. At least you'd stop unravelling."

Tilda was silent for a moment. She was slowly losing the negative thoughts about the plan, but logistical concerns were creeping in.

"What about Mike? I don't think I can lie to him."

Bea let the question hang for a moment as she considered how to answer. It was probably best to continue her silence on the man's apparent shortcomings. She reverted to half-truths and a lighthearted approach.

"Look at it this way. Everybody's marriage could benefit from an adventure. You take a brief break from reality for a day or two. Wake up, have a bit of a giggle catching up with your old friend, and then go home, reminded that life with Mike is far better now that Grady is all bald, fat and racist."

Tilda laughed.

"Bea! He would not be racist. Never."

"Well who knows what might have happened to him over the years. You could find out you had a lucky escape. Seriously darling, consider it. It's just a weekend and you need answers."

With her phone returned to the table, Tilda lay in the

bath. The water was long since cold, but she didn't notice. Her mind was playing the self-justification game. One weekend, one legal appointment, it was nothing bad. As lies went, it was tiny. Mike would appreciate the place to himself and she wouldn't be there to nag him about the vacuuming. She'd return on the Sunday evening, ready for the new week with a clear head.

Everything was going to be fine.

CHAPTER TWENTY-FIVE

Tilda. Monday June 10th 1996. Liverpool.

After an unconvincing start the new kettle started to show signs of life. The last one, that had served the house well since day one, had spluttered and died after Freya's mate Tony, attempted to boil Blossom Hill rosé the Saturday before. Wine and a cheap heating element were not compatible, it seemed. A life lesson learned for all concerned. An early morning Argos dash that morning had meant that the Going-Out kitty was down £5.99, with Freya feeling guilty and the rest of the house telling her she couldn't have seen it coming. Tony, it went without saying, would not be welcome back.

Kettle number two did its work. Tilda began to think about toast as Freya marched in.

"More leaflets for us. They're handing them out by the library now."

She strode over to the fridge and arranged brightly coloured information under already over-stretched magnets.

"They obviously think I'm smacked off my tits all the day is long. That's the third time since Thursday."

"Hmmm." Tilda wasn't listening. She was still thinking about toast.

"Do I look like a drug user? Tilds?"

Freya took a step closer to her friend, as if to offer up her face for scrutiny.

"Do I? They keep targeting me. Today it's all about Es."

"No, you don't look like a drug user and I can't imagine they are targeting you."

"I hope not. Exceptional quantities of voddy? Yes. Es? As if I can be arsed. I like sitting down too much."

Tilda had never taken drugs. She was completely frightened of both them *and* her utter naivety around the subject. Last year, in a Geology seminar, she had inadvertently taken the spare seat next to Stoned Steve and come away two hours later full of nausea and an insatiable need to wash her hair. As for other recreationally used substances, she was equally unknowledgeable and grateful that the majority of her friends were too. As much as she wished the Timid Tilda name hadn't stuck quite so firmly, it certainly suited her where illegal stimulants were concerned. Her only source of information about these matters came not from first hand experience, but the ever-growing literature clamped firmly on the fridge. She often scanned them with bored indifference, whilst waiting for water to boil or pasta to soften but they were wholly reminiscent of a travel brochure - one describing wild adventures in foreign lands that the occupant of this terraced house in the North West had no plans to experience.

Over the three years of making drinks and cooking her meals, there had been a drip drip drip of drug information going into Tilda. What started as a casual glance as she stirred soup had become a ritual. She could recite the main effects of each substance mentioned and was working her way to memorising all known names of each illegal drug covered. Now she had new pamphlets to fill her spare time. It suited her love of trivia and rote learning - cramming her mind with facts and statistics that she could retrieve whenever the need arose. It was why she was so good at exam revision. With all this in-gested substance information at her fingertips, she could have worked on a helpline if she'd wanted.

Lack of illegal high experience or not, it was only now, three months since meeting Grady, that she was finally able to understand the feelings of a comedown.

It wasn't his fault. It wasn't her fault either. Every-thing had been going brilliantly. It had amused Tilda to make comparisons between the developing relationship with the love of her life and her osmosised-drug knowledge of say, ecstasy. The feeling of being so in tune with her surroundings, of seeing colours and shapes in the world around her that may have always been there but were now enlarged, engorged, positively swollen as she moved from place to place, completing task after task and waiting for the next overwhelming rush of a letter or phone call. Tilda didn't need drugs to get high. She needed a letter to arrive with a York post-mark. It was that simple. And it had been that simple for three months. Until it had stopped.

"Tilds! Phone!"

A disembodied voice from the landing had screamed the information as Tilda emerged from her room and picked up the extension.

"Got it." Tilda had put the phone to her ear. It was too early for her Dad.

"Hello?"

"Tilda? It's me. Look, I'm really sorry…"

His voice, usually so reassuring, had been tight and measured. This was not their usual phone call time so something was wrong. A sudden panic had flooded over her as she heard the strain in his voice. Was this it? Was this what happened in relationships? Three months of the most beautiful and even erotic sentiments outlined by letter -

emotions, worries and dreams shared with no hesitancy or self-consciousness, building up to the time they could finally share themselves and their lives again, and now he was ringing her to end it. Was she being dumped? Ditched? Binned off? It had been hard to work out in those few seconds of thought, what would be worse - by phone or letter. This way she would be expected to say something back. Tilda knew that if she had tried to open her mouth even a little, all that would have been heard were heaving sobs and hyperventilating. She had started to struggle breathing already. Then he spoke.

"Tilda, something's happened. It's not a big deal really, but it's going to mean I have to rethink..."

From some inner core of strength that she didn't know she possessed, Tilda had found herself responding. Her voice had belonged to somebody else. A hardened tone almost bitter in delivery came out of her mouth. It unnerved her as much as him.

"No, don't explain. I get it. It's fine. See you around."

"What? Tilda, wait! Let me explain what's going on. I'm a mess here but it's nothing to do with you."

"Nothing to do with me? You're dumping me but it's nothing to do with me?"

The silence from the other end had caused her a brief wobble. Stay firm Tilda. Don't let him see you're completely devastated. After a lifetime of ticking seconds, he spoke.

"Tilda. I love you. I'm not dumping you. I just need to change our plans a little. It's my Dad."

Part Three

CHAPTER TWENTY-SIX

Tilda. Friday 7th October 2016. Stockport.

The days that had followed Bea's detective work had flung themselves between hazy and sharp depending on the stage of Tilda's mood. At times, she had even resorted to breathing exercises from the Introduction to Yoga course she had once been dragged to. She kept busy and could smother the rising feelings of angry butterflies when they made themselves known. At other times, she slept badly, grumbled through the day, and could just about manage not to throw a chair at Si if he looked at her the wrong way. It was hell. And now the day was here. Her much pondered, much stressed-over day of adventure had arrived and now *this* had happened.

"This will get the crowd behind him... 104 left, it's more than likely he's planning a treble 18. Will he do it? Yes he will! 50 left... goodness, this is not like Lewis at all. What has happened to him? Adrian Lewis, what is going on? Hamilton can't be worried about what he is seeing though. He wants double 16..."

One of the benefits of being dull and safe was that no one questioned the authenticity of the one lie you eventually told. At Bea's insistence, she'd taken an early dart at lunch under the pretence of a debilitating migraine and now had an illicit afternoon free to get ready for her York trip. No one had questioned it. In fact she had received quite a bit of sympathy and Tan Tights had half-smiled as she held the door open for her. Walking to the car park just after noon had felt wildly rebellious. But then as soon as she had walked into the house, an unexpected Mike had appeared, eating a pasty without a plate, and settling in for the afternoon.

It had been like this for the past two hours. Mike glued to his iPad watching YouTube clips of great darts moments, and Tilda being flustered in the background.

In terms of practical preparation, she had clothes and a sponge bag to pack. Yet mentally she was still at the 'To Do' List stage. Her tick list of feelings and thoughts were as rambling as the most disorganised packing list could ever be. So far today she could check off Fear, Embarrassment, Worry, Guilt and Insecurity. Still to cross out were Curiosity, Excitement and Closure. She was hoping she would be ready to tackle these before long. It seemed that she was dwelling on the negative somewhat.

"What is it you're doing again? I forgot." Mike stood in front of the coffee table, his tablet propped up against the tissue box, his arrow arm poised and the majority of his attention on Adrian Lewis' aim. "Weekend with Bea?"

"Yeah, with Bea. York."

"Nice one. That'll be fun. Bea's mad, in't she."

It was a rhetorical question but one that had been pondered by Tilda every day for the last week. Was Bea mad? Was this the most stupid idea anyone had ever had?

Probably.

Was this something that Tilda had to do, regardless of fear, guilt and embarrassment?

It seemed so.

It really bothered her that he was here. It irked her that he had also managed to wangle a free pass that afternoon. She wasn't even sure if he'd told her about it or not, such was the level of her distraction these days, but here he was. And at the exact same time Tilda had been planning to pack, soak in the bath and then set off on her little road trip, she had instead been subject to a non-stop barrage of PDC Championship Final excerpts from a previous Christmas. Apparently this was going to have some sort of subliminally positive effect on Mike's own darts prowess, which would enable him to play a blinder in the pub that night. There was going to be a trophy. That much she had gathered although Tilda had barely an idea about anything despite having been told about it several times. Mike being home had caused her a stomach-lurch of shame and prompted an outpouring of lies as soon as she walked into the house. Somewhere along the way the migraine story was peddled out, along with the early finish for the weekend with Bea, and the manufactured tour of a York street market. That one was another of Bea's ideas. Tilda had stopped question-ing the believabilty of these lies, she just told them, and this was the reason they had to be there on a Saturday. Her story, as well-thought out as Bea had planned, erupted like a gurgling mess of implausibility covering Mike and her home like an oil slick.

Her phone rang. It was Bea.

"Darling, how are you? HOW'S THE HEAD?"

"It's fine, you know it's fine, what's wrong?"

"Nothing. Just want to check you're all right."

Her voice dropped to an echoey whisper, implying she had taken herself to the tiny kitchen area and shut the door. Bea regularly remarked that the main clue that one of her colleagues was embarking upon a secret love affair was that they took their phones to the kitchen and shut the door. She often commented on it.

"All good at this end. Tan Tights even asked me to

ring you over the weekend to pass on her best wishes. You've got her exactly where you want her! She never does that when I have migraines. Although they do happen every time I've slept in, and most periods and usually when I've ..."

"Bea." Tilda had to interrupt or the monologue could have been never ending. "What's wrong? Are you still picking me up?" The concocted story continued to pour out of her mouth.

"What? Oh no, are you being overheard? I'm sorry, I thought you'd be alone." Bea's voice dropped lower, as though Mike's supersonic hearing were so great it would cover the council kitchen area, three miles away. "Can you talk?"

Tilda looked at Mike, still wholly engrossed in darts matches of yesteryear, still so wrapped up in his arm technique and his dreams of local pub glory. He was oblivious.

"Yeah, I can talk. What's up?"

CHAPTER TWENTY-SEVEN

Bea. Friday 7th October 2016. Stockport.

Tilda had never outlined clearly what had happened twenty years ago. Bea knew she shouldn't push, and she didn't. It had taken her almost as long to become someone Tilda had turned to in a crisis. She wasn't going to abuse that trust now. Too much prying would force the shutters to slam shut. As it was, they were only up an inch or two but the fact they were up at all was enough. She knew Tilda was a closed shop. She was fine with that. And yet then again it was all so maddening. So many questions unanswered about what went wrong. Where did Grady go? Bea had done some calculations, via an internal search of the council employee database, and found the date Tilda's employment began. February 1997. And in spite of the hundreds of parties, lovers and hangovers that Bea had experienced since then, she still remembered the frightened mouse of a child that started as a temp and never moved on. She had not been a person in love, nor someone lit up by the possibility of love. She had been empty. Bea had felt an immediate motherly concern for her that initially masqueraded as a simple makeover longing but eventually became what it was today. A bizarre hybrid of mother, mentor, friend and egger-on of deviant behaviour. As much as she enjoyed a healthy dose of hedonism in her own life, Bea also knew that she had been put on this earth to help Tilda. It was her one selfless act. It had just taken her twenty years to work out how.

"So why are you really ringing, Bea? I'm still packing." Bea heard Tilda mutter something to whoever was there - Mike presumably - and a door being opened and then closed behind her.

"I just thought I'd check you had everything. See if there's anything else you needed. I was worried about you."

"Bea, have you ever been married?"

Tilda's tone was firm and direct again. Bea paused. The temptation was to be flippant although she wasn't sure it was the most appropriate time.

"Oh you know, I was once for about five minutes. A hundred years ago." Bea couldn't shake off the habit of a lifetime.

"Bea." Tilda's voice was stern.

Chastened, Bea tried again.

"I was a child bride. I was ..."

"Bea!" Tilda was becoming exasperated.

Bea heard the tone. It was time to be real although this was not something that sat well with her. What was the point of reality when it was infinitely shitter than even the most basic fantasy or embellished anecdote? Nevertheless she took her friend's question seriously. It seemed only fair.

"I *was* married once. It lasted longer than five minutes but less than two years. I was nineteen so to me, it *does* feel a hundred years ago and also means I was a child bride of sorts. He was a perfectly decent boy from my school but vaguely satisfying sex and a mutual love of Bowie - God rest him - does not a marriage make. Last I heard, via another session of Internet research on work's time, he was married with four children to another girl in our year, Sarah Billington. I can only assume they are happy. As am I, because since my early scare I have been aware that myself and marriage are not to be, and I have steered well clear ever since."

Bea paused for breath, not used to sharing this much honest and unembossed detail from her personal life. No one usually asked her. They just liked hearing her Monday morning rundown of the weekend's escapades, fresh from their own domesticated lives of mundanity. Her epic adventures were a welcome break for her colleagues and friends, and even if they sometimes felt wholly unbelievable, no one minded. Tilda was different though, and regardless of the fact that this was the first time she had ever shared so much of herself with her, Bea felt it was appropriate.

Tilda's voice wavered as she spoke.

"I only asked because I'm feeling slightly shaky about all this. I know if I told you that, you would just tell me to go for it and find out how he is and ignore this horrible guilt that keeps making me feel like I'm going to spew any minute. But you see I'm married and this is against the rules. I don't like breaking the rules."

"The rules?"

"Yeah, the rules. The marriage rules."

"Tilda, who makes those rules? Are you talking about God?"

"Well, no not really. I don't know. My marriage vows I suppose. The legal contract. The promises we made. Everything I'm doing is against all that. I've got Mike in the lounge innocently practicing his darts arm and I'm here packing for a weekend away with a man I used to love and haven't seen in the flesh since I was twenty. The whole thing is ludicrous."

Bea listened and took a breath. She had to play this very gently, she could see that, but at the same time she knew some direct home truths needed to be shared. This might be the time. A quick decision needed to be made. Bea could continue to support Tilda as she had always done with calming words and supportive smiles. Or she could tell Tilda a few honest facts about life.

It took about five seconds for Bea to decide.

"Tilda, darling Tilda. Please stop worrying. You have done nothing wrong and more importantly you are *doing* nothing wrong. As it stands, you are going to spend the night in a budget hotel and have a meeting with someone you used to know. It might be a friendly reunion, it might be that he is married with kids and after catching up with you, says goodbye and you never see him again. It might be that he is, as you have already joked, gay and currently planning to convert his civil ceremony into a marriage at the first chance he gets. However, at no point is any of that wrong. It is human nature, it is satisfying your curiosity. It is simply life."

Bea stopped and attempted to gauge if Tilda's silence carried any hidden meanings. She couldn't find any so ploughed on, hoping she was still listening.

"Now, if as you seem to be imagining, you end up doing a little more than catching up, then that is completely your decision. If that's something you don't want to happen then just don't do it. Simple. If however, you find yourself hurtling towards a night of torrid passion with the gorgeous Grady, then promises, rules and husbands aside, ask yourself, why would it be happening? What is missing from your marriage that means you're contemplating a romp with someone else? And would it be a romp, which is all well and good, or is it the connection that you're craving? Something must be missing if you..."

"There's nothing wrong with my marriage." Tilda

spoke up. Her voice wavered and lacked a little of the determination from her earlier words. Bea heard the tremor and softened her attack. She wished she could make her see how exhilarating life could be if she could only prise herself away from her comfort zone.

"I didn't say there was something wrong. I just wondered if something might be missing." Bea spoke carefully. Tilda's voice implied tears weren't far away. Bea heard a couple of swallows and a blow of the nose before her friend spoke again.

"I can't cheat on Mike. I'm so much luckier than some women. He doesn't say cruel things to me, he would never hit me, he does his share of the chores - most of the time - he works hard. There's no reason to split up even if I wanted to. He's so... "

"Tilda, my goodness, stop! All these qualities, whilst admirable, are completely irrelevant. Do you think that being emotionally unfulfilled and not in love with your husband is NOT a good enough reason to end a marriage?"

Bea cursed herself inwardly. A silence descended on the conversation. So much for careful words, she'd gone too far again, she knew it. She'd pushed and pushed, and now here she was telling a fragile friend that her marriage was shit just because she was getting understandable last minute jitters about doing something so out of character she could have been the Dalai Lama throwing a punch over a spilt pint.

Bea quickly planned her apology. She needed Tilda to be aware that she knew she'd overstepped the mark. Again. This is what happened when you became genuine friends with Bea Charleston, she mused. It got horribly real far too quickly.

"Tilda, I'm sorry. I didn't mean to say that, just ignore me. I know nothing about your marriage and I

certainly can't give anyone any advice about proper relationships. Ignore everything I just said. I don't have a
clue what I'm talking about."

A few seconds more silence and then Tilda spoke.
Quietly, but her words were clear.

"It's going to be alright isn't it, Bea? I have to find
out, don't I?"

The resolve had returned. The inner strength that
had guided her through the death of her mother, the de-
cline of her father, the loss of her soul mate and the
ensuing years of boredom. She was not Timid Tilda. She
was a woman who used to be Tilda Willoughby and she
had to find out finally the answers to the questions that
had blighted her for too long.

"Bea, everything's going to be alright. Thank you. I'll
be in touch."

CHAPTER TWENTY-EIGHT

Tilda and Jim. Saturday 18th January 1997. Stockport.

The tiny bedroom she'd occupied all her life was now looking decidedly bare. There were irregular spaces on shelves - her clothes were packed in either the cases surrounding her, or in storage boxes on top of her wardrobe. Tilda opened the windows wide and let the curtains flutter in the breeze. Downstairs, she could hear her Dad pottering about, as she breathed in the gathering scent of freedom into her lungs.

In hindsight, it couldn't have gone any better. *Nice one Willoughby. You've thought of everything.* It would go down in history as the most rehearsed, well-prepared conversation anyone had ever had. One day it would be studied on a 'Maximise Your Business Through Effective Communication' seminar somewhere.

"*So how long are you going for?*"

"*I told you, two weeks.*"

"*And who are you going with, again?*"

"*Freya.*"

"*Did I ever meet her? I can't picture her.*"

"*Yes, Dad. You asked me why she had her hair the way she did.*"

"*And why did she?*"

"*Because when she gets bored, she twists her hair into Björk knots. I told you at the time.*"

"*Oh. And when will you be back?*"

Tilda had ignored him and opened the freezer door.

"*So, here are all the meals. Just bung them in the mi-*

crowave, they're all labelled."

"Microwave. Right."

"You managed fine while I was away for three years. This will be easy too."

"You came home for weekends."

"Not every weekend. You coped. You're more than capable of looking after yourself, you know."

"It's OK. You'll be back soon." He continued to peer into the freezer. Neat piles of frosty Tupperware boxes filled the entire top half of the space. There were an awful lot of meals.

"Where are you off to again? Spain?"

"Tenerife."

"Right. Winter sun. Well, don't worry about me. Two weeks will fly by. You'll be back home before you know it."

And with that thought, Tilda's father had almost smiled.

Her planning and organisation of the following fortnight had been painstaking. It had meant that the conversation she had been putting off for weeks had flowed reasonably smoothly. Apart from the sad half-smile he would offer now and then, she knew he'd manage to survive for two weeks. Two weeks of anything he wanted on the TV, not having to worry about how long she was spending on the phone each night, and not wincing with embarrassment any time he pulled a bra out of the washing machine. The two weeks would be over before he knew it.

Then it would be time to have the real conversation she'd been rehearsing for just as long.

Now in her room, making the final checks to her luggage, she forced away another pang of guilt. It was time to put herself first in her life. That was how Grady had put it. Time to live for herself. He'd used some sort of poetic, theatrical metaphor but she understood what he meant. For the last seven months she had been living her life for Grady. No question. Since that phone call, and the crashing feeling of the ultimate downer had encased her, she had ploughed on every day, thinking of this moment. The day that they would unfreeze their plans and start their adventures. The day where he would be free to join her in the next chapter of her life.

A shout from the kitchen interrupted her current bout of over-analysis.

"What do I do now?"

"Open the door. Give it a stir. Then another minute."

"Righto."

Happy with the instruction, her Dad carried on heating up his casserole.

She hadn't mentioned Grady to her Dad. He was the love of her life, the reason for waking up each morning and looking forward to the day ahead, and yet she hadn't spoken his name to her only blood relative. Another wave of guilt threatened to overtake her as she zipped up her rucksack. Perching on the edge of her bed, still covered in her faded New Kids on the Block duvet cover, she gathered herself together and picked up the little wooden chest by the bed. Inside was a neat bundle of letters, all written in the same sloping hand. Chronologically ordered, she selected the most recent, opened the torn envelope and removed the paper inside. Immersing herself in his words, Tilda re-read what in recent weeks had become her very own team talk.

'My Dad's heart attack has forced me to see how your life must feel every day. It's been difficult picking up the ropes and muddling through while he gets better, but the hardest thing isn't learning the ins and outs of the business,

but rather how selfless one has to be to put others first. You are the most selfless person I know. You've spent the first twenty one years of your life looking after others. You worry about your Dad when he only needs you to because he is used to it. You are always there for Freya, who relies on you for a calm head when she is having her latest drama. You were even the student who handed in assignments early to make it easier for your lecturers. It is high time you put yourself first in your own life. We've both got inside knowledge that life is too short and to live it watching from the wings is, to my mind, an absolute waste. When are you going to walk tall with your head held high, on to centre stage, and become the star of your own show? Because believe me Tilda, you are a star. It's time to do a bit of shining.'

And here it was. Her time to shine. Seven months after the phone call, Christmas was out of the way and she was ready. Bags packed, money saved, route planned. Now all she had to do was get herself and her rucksack down to the coach station. At 5.15pm this afternoon, Grady was going to be with her once more and their open-ended backpacking adventures were to begin.

Downstairs, settled with a cup of tea, Jim Willoughby lowered himself into an armchair. The taxi had thrown him somewhat, as he was unused to such extravagance from his only child. It seemed a bit steep but then she did have a lot of bags for two weeks in the sun. *Typical woman. Everything but the kitchen sink!* An indulgent smile transformed his face for a second, turning to sadness when the sharp memories of his darling Madeleine surfaced as they always did.

She had been a couple of years older than Tilda when

he had met her. Full of life and laughter. It only seemed minutes ago, but then there were times when he felt as if he were recounting scenes from a film, so removed were they from his own life. It had been 1973 when he'd been reading the free paper in the library and been distracted by her loud and demonstrative discussion with the librarian about an overdue fine. Even though she had been completely in the wrong, she'd managed to charm the helpless man into letting her off. It had been all he could do to stop himself applauding when she walked away, but instead he put down the broadsheet and ran after her, unsure as to what he would say. In the end it hadn't mattered. She took the lead in spite of her youth, and his life had begun. Jim swallowed the well-known lump away. The tightness in his throat was just part of his daily life now. Like an old friend that had overstayed its welcome - recognisable, reassuring sometimes, but he would still have preferred it to be long gone. It was the same with the tears. Remembering was always so bittersweet. That vivacious woman who did all the talking, who woke him up from his buttoned down life and showed him all the joys of the world, had been gone ten years later. Everything that was special, everything of beauty, everything that forced him to wake up each morning and breathe in and out always left him in the end. Two weeks without Tilda were not the end of the world. He knew that. It just felt like they were.

Whilst Jim faced the future alone in his house, Tilda was busy gathering her belongings from the boot of the taxi, palming coins on to the driver and looking around to see if she could see Grady. The bus station was busy today. Far too excited to concentrate on one thing at once, she dropped money, tripped over her smallest holdall and somehow managed to trap the seat belt in the car door as she slammed it shut. *Get it together Tilda. This is it. Your life is finally beginning.* White coaches were lined up in bays along wide glass windows, with matching logos splashed across their lengths. Short queues had formed by each one, comprised of students, families, couples and the single. All with their own stories, all with their own plans. Tilda grinned uncontrollably and wondered if anyone could possibly be as happy as she was at that moment. Illuminated signs showing destinations such as Grimsby, Leeds and Newcastle nestled amongst more exotic places like Bristol and Luton, as she scanned her eyes for the bay that would soon welcome the 1715 arrival from York. She dragged all her worldly goods to a nearby bench and settled down. She considered getting a drink, but wasn't sure she could stomach it. Butterflies impersonating baby elephants were doing a bang-up job of ensuring she wasn't going to be consuming anything soon.

As a coach arrived, Tilda squinted to see the time from the clock inside the building. Five ten. Too early for the York arrival. Rubbing her hands, she sat forward in an attempt to steady herself and her emotions. Her smile couldn't be controlled and as the minutes passed, she stopped worrying about how she appeared to others. This was her time. This was her life. She was firmly planted in centre-stage and she was definitely shining.

It was ten fifteen that night that Tilda had to accept that Grady wasn't coming.

CHAPTER TWENTY-NINE

Tilda. Friday 7th October 2016. York.

The Satnav told her she was mere minutes away.

"...and that's the way the roads are looking this afternoon. I'll be back here in half an hour."

"Thanks Debs. Just before our next record, did you know I'm reading a book on anti-gravity?"

"I didn't, Dave."

"It's so good, I just can't put it down! The time is coming up to ten minutes past four and here's Babylon Zoo with Spaceman."

Tilda rolled her eyes in the same way she imagined 'Debbie with the Travel' did every day. Poor woman. Whatever she was being paid, it wasn't enough.

Crossing the Pennines hadn't caused any problems, which was a surprise. Everything had run smoothly, easing one of several concerns that had plagued her that morning. Now she had finally found the courage to follow Bea's advice, and keep the phantom appointment that had been made, it would have been just her luck to be stuck on the M62, traffic at a standstill because of some unfortunate crash. As it happened, the journey had been a breeze. Just less than three hours. Had she been in a more relaxed state of mind, she'd have taken in more of the beautiful scenery as well. Once off the motorway, pretty villages filled with seasonal hues peppered the remaining journey. In spite of herself, Tilda couldn't ignore it all. The October sun had clung on for as long as possible. When she managed to stop thinking about the accompanying negativity, even for just a few moments, she could convince herself that she was having an unexpectedly lovely afternoon. Apart from all the nausea and stress that she was battling every second, obviously. Apart from all that.

The hotel had been easy to find and now here she was, sitting on the edge of the bed, with half an hour to go before her appointment. An appointment she was still mentally debating about keeping. She busied herself by checking her emails, scanning the briefest of messages from Freya.

"Tilds, a proper letter is coming soon. Loads of news. Love you x"

She smiled as her mind was cast back to her far-flung friend. Freya always had news. She was just one of those people.

She was immediately distracted as from the standard-issue bedside unit, her phone rang.

"Darling, it's me. Are you there?"

"Hi. Yes Bea, I'm here."

"Now, I don't want to panic you, but I thought you could do with my help at this specific time."

Tilda was suspicious.

"Help?"

"Yes, darling, my help." Bea was firm.

"What help? You're already responsible for me pulling a sickie, lying to my husband, driving across the country and faking a legal matter that will waste a company's time. What help are you going to give me now?"

The silence at the other end of the phone alerted Tilda to the fact she may have sounded a little harsh. The geographical distance from her real life was making her feel slightly flippant. Bea had only nudged her. She'd only needed to say no. As the silence continued, Tilda thought she'd better make it right. Sighing, she ploughed on.

"For all of which, I am very grateful. I know you are only trying to give me the gift of closure. It is much needed and appreciated."

The silence continued.

"Bea?"

A shuffle, perhaps a dropped phone and then the unmistakable sound of Ms. Charleston.

"Sorry about that Tilds, I was just topping up my mascara so I put you down for a moment. Right, where was I? Oh yes, time for my help. Now, consider me your very own Trinny and Susannah but without all the body-shaming. Tell me what you're wearing and I'll tell you if it's a good idea or not."

Tilda laughed.

"Bea, there's no point. I've not brought many other options with me." She looked down at her standard weekend uniform. Jeans, ballet pumps and a checked shirt. It was her favourite shirt. That was the only concession she'd made to giving her outfit some thought. The other shirts she wore were baggy and boyish. Comfy for the weekend schlep around Tesco, or hoovering the lounge with arms free to reach, but nothing that could be described as particularly flattering. This one, on the other hand, was fitted and slightly stretchy. It clung around her non-too shabby forty-year old lumps and bumps and always felt a little risqué. The popper-like studs that took the place of buttons always made her feel that there could be worse things happen than have it ripped open in an unlikely moment of passion. Discounting the contents of her underwear drawer, this was the sexiest item of clothing she owned. Actually, including the contents of her underwear drawer too. This was as good as it got.

Bea made wretching noises down the phone.

"You CANNOT seriously be telling me that you have chosen to wear a LUMBERJACK shirt to what could be the most significant meeting of your life? I mean, come on Tilda, I'm not saying you should be in evening wear, but would it have killed you to find a pretty wrap over top, or perhaps a camisole underneath a jacket? Have you learnt nothing all these years opposite me? For the love of God, tell me you've done your make-up."

Tilda smiled. Bea was just being Bea. It was normal. It was secure. It made her feel like nothing was wrong.

"Of course I've done my makeup, and yes, I've vamped up the eye liner a bit because I know you approve. Also, my hair is loose, just as it used to be. I've thought it over and I like this look. It is perfectly respectable, a little ordinary, but overall it is not that dissimilar to the way I dressed back when I knew him. I like me like this. It's reassuring."

Bea mulled over the information and mentally assessed what she was hearing.

"Right in that case, I have one nugget of wisdom to impart. To be honest, I should have told you this years ago, regardless of what you get up today. It's been bugging me forever. I mean, really, if this is my one lasting change I can make in your life then this is it. It's..."

"BEA. Get on with it! I'm going to be late."

Bea sighed and allowed the tension to build as much as she could with the three seconds she managed to stay quiet.

"Tilda, look down at your tree-chopping shirt and take a look at your buttons. If there aren't at least three undone from the top, then you might as well put a sign around your neck saying Ignore Me World, Nothing To See Here."

"You're saying I should flaunt my breasts so the world knows I'm up for it? Is that what second wave feminism really fought for?"

"Tilds, I'm not even joking and it's nothing to do with your tits. You are taking charge of your life, and making an exciting leap into the unknown. Just lower your defenses a little. Loose hair, a clingy top and smoking hot eyes are going to mean bugger-all if you walk around with your arms across your chest, your head down and every zip, button and stud tightly closed. View it as metaphorically opening up to possibilities."

Tilda replied firmly, although the smile in her voice was audible.

"Bea, you've been brilliant. I thank you for all your words of wisdom. I'm going to go now and see what happens. I'll be in touch at some point. And don't worry about me. I will judge all possibilities on their merits and consider them wisely."

A few more platitudes and the call ended. Tilda grabbed her bag from the bed, picked up the key card and office address, and walked towards the door. She took a final look in the mirror. In spite of everything Bea had said about her shirt - and she could forgive her as she'd never actually seen it in person - she felt wonderful. Not bad at all, she found herself thinking. She stood there a moment longer and assessed what the passage of time had done to her. A slight sag here and there, and the faint laughter lines she'd known for years, now firmly answering to wrinkles on a register. Small concessions to her advancing years but nothing horrendous. She could have looked a hell of a lot worse. She started to step away and open the door, but thought again and paused.

Looking down at her top, she counted the open buttons from the collar. Two. Not bad, but they were fairly close together. Words from the past echoed into her mind. Words she had once forced herself to forget, and yet now they were back and still as raw as they had been twenty years ago.

When are you going to walk tall, with you head held high, on to centre stage, and become the star of your own show?

It didn't take long to make up her mind. Opening the third one with a satisfying pop, she opened out the lapels, adjusted her bra and walked out into the early evening. Her 5.15pm appointment was almost here. It was time for her to do some shining.

CHAPTER THIRTY

Tilda and Rosie. Friday 7th October 2016. York.

As Tilda was giving herself a mental pep talk and leaving the hotel, the reception area of Grady and Son Solicitors was experiencing a flurry of activity. Mid-afternoon appointments were drawing to a close, with clients signing forms, leaving paperwork and exiting through the door, whilst end of the day appointments arrived alongside the daily cleaning team and couriers with documents. Rosie juggled them all in her smooth professional way, batting away the more trivial enquiries, and fine-tuning her boss' schedule for the following days. Although it should not have been a surprise, when the phone call came, it caught her off-guard.

"Good afternoon, Grady and Son Solicitors. Rosie speaking, how can I help you?"

"Ah, hello. Yes, I was hoping to be able to speak to Mr. Grady, son of William Grady."

"Can I ask what it's regarding?"

The caller had rung with a rehearsed spiel and wasn't going to reduce it in order to ease the burden of the listening PA juggling a busy afternoon.

"My name is Alice Chalmers and I am currently employed by a Mr. Grady of River View Heights to care for his terminally ill father over the last few weeks. I've been trying to get hold of him for some days now, on his mobile and landline but to no avail. It finally occurred to me to search online for his work number and here I am. Is it possible to speak to him? It's very important, I'm afraid."

Rosie knew she had strict instructions to field any calls relating to the old man, but there was something in the tone of Alice Chalmers' voice that made her stop. For all its calming sing-song manner, she could sense the matronly hint of severity that was barely covered by the froth. If Alice wanted to speak to someone, Rosie felt sure, she usually managed it. Besides, it was Friday afternoon and she was ready to go home. She buzzed through to the main office and waited for the pick up.

"Alice Chalmers for you on line two. Says it's urgent."

The slight interference on the line could not hide his irritation but she couldn't care less. One more client to go, a quick consultation and then the weekend could start. In her head, it already had.

The call came at 5.05pm.

She'd found the office easily enough. It had been a short walk across a pedestrianised square, close to the hotel, to bars and restaurants and in full view of the Lion and Lamb pub on the corner. Being slightly early, she found a bench and caught her breath. Tilda attempted to regulate the speed of her breathing which was careering off the charts. She was in full sight of the Grady and Son plate above the door. Using the last few minutes she had to herself, she ran over the lines Bea had told her to say, regarding a matter about money owed from a tenant. It was still clear in her head, but she felt a growing unease about the deception. So much time had passed yet here she was, sitting outside an office about to catch up with the man who promised her so much and yet never delivered. And all she could think about was a fabricated tenant and his backlog of rent.

It was too long ago to be angry now. Even back then, anger had taken a long time to arrive. It was the disappointment and heartbreak she remembered more keenly. Sitting alone in the bus station, all her belongings by her feet. Waiting hour after hour for 'one more coach' in case he'd caught a later one. The taxi back home had been perhaps the lowest point of all. She'd garbled an excuse about Freya breaking her leg and the holiday being off, and forced herself to ignore the look of relief on her Dad's face. And then even when she was back home, she waited. She waited for a phone call, she waited for a letter. The usual Friday and Monday 6pm phone chats didn't materialise, as every time she rang, no one answered, and when indeed she found the strength to write to him, his lack of reply was the final straw.

The ensuing days had been long and empty, eventually turning into weeks that felt equally lacking. She had seriously considered turning up on his doorstep. She'd found the coach times, set aside a weekend, and come close to buying a ticket. But there was something broken in her then, something irreparably damaged by the silence that she didn't trust herself to get there and back in one piece. He'd glimpsed a future with Tilda and he'd bottled it, simple as that. He had decided it was best to cut her out of his life, rather than let it fizzle. It had taken some months to accept that as fact, but eventually she had. There'd been little else to do except sink back into her old existence. An existence that felt a lot more painful than it previously had.

Freya was very kind to her, being the only person with an inkling of what had gone on. Then her regular Stockport visits became less frequent as her own life post-Uni took off. It was all so long ago. Tilda had kept breathing, had kept waking up and had kept trying to smile outwardly. At some point, she had managed to do it without having to force herself.

A chance meeting in the Crown with Mike coupled with the start of a council temp job forced her to shelve the feelings of rejection and hurt. Instead she concentrated on learning the ropes of the Policy Planning Department and distracted herself by dating the nice guy with the shaggy hair. It mostly felt like a lifetime ago and yet the memories of Grady had never truly faded. Just pushed away, deep inside, where they were buried far enough to be able to ignore most of the time.

It had taken some time to feel fondly about him, to look back with nostalgia rather than bitterness, to reminisce rather than dwell but time had soothed the pain. It needed to because there had been so much pain to begin with.

Nowadays, the image Tilda had of the smiling, Geography student cum artist was a hazy idea. A collection of images, short mental video clips that made her feel happy that *he* was happy. He might be camping in Scotland one minute or painting scenery in the sunshine another. She assumed he'd achieved his dream to make a living as a painter but she had no idea. These days it gave her comfort to think of him in a little studio in the Lakes, hanging his art and waving to the village butcher next door. She hadn't a clue if this was the case, but the passage of time was such that she gained strength from these fantasies. Whenever she found herself reminiscing - more and more frequently in recent weeks - she played whichever mental clip came to mind. Interestingly, they never involved other people. It seemed she was only willing to wish him happiness as long as it was solitary. As long as he still thought of her after all these years. She really hoped he was happy doing what he loved and what he had talked about back then. Which was why it was very confusing that she was sitting outside a legal firm, with an appointment with Grady - presumably a partner - for ten minutes time.

The ring of her mobile broke the spell as she rooted through her bag, desperately trying to mute *Blowing in the Wind* as she did. Too late she saw it was an unknown number.

"Hello, Matilda Rudd?"

"Yes?"

"I'm ringing on behalf of Mr. Grady of Grady and Son Solicitors. I'm very sorry but Mr. Grady is going to have to reschedule your appointment this afternoon. There's been a family emergency. If you want to come back on Monday, I can fit you in with our associate..."

The words continued, unheard. Tilda's face was burning. She took a few seconds to let the reality sink in. Was he doing this again? Standing her up without a thought to what she was going through out here? God, she was so stupid. How could she have let herself believe today was the day that she would get some answers? Of course she wouldn't. Nothing ever happened the way she wanted it to.

She spoke firmly.

"I'm sorry, is there no way he can squeeze me in quickly?"

"I'm afraid not, Mrs. Rudd."

The woman continued to make excuses as Tilda fumed. Nothing ever went to plan. She might as well have decided today was the day she would win the lottery or bump into George Clooney in the carpark. She was a deluded fool. Well no more. That might have been Tilda of old, but she was damned if she was going to be pushed around anymore. Time to be assertive. Time to stop being the victim of her own personality.

Tilda interrupted the woman without a second's thought.

"I'm sorry, but I've travelled quite some distance for this meeting. I need to see Mr. Grady himself. What kind of family emergency is it, exactly? Will he be available tomorrow?"

There was a pause at the end of the line. Tilda could hear the woman take a breath before attempting to deal with the latest annoying client of the day. She didn't care how she sounded. She wasn't going home without answers.

"I'm afraid we're closed until Monday now. We have a variety of other solicitors that can deal with your enquiry. If you would prefer to reschedule with Mr. Grady, then I will have to get back to you when he returns to work."

"But where is he now?" Tilda found herself getting quite demanding. It made no sense.

"He has to leave now." The woman paused before lowering her voice, implying 'he' was in earshot. Either that, or the Friday feeling was impacting on the clarity of her telephone manner.

"Look, he'll probably be away for a few weeks. He only just got the call. His father has passed away."

Amidst initial feelings of rejection, mirroring the same painful memories she'd white washed for years, were new arrivals of confusion and curiosity. Grady's dad had died today? That was terrible, although it surprised her to hear he'd made it this long. His heart attack was years ago. As soon as she had processed that, the next thought hit her. Dear God, he was about to leave the building. He was about to open the door, walk down the three steps to the pavement and maybe head towards the same car park where she'd left her Corsa. He would *have* to walk past her. He would *have* to see her.

As she mentally scanned the implications of this and almost reached a point where her brain had started to question the sense of staying in full view of someone who clearly had pressing matters with which to deal, the red door to Grady and Son Solicitors opened. A man, tall in stature, slimly built, and with a short goatee, walked sombrely down the steps. Tilda squinted in the early dusk. His dark curls, whilst greying, were still recognisable. The long nose seemed to be the same, and even his walk had similarities to the one she'd witnessed all those years ago. He walked away from the office and as she predicted, headed towards the bench, towards Tilda, and towards the town centre behind.

Tilda could barely look up. Sitting in the brace position she was doing literally that. Bracing herself to raise her head and take a good look up into the face of the man who had loved her, but had left her too. His steps grew louder, her breathing more shallow. She had to time this right. Slowly, paying close attention to the noise of his approach, she found the courage to raise her eyes and straighten up just as he was within touching distance. He walked hurriedly past, his face in clear view, his eyes straight ahead. The eyes were exactly as she remembered, the nose, too. The long shape of the jaw and the way he held his shoulders back confidently. All there in the fading daylight. All evidence that she had tracked him down. Her mission was accomplished. She should probably ring Bea and tell her the good news. Except for one small thing.

The man wasn't Grady.

CHAPTER THIRTY-ONE

William and Grady. Saturday 18th January 1997. York.

Winter sunlight swam through the window, making it clear the cleaners were up to their usual standards. No specks of dust or greasy finger marks to be found. It could be the study of an old stately house. In fact, the photographer from Yorkshire Homes had said exactly that. The photo-shoot for the March '96 issue had taken place over four days during the previous year and although there had been a concerted effort to tidy up and present the house as being particularly special, this room had needed little doing.

Large in size, and lined with floor to ceiling mahogany bookcases, it was a blur of emerald and burgundy leather bound journal volumes. Framed certificates and plaudits honouring the Grady name hung on what little wall space was visible, and created a dark, dense and fiercely masculine area of the house. At one end of the room was the wide bay window, the only source of natural light. Its views of the cottages and lanes running towards the valley had been one of the more desirable features of the home that had been specifically commented on in the article. The quote 'unparalleled rural beauty, encompassing rivulets of Yorkshire working life' had made Old Man Grady roar with pleasure. Whilst officially being nothing of the sort, owning the big house on the hill did make him feel like Lord of the Manor now and then. A feeling he was more than happy to accommodate and a feeling that John Grady was becoming increasingly embarrassed with, every day he remained living there. Luckily for him, that wasn't going to be for much longer.

With the unpredictability of the Yorkshire weather, the bay window alone was rarely enough to illuminate the room. A large lamp with its spotlights twisted outwards, stood in one corner, and in front of it, facing the impressive view was a desk. Not one of your flat pack, easily tacked together, sustainable wood, lightweight pieces of furniture. Not a discreet surface slotted into a narrow alcove for household admin and the occasional letter to a friend. Nothing like that at all. This desk was solid. Heavy in weight - it had taken three bulky men to move it into place several years earlier - it was going nowhere fast. Dark wooden planks, as thick as the beams supporting the roof, lay nestled together across the surface. Nailed into position, sanded down and covered in a thinner veneer of the same material, slick with shine, it was a wooden symbol of power. Sitting down in the high-backed leather of the office chair, looking out over the fields and beyond, Old Man Grady felt like he had truly made it. It amused him to feel as though he controlled everything he could see. The van driving up the hill to the stone cottage a few hundred yards away, the washing that was being pegged out on the line between two trees in the garden with the cobbles on the right. Everyday people getting on with their lives, but all hapless puppets in his empire. He knew it wasn't really his empire but he liked the idea that it was. All he needed was a white cat to stroke and his megalomaniac image would be complete.

His empire, in reality, amounted to far less. A reasonably successful firm of solicitors that had been handed down to him from his own father, ten years before, and of course the family responsibilities he'd had to assume fully upon the unexpected death of his wife, roughly a decade before that. Once the son, now the father. It would be the same for the next generation too. A rite of passage that would continue to be passed on through his ancestors, long after his death. He could hear his father's voice, strong and booming, in his head. *'It is your duty to instil the pride of hard work into your children, just as it will be their duty to instil it into theirs. Make the firm proud, William. Never settle for less.'*

Those words had been oft repeated and never challenged. William Grady had done as he was told. And now it was time for his offspring to do the same. Under his lead, he was sure his father would have been proud, even if it were something he would never have expressed in personal terms. The firm was a successful force with which to be reckoned and regularly made it into the top debt specialist lists for the area. The study boasted an array of awards and honours that recognised just that.

Perhaps he had become complacent, but that overblown incident back in June, had come as a huge surprise. He'd been dictating a letter in his office when the searing pain hit. Clutching his arm, he remembered dropping the Dictaphone and trying to shout, but with no breath. The next thing he knew he was lying in hospital wired up to goodness knows what, and feeling like a tethered bull. No one listened to him, of course. After he'd dismissed the nurses, even the male nurse - so ridiculous - he'd managed to insist that the consultant see him at once and transfer him to private patient status. There'd been some mix up and he'd been put in a ward with other people. There was nothing to make his blood boil and his heart pack up quicker than have his orders ignored, but he'd managed to convey his displeasure at the situation without bursting any more arteries. Since then, he'd been forced to take it easier. He wished he'd been as lucky as his father had been with him. He'd been a hard working and astute young solicitor who had been keen to learn the ropes and hungry for the chance to prove himself. Thirty years later, passing over the reigns of his business to his feckless waster of a son, had been the last straw. That had forced him to recover quicker than the doctors told him it would. It was motivational really. A good thing. Seven months on, and he was back. Between the staff, associates and his own offspring, there had been no massive catastrophes but this was more luck than prudent decision-making. William Grady was back, and able to control the puppets once more. As far as he was concerned, it wasn't a moment too soon.

As these thoughts were running through his father's mind in the study, Grady was lugging a heavy, bulging rucksack down the main stairs of the house. In the hallway, already placed neatly by the door, was a smaller canvas bag zipped tight with the essentials he reckoned he'd need for the foreseeable future. The planning for this trip had been both meticulous and dizzyingly exciting. Once it had become clear that Tilda was of a similar mind, and that like him, she wanted her future to be a joint adventure, it had been easy. They'd planned their route, what money they'd need, and how much to budget until they got casual work along the way. Everything else could be worked out later. It might not have been planning careers, weddings and kids, but it was just as full of commitment as those events would be to others. And he couldn't wait for the day those milestones would also be of concern for them both. The setback with his father, just as their plans had been ready to roll,

had been a real blow. Now it didn't matter in the slightest, and had given them more time to work out the
details of their big adventure. Back then, however, it had
felt like the end of the world.

Never especially close to his father at the best of
times, having to help deal with pay slips, billing and staff
problems whilst battling with the loss of his own plans
and the potential death of a man for whom he had very
little respect, meant that Grady's inner world felt more
like a swirling vortex rather than the calm and peaceful
space it usually inhabited. So, just as promised back then
- to a wide variety of distant family members, firm associates and doctors - he had paused his own plans and
delayed his future for the good of his father. Tilda had
been as amazing as he knew she would be. Never once
complaining, and actively going out of her way to make
him feel better when the frustrations about the situation
were clouding his mind. And now it was here. The day
to which he had been counting down, since before he
could consciously understand. The day he was going to
start living.

The first day of a future of happiness.

Bags by the door, money and bus ticket in his pocket,
Grady debated his next move. It would be far easier to
pick up his bags, open the front door and stride down
the hill never looking back. He'd said his goodbyes to
everyone that mattered. But an annoying sense of obligation seemed to be twisted around him inside, making
him pause and question whether that would be the right
thing to do. One moment of indecision and duty won
over. He found himself pushing open the door to his father's study in spite of the pointlessness of what he had
to say. Deaf ears and pigheadedness would be all that
was waiting.

"All right?"

Silence.

"Hello. Dad?"

The swivel chair shifted a fraction whilst the old man's eyes stayed firmly on the case file in front of him.

"Hmmm?"

"I'm off now. I just wanted to say goodbye."

There was no sound. Grady shifted nervously from foot to foot. It made him mad how ineffectual he felt whenever he attempted to engage in the briefest of conversations with this automaton. Not for the first time he wondered what on earth his mother must have seen in him. All his understanding of goodness and light and *even love* must have come from her. Nature over nurture, no question about it.

"Dad?"

Time was ticking. This was pointless.

"I'm off now, like I told you. I'm not sure when I'll be back but I'll get in touch at some point, I imagine."

Grady looked out of the window. A little speck at the bottom of the hill caught his attention. A child, no it was two children in fact. It wasn't the children that caught his eye, rather the red kite that they were flying. It soared high in the air, dipping now and then before rising once more. The occasional wobble and fall and a long length of string could not disguise the fact that it was ultimately free. Far freer than Grady had ever been. His resolve strengthened as his voice calmly sliced through the tension.

"Be like that then. It's your choice."

Finally movement. The document was placed on the desk and the chair slowly wheeled backwards, rotating as it did. The old man, flint-eyed and pale stared up at his son through the gold-rimmed spectacles on the end of his nose.

"We've had this conversation. I made it clear then, and I'll repeat myself now. You're not going anywhere. You will stay here and make the firm proud."

Grady breathed in. He had known this attempt at communication would result in a confrontation, but he didn't think it would be the second he'd spoken. He should have left after all. Breathing out, he allowed the seconds that passed to temper the anger that was building up inside. Nobody had ever stood up to his father. No one dared. The fact that it had fallen to him - chilled out, pacifist, live-and-let-live John Grady - was ironic to say the least but it had to be done. Bullies needed to be confronted and that was what he intended to do.

"I know what you said, *Father*, but I didn't agree with you then and I don't now. I'm leaving now, to meet my girlfriend, to travel and work and paint. I agree with you on one thing. It's not the start of a career, I know that. But I'm twenty-one. I have the whole of my life ahead of me and I can use this time to work out what I want to do. All I know is, with respect, I do not want to be a solicitor. I don't want to work in the firm and I don't want to live here any longer. I'm not rejecting you and your life, I'm just making decisions about my own. It's as simple as that. I'm sorry you don't approve but I don't actually need your approval. Not one bit of it. And so, I'll say it again. I'm leaving now but I'll be in touch. It's your choice if you accept that or not."

It had possibly been the longest period of uninterrupted speech Grady had ever had with his father. Usually there were decrees, orders and condemnations bounced back from the old man whenever anyone spoke, especially when it was one of the puppets. Perhaps the heart attack had slowed him down somewhat, but by the time he'd got to his feet, Grady was already through the door. With his rucksack being hoisted upon his back, the old man let his feelings be known. His anger was clear.

"Now you listen to me, you good for nothing waste of space. I forbid you to walk out of that door, do you hear me?"

It was easy for Grady to keep calm now. There was nothing to keep him here, nothing of beauty in this ugly house.

"I hear you but I've made my position clear. I am an adult and as such, am more than capable of making my own decisions. I'm going now, regardless of what you say."

Grady looked at his father's red face and bulging eyes." You should go and sit down before you have a relapse."

Although meant with concern, this observation seemed to add oil to the already growing flames.

"Sit down? SIT DOWN? How DARE you talk to me like that. I am your father and I decide where you go and what you do. Just because you've been blindsided by some trollop who's been charitable enough to open her legs does *not* mean you turn your back on your responsibilities and family duty. You will not leave this house, do you understand?"

Grady, backpack hoisted in place and small holdall in hand, stopped what he was doing. Removing his free hand from the front door latch, he slowly closed it shut in front of him. Turning around, he saw his father, his stonehearted, cruel beast of a father walking back towards the study, head held high. The final demand from his lips had been uttered and therefore the conversation was over. He expected his son to turn around, put his bags down and do as he was told.

He could go and fuck himself.

"Excuse me, what did you just call Tilda?"

The old man looked back, confused.

"Who?"

"Tilda, my girlfriend. What did you just call her?"

William Grady cast his mind back.

"I can't remember the exact terminology, but I imagine it was something like slut, slapper, tart or trollop. It sounds as if she's got you exactly where she wants you. It'll only be the money she's after, not that you'll get a penny from me if you carry on the way you've been acting. Does she know that if you follow a fool's plan such as this, then you'll be as poor as she is? I bet she hasn't factored that into her plans, scheming little bitch. I bet she..."

William Grady didn't get any further into his rant. His son charged at him, hands outstretched until they grabbed the lapels of his jacket. Peaceful, placid Grady had been pushed to his limits.

"Don't you ever, EVER say anything about Tilda. She is the only good thing in my life and I will not let you talk about her in such a disgusting way."

His father wriggled out of Grady's clutches, hampered as they were by the canvas weight on his back, and took his chance to grab his shoulders. His voice, when it spoke, was low and ominous.

"Watch it boy. You're treading a fine line. Anyone would think that you *wanted* to be cut off. I'm warning you to put a stop to all these stupid, beatnik ideas and remember who you are."

"I know what *you* are. You're a bitter and twisted old man, and one day soon, you'll have another heart attack and it will finish you off. And the world will be a better place for it. Now take your hands off me, you bastard."

It would have been unclear had there been any onlookers present, the exact order of events that followed this exchange. Did the old man let go of Grady a little too forcefully? Or did the momentum of Grady's efforts at pulling away from such a grip, add to the power of the fall. Whatever the truth, it made no difference to the outcome. As William's grip of Grady loosened, his son stumbled backwards into the room, falling with some speed as the luggage on his back dragged him down.

The crack of his head on the corner of the desk was the only sound to be heard. It reverberated around the room with a sickening echo.

It was at this point, that a tall man with curly hair and a long nose came downstairs to see what was going on.

CHAPTER THIRTY-TWO

The Solicitor and Tilda. Friday 7th October 2016. York.

Of course, he'd *intended* to go home. When he left the office, his ears ringing with manufactured sympathy and fraudulent pity, he'd fully intended to head straight there. Not to the *apartment* he called home, obviously, but rather to the cold grey building of his childhood. The one with unwelcoming gates and icy memories. The call had caught him unawares. Having studiously avoided all attempts at contact from the *Alice woman* since her appointment, he'd begun to forget how serious the situation had become. Whilst not made clear in their one and only conversation back at the start, he'd assumed that all responsibilities had been handed over to this Alice... *he glanced at the card she'd given him...* this Alice Chalmers and her team upon engagement. The fact that she'd managed to find him, and expect his immediate presence now, irritated him beyond measure.

It had been Rosie who was the only one with an understanding of the situation. Rosie, who remembered what a bastard the old man had been, and how much pain he'd caused when he ran the firm. Rosie, who had been loyal to the company when everyone else had melted away, sick of the tirades of verbal abuse and the general lack of respect that had been bandied about. Good old Rosie. Like a glamorous, yet kindly aunt, despite not being much older than him. She had kept her head and been a clear voice of reason when everything seemed overwhelming. Without her, there would have been no firm left, so invaluable she'd become over the years. And today, it had been Rosie that gently pointed out that there were funeral arrangements to make, people to notify and a whole host of responsibilities that the private palliative care team he was currently paying, should not, nor would not do. It was time to take over.

With those words spurring him into some sort of action, and with a hurried gathering of his briefcase and coat, he was now walking towards the town, on a mission to flag a taxi and take him, however briefly, into the mother of all head fucks. But then he passed the Lion. The sweet aroma of beer fumes and wafts of outdoor tobacco filled his lungs, causing his pace to slow. Surely he had time for one quick drink? He'd had bad news. This was highly appropriate under the circumstances. Alice Chalmers and her band of merry men could probably wait a little longer? Without thinking it through in any greater depth than the most superficial of mental debates, he turned back on himself and entered the pub. He'd only be ten minutes later than he'd planned.

From her bench, Tilda had watched, bewildered. To her left sat an elderly man feeding pigeons, and to her right a gaggle of school girls gossiped and screamed at anything and everything, but her tunnel vision blanked all that out. All she saw was the man that walked past her. The man, who at one time had been her reason for living and yet now looked like the living dead. It was too much to comprehend and her mind was struggling to make sense of it. Instead she focused on what she could see.

The man passed her, stopped for a second and retraced his steps before striding purposefully into a pub.

A painting of a lion and lamb swung from above the door as he entered the darkness beyond. Her head was all a swirl as she considered her next move. Wait for him to come out? Follow him wherever he ended up? Force her legs to carry her weight and walk in there after him? She didn't need to think too long. She didn't even need to try. Without consciously making a decision, her legs took charge. She stood, and without knowing what she was going to do when she got there, walked slowly towards the pub.

It was much busier than his usual drinking sessions got. The Friday post-work, early evening drinks were well underway, and he'd had to wait to be served. Not usually the case mid-morning, between hearings.

"Usual, Sir?"

"Yes, thanks."

The barman, whose name was still beyond him, stabbed the optic with the glass, and placed the amber liquid in front of him. Since the panic attack, the barman remembered him, and he hadn't had to ask for a double scotch, no ice, since. He sipped it. It wouldn't do to throw it back and immediately require another. Not when he had to create some sort of semblance of respectability when he finally left here and went to face Alice Chalmers' particular style of music.

He was concentrating on sipping rather than downing, when he became aware of her. A skinny blonde woman, just out of the corner of his eye. Not his type in any way - under normal circumstances he would never have noticed her. If he were ever forced to pick a type, his eyes were usually drawn to the curvier of brunettes. This woman would not be on his radar at all. However, she was definitely staring at him. Not an appreciative glance. Not a longer-than-strictly-appropriate moment of mutual eye contact to signify shyly she was interested. No, this was out and out staring. Her face was pale - pinched and hollow as if she'd not slept for days. Her eyes, whilst probably quite pretty under the right circumstances, were crazily wide. Was she staring at *him* or something *behind* him? He didn't know her, had never met her, and was becoming increasingly unnerved by her gaze. Casting his mind back over recent cases, he could dismiss all thoughts that she was a past client. And he'd never seen her face across a table in a meeting or hearing. Booze courage, or just a lack of tolerance at this mentally tumultuous time, forced him to respond. He put down his glass and turned to face her. It was time to tell her to stop.

"Is there a problem?"

His irritation was more than obvious. Everyone within earshot would have sensed it. She blinked once or twice in quick succession as if he'd broken her trance, coughed slightly, and looked down shaking her head.

"I'm sorry... I just..."

She appeared lost for words. He continued to be annoyed by her although he simultaneously managed the thought that at least this was distracting him from what he should really be thinking about now.

"What is it? Who are you and why do you keep staring at me? Have we met?"

Tilda knew this was not going to plan.

"I'm sorry...no, we've never..."

She continued to splutter over her words, struggling to formulate her scrambled thoughts, almost startled at his direct tone. *Get it together Tilds*, she urged herself, evoking motivational images of the far stronger Freya and Bea in her choice of nickname. How strange it was that her closest confidants were so similar. When she wasn't living this exact moment anymore, she'd consider what that was about. But for now, she had more pressing matters in hand. She'd come this far. She was not going to balls it up by chickening out and leaving with less information than she'd started. She took a deep breath and tried again. Calmly, chest rising and falling, she took control.

"I'm sorry to stare. My name is Tilda Willoughby. I thought you were someone I used to know, but you're not. You're not Grady. I apologise for interrupting you. It seems I've had a wasted journey."

His eyes continued to return her stare, pooling a mixture of sadness, annoyance and apathy of life in general. She had no idea what was running through his mind. Surely she couldn't have got this wrong? The height, the hair and the nose were all spot on, but this couldn't be Grady. Her lovely, mellow, happy, carefree soul mate, who had opened her eyes to how wonderful life could be. This jaundiced, sweating, alcoholic stranger could never be her Grady from all those years ago. What was going on?

Finally the man spoke. There wasn't a dawning realisation, or clear sign that the penny had dropped. His voice was imperceptible at first. A mumble. Fragments of words under his breath, nothing clear or coherent.

"I'm sorry, could you say that again?" she whispered.

The man sighed, weary with the almighty effort this was taking. Knocking back his drink in one final motion, he placed the glass on the bar and tried again. This time there was no mistaking what he said. Tilda heard him loud and clear.

"I think you mean my brother."

CHAPTER THIRTY-THREE

Stewart and Tilda. Friday 7th October 2016. York.

Twenty minutes later and her glass of wine was largely untouched. In front of him, were a couple of empty tumblers. Now that he was thinking, his rate of consumption had slowed slightly and number three was lasting a little longer. Tilda was glad. There were too many unanswered questions. She needed to know she was getting the undiluted truth. They continued to face each other across the padded booth, the coloured glass of the window not helping the overall dingy atmosphere one bit, as Grady's brother silently sought the words he needed.

Although saying nothing, his mind was dancing. Images flashed before him with no order or logic. *A large, green birthday cake shaped like a train... two boys tentatively poking a beehive with a twig... rolling down a hill gathering stray grass and leaves as they tumbled.* Like littered fragments being swirled on water, they made no sense mixed up together. He needed to focus. He needed to remember something whole. His glass rotated in his hand. He let the scotch swirl around in every direction, as he struggled to pinpoint the correct starting place for what he should say.

The snapshot of a bunk bed floated into his head. *A ratty old blanket tucked under the top mattress, falling down to conceal the top-secret headquarters below. Two little boys giggling behind the duvet on the bottom bed. Their dark curls identical, the older of the two looking after his baby brother who'd only just been able to haul himself up onto the mattress. A young woman peeking around the hanging blanket with a biscuit for the intrepid campers.*

His happy place.

"I'm sorry. I'm not very good at… I don't know where to begin."

Tears welled up in the eyes of forty-four year old Stewart Grady as he looked at the woman. The woman he had known was going to turn up one day. She looked straight ahead and didn't blink.

"How about the beginning?"

Wiping his eyes, he started to talk.

"He was just like our mum, John was. I suppose he was Grady to you, wasn't he?" Stewart Grady looked at Tilda for agreement. "He always said there were too many Johns in the world."

Tilda smiled on the outside as inside she ached at the stab of the memory. She wanted him to keep talking, but knew she'd have to battle the rising dread inside.

"I was five when she died and he was one. And it's awful because I can't remember her voice or her smell or anything tangible about her. But when I force myself to come up with something, it's a vague feeling of some-one who was floaty and carefree. I felt happy when she was there. She made everything an adventure. And that's just like John. Like your Grady."

"My Grady." Tilda whispered the words as an echo. Tears pricked her eyes. Someone who knew Grady also knew he was hers.

"Where is he now? Where's Grady?"

She didn't want to force the issue, but felt as though Stewart needed a gentle nudge in the right direction. She watched him take another swig of scotch. Then he picked up a beer mat and started to fiddle with that. Finally he spoke.

"Did John, I mean Grady, ever say anything about our Dad?"

Tilda remembered with a start, physically jumping back as she did.

"Oh my God, I'm so sorry. He died today, didn't he? They cancelled my appointment. How could you stay here with me and my daft questions, you must go to him." She lifted her bag over her shoulder and began to shimmy out of the seat. "Come on. You have to leave."

Stewart Grady remained where he was.

"Tilda, sit down." He didn't look up from his glass as he spoke. Just uttered the quiet command as if knowing it would be followed. A glimpse of the accomplished legal expert before the alcohol and self-loathing took over.

"Please, just sit. There's no rush, he's not going anywhere."

Tilda looked down at the troubled expression. It wasn't grief as much as resignation. Taking his advice, she settled back into her seat, and replaced her belongings. Now it was her turn to take a steadying drink of wine. She had to know, but she knew she didn't want to. She replaced her glass and finally answered his question.

"No, Stewart, Grady told me very little about his father. I got the impression that they did not get on, and that when your dad was ill, and Grady helped with the business - back in 1996 - it was not what he'd rather have been doing."

Tilda was almost quoting him verbatim. She'd re-read those letters many times over the last few weeks. Stewart listened grimly and waited for her to finish. His expression had become more determined. He had things to say, and now it seemed he had found the words.

"You're right. They didn't get on at all. Our father didn't really get on with anyone. He had no friends, only work acquaintances, and tended to make sure he could control anyone he had dealings with."

Tilda listened but was already confused.

"I can understand how he could control people he employed, but how could he have such a say in your life, or in Grady's? Surely you could have refused to do what he wanted?"

The solicitor smiled sadly to himself and took another sip. It was impossible to explain to anyone who hadn't lived through it.

"It was always easier for me. I took after our dad in lots of ways. I don't mean I was a bully, well, on reflection maybe I've had my moments, but I was happy to do what he wanted. A career in law was something that appealed, regardless of whatever pressure my father would have put on me. He didn't need to, as I was already on board. John was the complete opposite of me. He preferred being outdoors. He was always sketching beetles, or leaves, or some broken piece of twig he'd found in the garden. Our mum was long dead but I always got the impression she would have approved. Our father, however, did not. He used to lose it with John, berating him for his latest art project, or criticising him for wanting to have the final say in the subjects he chose. It was pathetic really. John was never going to be a solicitor, never in a million years. Yet Dad was hell bent on forcing him into the most uncomfortable of lives, just so he could be in control."

Tilda was silent for a moment as she digested the information. She still didn't understand.

"So if he didn't become a solicitor, what did he become? What's Grady's job?"

Stewart paused, as he thought back. Half cut, he was becoming less guarded about the information he was sharing. He'd only just met this woman, but he found himself opening up to her. A new sensation. Smiling he replied to her question, whilst never fully answering it.

"You know when you see these documentaries on TV? That crocodile guy from Australia, or Bear Grylls or someone like that? I always think Grady would have enjoyed working on one of those sorts of programmes. He'd never have wanted to be in front of the camera, but he'd have been great at checking out locations, and writing scripts. He was always good with words. Actually, he could have made a good lawyer if he'd put his mind to it."

He took another sip. Tilda was getting impatient.

"Stewart. Where is he? Where's Grady now? Does he have a family? I know he's probably married. *Is* he married? Is he gay, even? You can tell me, I can take it. I just need to know."

Stewart Grady tipped the last mouthful of his scotch deep into his throat. His eyes were pricking with tears again. He'd kept this buried for so long. It was long overdue to be unearthed, and there was a particular sweetness to the timing of this, what with his Dad's eventual demise just a few hours before.

Stewart looked at the skinny blonde woman straight in the eye. It was time for the truth to be heard.

"Grady's dead." He touched her hand. "I'm so sorry."

CHAPTER THIRTY-FOUR

Ron and Jean. Saturday 18th January 1997. York.

The call had come at an early point into the shift. *Head injury, white male, 21*. It was never easy being the first at a scene. As much experience as the job gave you, there were always nerves when faced with a new situation. It was a relief when the adrenaline took over and the practical nature of what needed to be done became the driving force. After twenty-five years as a paramedic, Ron had seen it all. Women in labour in laybys, hyperventilating husbands nearby, schoolboys' heads stuck through railings during particularly mischievous and illicit climbs. And amidst all the humorous or life-affirming anecdotes that he shared with Jean and the boys, there were the truly horrific and heartbreaking. Today's call fell squarely into the latter category. It was a tragedy, plain and simple. A terrible accident and extreme bad luck. The heavy sadness had stayed with him all day.

"And so then what happened?"

Jean probed as he passed her the plate to dry. After so many years, she could instinctively sense when he needed to talk. When the day's trials were weighing him down, when one glass of wine wasn't going to be enough this evening.

Ron rubbed the plate absentmindedly.

"Well that was when it hit me. The guy was probably

my age and he just sat in the corner on a chair, shaking his head as if he couldn't believe what had happened. We put the shock blanket round him, and someone made him a cup of tea, but he became a shell of a man in front of our eyes. He just kept saying 'No, not my John, not my John' over and over."

"How had it happened?"

Jean stacked the dishes neatly as she spoke. Best to let him get it all out now rather than not sleep tonight.

"It was a complete accident. Just bad timing. Turns out, he was on his way to start a gap year with his girl-friend. He picked up his rucksack that was jam packed with all his belongings, and the weight of it pulled him back and he stumbled, cracking his head on the desk."

"Oh no. That's terrible. Was there anyone there?"

"No. An older brother was upstairs, and the father had been on his way in from the garden when he heard the noise. He just missed witnessing it."

"What a terrible tragedy. The poor man. Must be so hard to lose a son like that."

Jean moved on to the cutlery as Ron continued to wipe the worktops aimlessly.

"The man told us how proud his son had made him. Apparently he graduated last year, and was going travelling before returning to work in his solicitors' firm."

"Oh dear. And just after Christmas too." Jean's comments had started to become a regular beat in the oral retelling. "How will he manage now?"

"I don't think he had grasped what had happened, to be honest, love. It was as if he still thought it possible that his son was going to get up off the stretcher and tell us all to stop making a fuss. The man had no idea what was going on. And as for the other lad, he just stood in the corner of the room looking terrified. It'll take some strength for them to get through this. At least they have each other, I suppose."

Ron folded the tea towel as Jean recognised he'd exorcised a few of the demons that would have troubled him later, if he hadn't shared. With a cup of tea made, they sat down in their living room and turned on the television, to drown out the rest.

Ron's account of the aftermath had been mostly accurate. William had sat in the corner for some time after Grady's body had been removed. With a silver foil blanket around his shoulders, he continued to mutter under his breath, although in spite of Ron's assertions to the contrary, no one could make out the words. Hot, sweet tea had been brewed although remained untouched by his side. Stewart had stayed on the other side of the room. He stood in the facing doorway, paralysed with the shock of it all. His eyes had taken everything in, but he didn't move or speak. The paramedics milled around and packed away their unused equipment as the police had arrived. Statements had to be taken, as routine an accident as this was. The police made the impersonal formality sound as if it would be a matter of moments, and they'd be out of the way as soon as possible.

It was as the officers busied themselves with finding a couple of chairs, that Ron had missed it. Almost imperceptibly, and for just a brief movement, William Grady held his finger to his lips and made clear to his remaining son that the secret they now shared was to remain exactly that. A secret.

CHAPTER THIRTY-FIVE

Alice, Flo and Gregor. Friday 7th *October 2016. York.*

Today, the big house on the hill seemed far less austere and unwelcoming. Not that the passage of time had done anything to soften its coldness. It was more to do with the wholly expected events of the morning. Officially, the death of William Grady was a sad occurrence. Everyone knew that. And yet, regardless of the solemn tasks in hand, and the utter professionalism of all concerned, there was a slightly different feeling in the air. Barely perceptible, nothing that could tangibly be put into words, yet a sense of freedom was filtering into the consciousness of everyone. A feeling that comes with the first spring day after months of grey clouds or the hint of an unexpected surprise, catching one off guard and lightening the mood. The tension had appeared to evaporate with the old man's last breath. No one behaved any differently from how they should, but the atmosphere could now be described as *not unpleasant*. The eggshells around which the team had navigated the past few weeks had been swept away, giving them all a slightly inappropriate spring in their step - a spring that they were working hard to subdue at this *sad* time.

Gregor was finding it the hardest to hide, lightly smiling as he took his part in the last offices of their most recent client. Just a hint of an upturned lip, and not one directly associated with the passing of the man he was currently washing. Rather a sense of relief that the awkwardness and uncomfortable nature of this gig was behind them. As soon as the son arrived, he had a date with a cold beer and last week's *Strictly*. It couldn't come soon enough.

Flo also felt flushes of relief, but this was tempered with the guilt of feeling such a way in the face of the work of the Almighty. Sure, the old man was bigoted and cruel, but no one deserved to die alone. He was one of God's children, just the same as she was. Her mind skillfully avoided recalling the times she escaped at the end of her shift, ranting about the fact the old man deserved nothing less. A fiery eternity was all he had been good for back then. It was just easier to be charitable now. Now he could do no more harm to anyone.

Alice was the one, who once again, was seeing the bigger picture. Her illicit online snooping had finally paid off, and whilst being frowned on by their strict policies and working protocol, had at least meant the Next of Kin had been informed about the situation. The receptionist had assured her, when she'd rung back, that he had left and was on his way. She looked up at the clock for the fiftieth time since that call. Three hours later she was still waiting.

Flo broke the silence.

"What next? He's all clean now."

"Check the Care Plan," Alice said. "I think it specifies a particular suit."

"Leave it to me, I'll find it."

Flo marched out of the room in search of her copy, renewed energy pouring out of her. Alice checked through her bundle of papers for hers. It had been the briefest document of its type she had seen. Emailed through to her, after their services had been engaged, she'd been taken aback by the blank spaces or 'not applicable' options chosen. It should have given her a hint as to how this would go, but after caring for William in his final weeks, she had started to see why his nearest and dearest were giving him a wide berth. It was still sad, but completely understandable now that she'd spent some time here.

Gregor spoke his thoughts aloud as he emptied the bowl into the sink.

"I wonder what he did?"

"What who did?" Alice said.

"William. I know he was horrible to us, and probably with everybody else too, but I wonder if he did anything really bad that meant his family disowned him."

"What are you talking about?" Flo returned to the room with a collection of immaculate suits on padded hangers.

"I've no idea which one is the right one. I'm going to lay them all out and check."

Flo busied herself with the task, while Gregor continued to ponder.

"It could have been emotional cruelty over years and years. You know, picking on everybody he knew until they'd all had enough."

"I can believe that," Flo spat. Her charitable nature remained passive for the moment. "I never heard him say a kind word about anyone."

"To be fair, we heard him say very little. Let's not judge him too harshly." Alice continued to smooth the ruffles, intent to remain as respectful to the client as possible. At least until she was with her takeaway and bottle of Rioja that evening. Martin would be putting up with some stories then, poor guy.

"He could have been a Mafia boss, you know, like the Godfather?" Gregor's ears pinked in excitement as he warmed to his theme. "Yes, I can just see it. He sits at that big desk, looking out of the window as local business people, and poverty stricken neighbours and... and all the other mafia bosses all come to pay compliments and ask for money at his daughter's wedding. Oh, God, that's definitely it. He's Marlon Brando!"

Gregor was pacing up and down with childish glee as he worked out the details of his suspicions. What a great tale he'd have to tell his nephews and nieces when he was old. He'd cared for the North Yorkshire don known as William Grady and been there when he died. It would make him seem powerful and brave.

"Gregor, calm yourself and help Flo find the right suit. You're like a big kid at times"

"I'm just saying..." he protested.

"Shush, we need to get him dressed and then we can wait in the other room. The son should be here any minute. Hopefully."

As her mind wandered back to the clock a funny thought struck her. It wouldn't do to indulge Gregor, and she had to remain visibly in charge. But still, this had been a tough job, and maybe it was all right to be able to let her guard down once in a while. It would show to the staff she was capable of being relaxed and having a joke along with the rest of them. She threw caution to the wind and went for it.

"He can't be the Godfather. Not even close. If he were, Michael Corleone would be here with all the businessmen paying their respects, Kay would be pacing around downstairs with the kids, and Tom Hagan would be making calls in the kitchen."

Gregor was taken aback.

"You know the Godfather? Alice, you legend."

Alice tried to purse her lips but smiled regardless. She *loved* the Godfather.

"I'm not completely devoid of cultural references. And call me crazy, but I even enjoyed the third one."

"Well now you've gone too far, but I'll let it go as it's your first faux pas with me. I might even see if it's on Netflix tonight as a sign of respect."

Alice smiled as thoughts of the doe-eyed and beautiful Michael of the first film flitted into her mind, causing a slight increase in heart rate and a rosy glow to settle on her face. Wouldn't it be wonderful if William's next of kin was a boyishly handsome Al Pacino.

Ten seconds later her fantasy was swiftly punctured as a tear-stained and dishevelled Stewart Grady knocked on the front door.

CHAPTER THIRTY-SIX

Tilda. Friday 7th October 2016. York.

The budget hotel in which she currently found herself seemed entirely appropriate in the circumstances. Its particular essence of magnolian bland was being gamely enlivened by splashes of lilac on the faded furnishings adorning her perfectly average and utterly non-descript room for the night. Nothing stood out as pleasing to the eye, but nor did it offend. A bed, desk with chair and slim wardrobe were all the furniture that had been deemed necessary. Apart from the telephone and desk lamp, the only other items of interest were sitting on a neatly arranged tray. Coffee sachets, two mini milk containers, and a pair of Morning Coffee biscuits that had been carefully placed next to Gulliver's own kettle. A kettle that looked like it hadn't been boiled in months.

Grady was dead.

It was hard to imagine much of any interest happening in this room. This room, or one of the other hundred identical ones in the hotel. A conveyor belt of travelling reps, casually contracted workers, the occasional budget hen-do? It was difficult to picture passion, rage, pleasure or heartbreak. Impossible to imagine anything of emotional worth being contained within the four walls, walls that would wobble and fall to the ground in the face of such depth of feeling. Indeed, her self-containment and lack of response suited her surroundings perfectly. There was no distraught wailing to be done, no beating her breast as she sank into the gold and cream opulence of a king sized boudoir. She was not the tragic heroine in her own life story, tossing between one adventurous lover to the next. There was nothing so full of feeling as that. Instead, she perched on the edge of a neatly made bed, straight backed and open eyed. Her occasional blink and the metronomic rise of her chest were the only movements she seemed able to make. Not for her, luxury or abundance. Not for her, passion and excitement. Not for her, love and companionship. *Breathe in, breathe out, same as always. Nothing has really changed.*

From her central view, something caught her eye. A smudge on the wall, maybe a smear of grease that was catching the light from the lamp. It was a small mark in an otherwise uniform wall. A blank wall devoid of interest. There were no patterns, no textures, no contrasting colours to create an effect. But, still, that smudge was there. That smudge was the most fascinating part of the whole room. Tilda focused on the smudge. A beautiful idiosyncrasy in an existence so empty of unique quality.

Tilda looked at the smudge for a long time.

Hours passed. It felt like hours, Tilda wasn't sure - a clock being an item of hotel décor that had been ruled as unnecessary by this particular chain. Her mind had gradually begun to awaken from its numb inertia some time ago and was now ticking and whirring once more. Random thoughts that whilst making themselves known, didn't mean she had the presence of mind to do anything about. They just bounced around her brain, settling nowhere but always moving. She should ring Bea, but couldn't find the words. She needed to text Mike to pretend she was having fun but knew that was beyond her. It had been seven hours since she'd eaten but she wasn't hungry and didn't know where she could find food at this time. What should she eat? Should she get drunk? What time was it anyway? Grady was dead.

Lying back on the bed, wide-awake and fully clothed, Tilda continued to stare ahead as the thoughts kept moving. She let them form, unencumbered by censorship or attempts to organise them into finding answers. That could come later.

Through the open curtains, the sky was slowly changing. The slightest sliver of turquoise was emerging amidst the blue-black backdrop of night. Tilda's eyes remained open. Still dressed, still in the same position as earlier, she saw the sky and decided it must be five o'clock. That was about right for this time of year. The lamp was still on, the smudge still there. Tilda focused on it again, as less frantic and uncontrolled thoughts seeped into her now conscious mind. Perhaps it was time to think about what had happened, time to let the thoughts be laid out and filtered. To be considered and dealt with. Time to begin to grieve. For the first time since she'd left him, Tilda's mind turned to Stewart.

He hadn't coped well with their conversation. It was understandable, coming as it did, hot on the heels of the news of his father. Initially, Tilda had assumed the emotion was for the old man, but it transpired not. As soon as he had started to talk about his little brother, the tears fell. It had fallen to Tilda to comfort him the best she could. An initial hand on top of his which ultimately led to her moving to sit next to him so she could hold him as he crumbled. It appeared she wasn't the only person who had shelved feelings from the past. That thought had made her feel closer to this grey solicitor than anything else they may have had in common. As he talked and she listened, her own feelings of loss were dwarfed by the colossal burden he had been carrying for years.

She'd had no idea what happened to Grady, so had been able to imagine him living a full and happy life, exactly as he'd always planned. She wasn't sure who had it worse, her not knowing, or Stewart knowing everything. The truth had eaten him up for too long. It was right to let it out, but she was worried about him now. There had been so much he still hadn't said. Thoughts half realised, sentences half formed, before his voice cracked and he'd had to stop. It had seemed right to leave her phone number. It had been her arrival under such a flimsy pretext that had prompted this. He hadn't been prepared. He hadn't known it was coming. She felt responsible for him.

Stewart and his unearthed feelings faded from her mind as she sat back on the pillows. Drawing her knees to her chest, she continued to look at the sky as it continued to dawn.

Soon it would be time to think about Grady. And all she knew was that Grady was dead.

Part Four

CHAPTER THIRTY-SEVEN

Bea and Tilda. Monday 24th October 2016. Stockport.

It was starting to become a habit. For the second Monday morning in three weeks, Bea looked across at the empty desk in front of her. Tilda was late. Again. Si ambled over, throwing a half-hearted hand gesture as he finished a mouthful of toast.

"What's going on with her? What's the craic?"

Bea's already arched brows were further raised towards her hairline with his accusatory tone.

"Pardon?"

"What's going on with her? Your mate. Why has she gone all... I don't know, all un-Tilda-like? Is she taking advantage of Tan Tights' conference? I told Alex *we* should have done that."

Bea sighed. She had no intention of answering Si's prying questions about things that were none of his business, even if he *were* voicing thoughts she'd started to wonder herself. What had happened this morning to cause the latest display of out of character behaviour from the woman whose thrice-daily tea breaks could be used to set the speaking clock? Something must have gone on. It was obviously linked with the fallout after York.

Alex walked past, as Si continued to hover.

"What're you doing?" he said to no one in particular. Ignored by Bea, Si answered for everyone.

"*I'm* on my way to do shredding, Bea is being cagey and unusually lacking in the goss, and we think Tilda is having a torrid affair which is upsetting her usual

8.46am office arrival time. Or she's just enjoying a boss-free office for change. I was in two minds to come in myself today. But then I remembered, it's fresh batter day at the chippy, so lunch will be ace."

Alex had tuned out long before Si had finished, as his interest waned. He was also on the way for his morning toilet session. Why get up early and have to use your own valuable sleeping time, when there was a perfectly good staff toilet at work that could play host to his bowel movements on his own timescale and be paid for it. Between 11am and 11.25am usually, like clockwork. It wasn't just Tilda who could be consistent. He moved on, keen to stick to the schedule, as Si continued to stand by Bea's desk.

"So do you think she's alright then? I mean, she'd let you know, wouldn't she, if anything was wrong?"

"Course she's fine," Bea breezed, airily. "She's just having a few personal issues, you know?" She left it hanging in the air without explanation. He received the information in the way she had intended - a knowing nod, and a physical step backwards. Personal issues could mean anything. From rows with the hubby, resulting in emotional outbursts at work of which he wanted no part, to worse still, vagina-related atrocities, where graphic details would be discussed over mugs of tea by the photocopier. Si couldn't handle any of that. Time to stop asking. He was only just getting over his Auntie Doreen's hysterectomy, and that had been three years ago.

Chuckling at how predictable he was - the 'women's troubles' kryptonite never failed - Bea turned her attention to her screen as she shook off her own concerns. She was worried of course, just as she had been the Monday after York. And just as it had been two weeks ago, she knew texting or ringing was pointless. If Tilda didn't want to talk, she'd ignore any attempts anyone made, including those of her best mate. Bea had tried her hardest last time, and got nowhere. She pushed the memory out of her mind, and focused on distancing herself from Si, whose looming shadow had reemerged and was starting to irritate her at this early point of the working week. Sighing she turned to face him, slapping on her brightest smile.

"Tilda's absolutely fine, Si. Nothing is going on so don't worry your pretty little head about it. Now, if you are going to the shredder, will you be a love and pop these through as well."

She heaved a dead weight of old papers onto Si's ill-prepared outstretched arms. Focusing on his new burden and relieved that there was an end to any potential uterus conversations, his attention moved away from Tilda's empty desk, and onto the immediate problem of shredding several reams of paper into the overflowing plastic bin attached to the machine. He staggered off, glad of the excuse, but feeling used nonetheless.

Bea looked at the clock. Five past eleven. Something was wrong. She knew it now, like she knew it two weeks ago.

"Has anyone seen Tilda?" Tan Tights had enquired to the office in general, almost a fortnight ago to the minute.

Bea had squirmed in her seat. Her texts were being ignored, her calls unanswered. This whole weekend reunion had been because of her meddling, and now look what had happened. Tilda was missing, no one knew where she was other than Bea, and that could mean only one of two things. Tilda was lying in bed with an exhausted but sexually satisfied Grady, having spent the weekend catching up in

the best way Bea could imagine. Or, perhaps more realisti-
cally knowing Tilda, she was lying in a ditch, the victim of a
mugging or car crash or axe murderer. And Bea was the
only one who could tell the police who she was and where
she'd been. Maybe it was time to ring someone. Bea picked
up the phone but paused. Who on earth was she going to
call? Tilda? Mike? The police? She put her phone down.
There was nothing she could do. It was just agony to have
to wait.

It hadn't been long in reality, but felt like hours to Bea.
At twenty past ten, Tilda had walked in and headed
straight towards Susan Donaldson's room. If the lateness,
and the immediate meeting with the boss hadn't already
alerted Bea that something was wrong, she only had to look
at Tilda for alarm bells to ring. Her eyes were dark, her
skin washed out and pale, and the recently flowing locks
that had suited her so well, were scraped right back into
that sensible-height of a pony tail that had been her staple
look for years. And if that wasn't enough to cause alarm,
the expression on her face was unlike anything Bea had ev-
er seen. Hollow, blank, and empty. As if she were running
late because she'd just dashed from a quick lobotomy pro-
cedure, the way someone else - well, Bea - might squeeze in
a bit of Botox before work. Nothing appeared to be going
on inside her mind. Instead, just walking with one foot in
front of the other was taking all her energy - as if she'd got
herself ready, driven to work and walked into the building
on auto pilot, because she wasn't capable of processing any
other information or emotion herself. Bea's hand covered
her mouth, in alarm. She spied through the open blinds of
the boss' office as the brief meeting drew to a conclusion.
The worry intensified as she saw Tan Tights pat Tilda's
arm, in a manner that only highlighted how devoid of actu-
al empathy the woman was. A hydraulic crane might have

done a better job of making an employee feel better. Bea continued to muse about robotic bosses as the door opened and Tilda emerged. Head down, she went straight to her desk and switched on her computer. Bea couldn't stop herself.

"Darling, are you alright? I'm so sorry about whatever went wrong. It's all my fault. What happened? No, don't tell me, it's none of my business. But tell me if you want to. Was he a complete arse? Was he racist? Was he married? What can I do? Tilda?"

Tilda lifted her head slightly so she could be seen above her monitor, but eye contact was still a struggle. She knew she was going to have to fill in all the details for Bea. It was only fair after all the trouble she'd gone to help her find some answers. And yet saying it all out loud was still some way off. She'd not had to speak for a whole twenty-four hours after finding out the truth. A couple of 'I'm having a great time' texts to Mike had been hard enough to send, so after that she'd turned her phone off so that Bea's inevitable questions wouldn't even register. It was only now she was back home that she realised how difficult this was going to be. Delayed grief was no different from actual grief. That had become immediately clear. Regardless of what had happened in the past, thinking that Grady was still living, breathing, laughing and hopefully loving her after all this time, made the news of his death two decades earlier, utterly devastating. It may as well have happened that weekend. She could have witnessed Grady's Dad knock his son to the ground in front of her very eyes two days ago and the feeling would be just the same. She swallowed a few times and raised her head a touch further. She just wanted to be left alone but knew she needed to explain, however, briefly. She coughed slightly. It made no difference. The heartbreak was still lodged and going nowhere.

"He's dead, Bea," she whispered. "Soon after I knew

him. That's what I found out."

"Oh my God, no." Bea's face fell.

"I've told Susan my cousin has died." Tilda swallowed again, not looking at her friend, knowing if anyone was nice to her at this moment she would start to cry and never stop. "I don't have any cousins, so it's OK to say that, I think."

"Oh my darling, Tilda, sweetheart, I'm so..."

"It's fine. I need to stop thinking. I..."

Tilda's voice started to crack and she had to give herself a moment. A quick swig of a water bottle and a couple of deep breaths and she was able to continue.

"I'm grateful, Bea, I really am. You gave me a chance to find out and that was so kind of you. But it didn't work out the way I thought it would. I thought my biggest disappointment would be that he was happy with someone else. And I thought that would make me sad. But right now, I'd take that over anything else in the world. He's dead. Which means all my memories are dead too. Because I only ever remembered him so I could imagine what he'd be doing today. I liked to think of him painting, or just lying in a tent reading. But all that's over now. He never got to do any of those things. He didn't even get to do anything mundane or boring like work in an office. He didn't get to marry someone he didn't truly love, or wonder where the years went, and how he'd ended up in his rut. He had no life at all."

Tilda paused again, another sip of water and another steadying moment before carrying on.

"I will be fine, Bea, I'm sure I will. But for now, everything feels over. My dreams about him are fake. They mean nothing and without them I'm not sure what I've got to keep me going."

"Oh darling, don't say..."

Tilda cut her short.

"I will be fine. Honestly. I just need to stop thinking."

As if to signify the one-sided conversation was over, Tilda lowered her head and moved her chair further into the desk. She stared at the screen, looking to the outside world like she was hard at work.

That had been a fortnight ago, and Bea was getting that same feeling of nausea in her stomach that she'd had on that day. Since her return from York, Tilda had been unusually quiet, even for her. She'd not raised a smile, or rolled her eyes the way she used to, whenever Si and Alex were being particularly annoying. It was as if she'd regressed into the frightened mouse of a girl that had been sent as a temp, way back when, who jumped when someone spoke to her, and had been over-whelmed by almost all aspects of Bea's personality.

It had been rather satisfying to see Tilda blossom over the years. To the untrained eye, the change hadn't been obvious, but to Bea it had been clear. The panic in her eyes whenever Bea made conversation had subsid-ed, and her body language had gradually downscaled from being 'uptight' to 'sensibly cautious'. It had been quite a revelation when she had first openly laughed. Bea had been relaying intimate details of a particularly adventurous tryst she had experienced...

"... and somewhere between the exploding tube of lube and Gerry's friend turning up, we just decided to ménage a trois it to fuck!"

...and Tilda had laughed. At the time, Bea hadn't been sure if she had assumed she was joking, when it had been a deadly serious recount of an exhilarating Satur-day night experience. But it hadn't mattered. The quiet girl that sat opposite her had laughed, and shown that hidden deep down inside, amidst all the tightly con-trolled feelings, there was someone there appreciated a good sex story. Bea had a new friend. And now twenty years later, that friend was in trouble and Bea was beside herself with worry.

Bea straightened her work face as she wavered between feelings of intense guilt and a desperate urge to do something. But there was nothing to be done. Grady was dead, Tilda was devastated, and that stress had made her go AWOL again.

But most of all, the one feeling she couldn't shake, was that she wished fervently she'd left the whole thing alone.

CHAPTER THIRTY-EIGHT

Tilda. Saturday 15th October 2016. Stockport.

Auto-pilot seemed too human a description for the way Tilda was feeling. Tilda wasn't feeling anything at all. Just functioning, and not particularly well. Whilst the office had been problematic and the family bereavement excuse, coupled with a heavily air-punctuated 'women's issue' implication allowed her to just about get away with her current state, home had not been so difficult.

"Did you get butter?" Mike said, as he delved into the back of the fridge.

"Erm no, I mean, yes. Top shelf, by the cheese."

Mike searched through the assorted dairy items at his immediate eye level.

"Nope, defo not here, love. Whereabouts do you mean?"

"Top shelf, by the cheese. Towards the left."

Tilda's voice was flat and monotone. She hadn't looked up. Mike continued to scan. The modest, slimline four-shelf refrigerator was not a place for a tub of butter to remain hidden whilst being actively sought. Mike kept looking.

"Do you mean *this*?"

He held up a tub of butter. Tilda's eyes flickered across momentarily, still red from lack of sleep, and sporadic crying.

"Yes."

Mike smiled ruefully.

"Oh, now I get it. It was saying *lightest* on it, so I

didn't think it was proper butter. Will it be the same?"

"Yes." Tilda continued to pretend to read the paper as she stared at the open page.

"Well, I'll give it a go, but to be honest, I think I'm going to want normal butter next time. Is that alright?" Tilda's eyes remained looking down.

"Fine."

Buttering the piece of toast, with the thickest slick of fat he could balance on the knife - he had to because it was *lightest* - he walked towards Tilda, sitting at the kitchen table, and bent down to kiss her head as he passed.

"You're bad this month aren't you, love?" he said as he walked passed. "Right, got to go, the footy starts at three."

The door slammed behind him, and silence descended once more. Tilda continued to hold the newspaper open in front of her. It was a week since her sleepless night in a hotel room. She had the house to herself for the rest of the day, and yet all she could do was stare.

CHAPTER THIRTY-NINE

Tilda and Mike. Friday 21st October 2016. Stockport.

The first seven days had passed in exactly the same way as each other. Wake up, go to work and come home. One week done, and before she knew it, another. Her routine gave her a rigid focus to cling to, until she could make it to the one part of the day she was alone. What used to be her hour of solitude with a cup of tea before Mike returned was now becoming her hour of emotional freedom. She needed it. It was essential. Not having to keep it together and pretend to be all right was as sweet as it was painful. She had a window in which to fall apart before it was time to suck in her insides once more. Since technological advances in recent years had meant Tilda relied on her phone and almost redundant DVD clock for time updates, there were no mournful tick-tocks punctuating the air. Because the kitchen was relatively new, and the plumber had done a professional job of installing the sink, no dripping tap kept a monotonous beat to soundtrack Tilda's daily hour of despair. Instead, she was left with an occasional car dawdling by, and just before 6pm, the sound of the ice cream van. Greensleeves could try all it liked, the hour was weighted with an oppressive air. And yet in contrast to this, it was when she could feel her most real. She could let the tears flow. She could grieve for the fantasy that was lost. And now it was the Friday of the second week since the bomb dropped, she made another decision.

For the second time in two decades, she was going to

unearth her buried treasure from the loft.

This time there had been no nostalgic tingles as she climbed the ladder. No churning guts wondering what past emotions she'd be facing. Nothing could make her feel any worse than she did already. This time was simply a way to pay honour to Grady's memory. His doodle on the beer mat, the sketch he'd sent of her eyes, the York postcard scrawled with his kisses. These needed to be seen once more. They were all she had left of him, and they needed to be aired. Unlike the last time she did this, she hadn't needed wine as a motivator. This time she was ready to do this on her own.

Mike barged the front door open with his full weight. He should really do something about that.

"Alright love, I'm gasping." He strode in and pecked the top of his wife's head.

Tilda remained silent. It seemed she was engrossed in some sort of book, and didn't look up.

"Alright love? I'm back." Mike unwittingly stated the obvious as he repeated himself. His eyes settled on the wooden box and old rubbish lying across her lap. He didn't know what to do next. He had never had to announce his arrival before.

"Oh, sorry. I didn't hear you come in." Tilda returned to her reading, and the silence resumed.

Mike was unsure of his next move. It didn't bother him having to make his own cup of tea. He was perfectly capable, and he certainly didn't *expect* it from her. But still, it was what had always happened. Why was Tilda being weird?

As Mike trooped off to the kitchen, wondering what other surprises were in store, Tilda continued to read the volume of Emerson she had in her hand. It had arrived in the post at her Dad's house, soon after her week in the Lakes. At the time she had devoured it. She ingested every line as if Grady himself had written them just for her. Here and there were notes in pencil. Small comments he'd added so she could see the world as fully as he did. For a few moments, until she'd been interrupted, it was as though he were alive again.

Tilda came to the end of the passage and sank her head back into the cushion. She returned mentally to the room. A check of her phone told her today's hour of uninhibited wallowing had spread into two. This time two weeks ago, she'd been seated opposite Stewart Grady as her world fell apart.

To her right Mike was sitting on the settee, playing with his iPad. A half-drunk mug of something brown was balanced on his thigh. She wondered if she was right to feel miffed that it hadn't occurred to him to make her a drink too. She wasn't sure, and she didn't really care enough to mention it. Too much swirling was still going on. With a visible effort, she forced herself out of her chair, papers falling to the ground as she stood. She swept them into the box and closed the lid, whilst simultaneously replicating the action internally with her own emotions. She took the box to the bottom of the stairs, ready for its return to the loft later, and then headed to the kitchen. The evening routine kicked in once more.

From the kitchen, the unmistakable smell of sizzling chicken wafted through to the indented sofa he was still plonked upon. Hunching over Clash of the Clans had kept him pretty busy whilst Tilda was being strange. There were always more villages to raid once you got into it but it was time to stop. The ache in his back, coupled with the aroma of impending food meant a move was necessary. As he stood and stretched himself to his full height he spotted a piece of paper on the floor. It was sticking out from under Tilda's chair. He picked it up and scanned its content, proud of having the fore-sight to keep the house tidy in Tilda's hormonal-induced absence. Handwriting almost identical to Tilda's was scrawled across it in faded loops and swirls.

April 14th *1996*

My thoughts are worthy of attention. My body is desired and responsive. I am nurtured, encouraged, cared for, wor-ried about and loved a hell of a lot. I have a new friend and champion. Nothing is too pointless to share, throwaway lines are explored and challenged, compliments are meant, and not overused causing them to lack value. Every word has meaning, every idea is considered, nothing is out of bounds or off limits. Flippancy can backfire, but respect has become deeply rooted. I am important and not because of false bravado, alcohol induced confidence or pretending the barbs of self-deprecation are not inwardly stinging. I am important because I have value, I am unique, I am beauti-ful, I am me.

Shrugging, Mike balled up the scribbled note and bowled it expertly into the wastepaper basket. It wasn't as if she was going to want an old piece of copied-out poetry after all this time.

Nice one Mikey boy! Brownie points for helping with her tidying.

From the slither of open doorway, Tilda witnessed this act of intense sacrilege. Her face burned. How dare he be so dismissive of something so personal. How dare he throw away something of hers - it could have been last week's shopping list for all he knew, it was still thoughtless. Looking at him now with his shaggy hair and skewiff tie, the childlike qualities that had once seemed sweet were becoming downright irritating. What was wrong with looking and acting like a forty year old? She did. She had wrinkles and grey hairs and sagging bits of flesh all over her body. She was a responsible adult. She didn't need someone reminding her to put the dishes in the sink or having to flag down her reversing car most mornings because she'd forgotten her lunch again. Why couldn't Mike run a comb through his hair now and then, or straighten his tie with the button fastened as he left for work. Why was she always having to be the grown up? Snippets of a recent conversation with Bea flitted across her mind.

"But do you still love him, do you want to stay with him? Aside from not being the love of your life and him clearly having some dependency issues, does he still do it for you?"

Bea had been eating a banana, which seemed to make the whole exchange highly comical at the time. Now she was remembering it back, it didn't seem as funny.

"Of course I love him, and yes, I'm going to stay with him," Tilda had replied. *"He's a very good man."*

"Well that's the most ridiculous answer to that question I've ever heard. A very good man? Stop it, Tilda, you'll make me moist."

As if to emphasise her exaggerated sarcasm, Bea had rolled her eyes for a full five seconds, making Tilda laugh despite herself.

"Don't, Bea. I mean it. He is a good man. I can't leave him, there's no reason to. We share a life, we've been together for a long time. He remembers to pick the milk up when I text him that we've run out." She added an afterthought. *"Usually."* Tilda had continued in earnest. *"He's a*

great husband and I'm very lucky really. So yeah, I must love him, mustn't I? There is no good reason to leave."

Bea slowly put the empty banana peel on her desk and wiped her hands on her thighs. She'd paused for a second or two before speaking, but continued.

"So you don't think that you deserve more? Someone that gets you on every level? Someone that understands what makes you tick, and loves you for it?"

And that had been that. They'd been interrupted by Alex and Si behaving in as daft a way as Tilda assumed her husband did in his place of work, and the conversation had ended. But every now and again, Bea's question that she had never answered at the time, floated into her head. Did she think being emotionally unfulfilled was NOT a good enough reason to end a marriage? Well did she? Standing in the kitchen, looking at Mike throw away a fragment of herself so thoughtlessly, she knew she had to come to some sort of answer, and fast.

The evening continued in a blur. Whilst going through the motions of her routine with apparent ease, Tilda took it upon herself to think.

The following day continued in the same way. Outwardly vacuuming the stairs, whizzing around the supermarket, filling up with petrol - she managed to do all her chores as the internal dialogue between Sensible Tilda, and Un-Tilda-like Tilda raged within. An unexpected letter from Freya provided a glimmer of calm amongst all the turmoil. But even that had its moments. She needed to order herself, she needed her brain to stop whirring, and she needed it soon.

By the end of the weekend, a peace had descended. Sunday evening had arrived. A notepad with an archive of 'to do' lists lay by her side. Scribbled notes, and half-formed ideas were crammed into the spiral bound pages. It had helped to write it all down again. Her journal that had once been such an important part of her routine had been neglected for years. Now that habit had been resurrected, things seemed clearer already.

She knew exactly what she was going to do. Well, she was pretty sure she did. She'd sleep on it, and decide for sure in the morning.

CHAPTER FORTY

Freya. Saturday 15th October 2016. Fremantle, Western Australia.

It was finally quiet upstairs. The last few days had been far too exciting for the boys. They'd eaten crap, had too many late nights and generally pushed every boundary going. It was no surprise they were a bugger to get to bed. Riley was looking particularly flushed when she put the light out. But peace had descended. It wouldn't last, but every moment of sanity counted. She could curl up on the deck with a glass of wine and write to her oldest mate. It had been far too long and the guilt had become impossible to ignore.

Freya found a pen, got some paper from the printer tray, and settled down to her long overdue task.

Saturday night, Down Under!

Tilds!

I know you can hardly believe your eyes. A letter through the post! Can it be? Are you hallucinating? Is this a mirage? (Or is that to do with deserts? I never know how to use that phrase correctly.) Anyway, yes it is I - Freya the Aussie. Greetings from Down Under! Greetings on real paper written with an inky pen, no less. It's like it's Victorian times! G'day!!!!

OK, I will now calm down and try to communicate

properly. And first you must let me gush and grovel about how long it's been since I emailed. I've just reread your last one and it's well over a year. I know! I am the shittest friend that ever lived, but I will make it up to you now with all my news, and a little bit extra. Have you even opened the brown envelope that I've enclosed? I bet not. It's probably resting on your lap, waiting its turn until you get to the end of all my waffle. I can picture you now, Tilds. You will be calmly reading, line-by-line, and sitting up straight and smiling at how accurately I've described you. I BET I'm right. Everyone else would rip it open the second they saw it, but I know you'll be waiting. Ha, I'm going to make you wait even longer and write pages and pages and pages, just to wind you up.

A change of plan. Riley has just been sick. I've sorted him out and put him back to bed, but maybe I should just get on with my news rather than teasing this out. I have a feeling it's going to be long night. Booooo.

So, there were a couple of reasons for getting in touch this way. I know you still refuse to engage with the whole Facebook thing so you will have missed my recent status outpourings about my 40th present from Aiden. (And if anyone asks, I'm sticking with 34 for as long as possible. I think I can get away with it for another decade at least.) Anyway, he only went and bought me a bloody sky dive session!! Yes! You read that correctly. I had to jump out of a plane FFS. (That's means for fuck's sake BTW. I speak fluent Teen now that Finn is nearly seven. Seven is the new twelve.) This is what happens when you marry an Aussie male. All your significant birthday presents suddenly become outdoorsy and tinged with danger. But still, I did it! Yes, I did!! And I wanted to tell you because I felt bloody proud of myself. I'll email you a load of pics if I can prise the lads from the computer. If you get a photo in your inbox of me in an unflattering Challenge Anneka jumpsuit, you'll know what it's about.

The other reason I am writing is really lovely actually. I have some proper photos (as in hard copies) to send, so wonder no longer what is in the mysterious brown envelope. They aren't from me, but Jonathan. Do you remember mature Jonathan from Uni? He came to stay for a few days, last week. Apparently he's sold his wine shop, and is having a sort of gap year/mini mid-life crisis, and seeing the vineyards of the world. He looks exactly the same, apart from a bit of silver in his beard, and is nearly 50. Yes! 50! On a sort of related (well not really related at all) topic, did you know he was gay? He mentioned that he'd split from his last boyfriend a couple of years ago, and I just thought 'God, of course.' It makes loads of sense. It especially explains why he knocked me back in 2nd year. That's when I should have realised. Anyway, the kids adored him, and treated him like a long lost Uncle that I'd been hiding somewhere, but now he's gone they are all stroppy and confident and say phrases like 'I think you'll find, Freya, carrots are not my bag,' when I'm asking if they want veggies. Damn him for giving them self-confidence. Anyway, he slept in Finn's room whilst Finn bunked in with Riley, he bought us loads of decent wine, and he stayed for five days before buggering off to the Barossa, across in the South. While he was here, we had some gorgeous evenings. When the kids were finally asleep, we'd sit on the deck, and open the wine. He had brought hundreds of photos with him - all in a big padded envelope - and we spread them across the floor and played 'How many of Freya's conquests can we see?' Ha ha. And also, now I remember, why on earth did you let me go out with that terrible hair? The Björk knots! Why, Tilda? Why?

Anyway, back to the point of me writing, because I just

know there will be more kiddie-vom at some point. There were so many pictures, and Jonathan had no idea about who some of the people even were, so I sneaked a few for you, just for old times' sake. Hence the envelope. I wish you could have been here because I think you'd have loved it.

So, a quick round up of the goss I am party to, since Jonathan came. Did you know Kenny is married? Bleugh, that poor woman! Apparently they are very happy and have four or five kids. I can't remember. He is Facebook friends with Jonathan so he knew all about it. I just felt nauseous. And Dhanesh is living in London, somewhere near to the wine shop, so they are still in touch too. He got divorced a couple of years ago, and doesn't have kids. Jen has her own business, which J seemed to think was something to do with organic ready meals, and last he heard Sam was living in San Francisco. It highlighted how bad I was at keeping in touch with them all, and also made me feel determined that I needed to write to you and remind you I still exist. Ha.

So what is new with you Tilds? Keeping busy? How's Mike? You are always welcome to come and visit, anytime you are passing the Southern Hemisphere, you know. I'd love Aiden to meet you. He never seems to believe all my wild tales from before him. You could back up all Jonathan's crazy (true) assertions! It really was good to be able to talk about the old days with him. We had some good times, didn't we?

So enjoy the photos. Don't judge my fashion mistakes too harshly, and stay well. I've missed you loads recently.

Loads of love
Freya x

PS. My favourite photo is without doubt, the one where we are in the big group - all hunched around the pub table?

I look shocking but you look stunning - all sparkling eyes and glowing skin. And that guy you were mad on at the time! He had a G name? Gregory? Gordon? Such a long time ago.

Christ, Tilda. We're fucking 40. Where have our lives gone? I guess if we don't start jumping out of planes now, we never will.

CHAPTER FORTY-ONE

Bea. Monday 24th October 2016. Stockport.

Midday had arrived. The recent data on social housing had kept Bea occupied for the last couple of hours, but she needed a break. With Susan at her conference, it was still a much more relaxed working environment than usual. This was being fully utilized by Si and Alex who had spent the best part of the previous hour moving their computer monitors in order to create a makeshift table tennis court for the office to enjoy. Bea had been alerted to this fact when a ping-pong ball hit her head minutes earlier. Luckily for her, she had been particularly effective in her backcombing skills that morning. The ping-pong ball had been the signal though. She took it as her cue that the morning's work was done, and it was time for lunch.

"Oi Bea," shouted Alex who was easily within earshot and did not need the volume. "Bea, if Tilda's not here this afternoon, will you work somewhere else so me and Si can have a full length court for our tournament?"

"No. Piss off."

"We'll put everything back afterwards."

"You can bugger off, I'm not moving desks. Anyway, Tilda will probably be in this afternoon."

"Nah. She's pulled a sickie without ringing in sick. She won't be in today."

"You're not having my desk."

"Right, well if you continue to stand in our sporting

way, don't have a go at us if you keep getting hit. This is the Policy Team Ping-Pong Championships and it's going to get COMPETITIVE."

So as to demonstrate just how competitive it was going to get, Alex tensed his muscles and growled. He looked ridiculous. Bea managed a smile and turned away to her computer.

She had an email. From Tilda.

A quick mouse scroll downwards told her this was not a quick note. This was long. It was epic. Without thinking too hard, she pressed print and sprang up to retrieve the pages from the printer the second they were out. Taking the papers to the meetings room, along with her cup of tea, she passed Si on the way.

"All right, you can have my desk for a bit, but make sure everything goes back. I'm going to work in here for a while."

Si looked after her openmouthed. Bea never did what they wanted her to do.

"Erm... thanks," he managed in reply, as he watched her leopard-print ensemble swish past him and into the small room nearby. She turned back as she stood in the doorway, realizing she needed to make her point clear.

"Si, I'm shutting the door, closing the blinds and booking myself in here for an hour. You are under strict instructions to leave me alone. If I had a Do Not Disturb sign from a hotel, I'd be using it now, get it?"

"Got it Bea! If you hear a knock, it'll just be the ball. Ignore us."

With that, Bea kicked her shoes off and curled up in a padded chair under the window. The sun warmed her back as she read the words Tilda had sent her.

Hi Bea,

I'm sorry for emailing, rather than calling but I need to tell you a couple things and it's easier if I just type without interruptions. You know what you're like! I'll never get it all out.

First of all, I've just got off the phone with Tan Tights - I think I interrupted her free buffet - and I've told her I need to take two weeks holiday as of now. I know! Timid Tilda stood up for herself. I told her there was a lot of family paperwork to deal with, what with my fake dead cousin dying so suddenly, and she didn't ask too many questions. Well done me!

Bea's eyebrows automatically rose. The tone was that of old Tilda, not red-rimmed, tear stained Tilda of the past fortnight. In fact, it wasn't even old Tilda. The writer of this email had a spark that old Tilda rarely exhibited. Bea kept reading, as some of her worries began to slip away. She was intrigued to know what was going on.

'*The second thing I need to tell you is that this is not the whole story. Yes, I'm on leave for the next two weeks, that's true. It's become clear to me that I needed a break. I'm not sure if you noticed it, but I've been a complete mess since York...*'

"No shit," Bea muttered under her breath.

'*...and I've tried to keep my head down - get up in the morning, go to work, come home and act normal, but it's not really worked. Last week, after I came out of Tesco, I got into the car and couldn't find the energy to drive myself home. I just stayed in my car, in the carpark for hours. It was as if I were paralysed. My thoughts were overwhelming my whole body. I couldn't move. I thought about the things I wish I'd experienced, and the things I'd planned to have done with my life by now. I cried, (obviously), and I got really annoyed about what I have come to accept as being* *acceptable. When did I begin to think I didn't deserve to be happy? When did I decide I was happy with a man that has never once made me light up with joy? I don't understand why I started to treat myself so badly. So I've started to think again.'*

Bea fanned out the printed pages across her lap as if by scanning quickly, she might spot a clue as to what Tilda was building towards. It was no use. She would need to read this properly. She sipped her tea and returned to the next paragraph.

'The trouble is, now that Grady is dead, it's as if everything else has died with him. I can't dream anymore, I can't close my eyes and picture him being happy. Whenever I wanted to, I had a lovely, reassuring fantasy that he was doing well, and that he was happy with the choice he made. Now I know he never got that chance. And that seems to be the saddest part of all.

I've cried a lot in the last couple of weeks - not sure if you realised...'

"Hmm, I had an inkling," smiled Bea.

'...and I've thought a lot too. Finally, I've decided something. I don't want to be sad anymore. Not even a little bit, not ever again. I lived with my Dad who was sad, I lost Grady and I was sad, I settled down with Mike when I was sad and now I've lost Grady again and I'm still bloody sad. Even if I hadn't been sad, I'd have just BEEN. Does that make sense? Just existing. Just going through the motions without even thinking about what I was missing. There'd be no joy, no excitement and no living. So this weekend I came to a conclusion. It is simply not good enough.'

Bea's smile faded as she read. Her stomach ached for the years her friend had lost. She could never turn back the clock and get back all that time. And yet, in spite of this, she was in awe of the sense of purpose she could feel in Tilda's words. Bea kept reading, her legs curled under her, as an occasional ping-pong ball bounced against the window.

You are the first to know. I have decided to adopt a new outlook. I am going to devote the immediate few weeks to seeking out pleasure and trying to find happiness. Not happiness for anyone else, just for me. Grady packed more positive energy into his twenty-one years than I have in nearly twice that. It's time to start noticing and experiencing the beauty all around, in the world beyond the office. It's time to live.

Bea wiped a tear as it rolled down her cheek, and turned over to the last page. Her smile was resurfacing, in spite of the emotion.

'Don't tell Tan Tights yet, but I'm handing in my notice. I'll let her know towards the end of my leave. I'll keep in touch with you, Bea, if I can. You have been showing me for years what happiness and the joy of living actually look like. It's time I stopped watching you, and experienced it for myself.

Don't worry about me. I'm going to be absolutely fine.
All my love
Tilda xxx

Bea's smile now shone through the trickle of tears. She wanted to punch the air. She wanted to go out into the office, stand on a desk and announce to the world that Timid Tilda Rudd was a bloody marvel.

"You go, girl," she found herself saying, as she drained her mug, blew her nose and attempted to read it all over again.

Soon she would have to walk back into the office as

if something wonderful and momentous had *not* just happened in the world.

Stewart and Rosie. Monday 24th October 2016. York.

Stewart looked at his watch. Five thirty. From his office he could see Rosie firmly leading the last client of the day towards the door - definitely a chatterer. It had become clear over his career that working in conveyancing did not automatically protect you from hearing the grim details of a couple's divorce if that divorce was the reason for their house sale. Rosie was wearing her perfected mask of polite non-response. A big smile, courteous nods of the head, but no actual words as she steered an elbow and walked them towards the exit. He had to give her credit - she was good. She made his working life a whole lot easier to manage and these past weeks he'd been especially grateful for her role in his home life too.

He'd only been back for a day, and yet it was as if he'd never been away. As if the old man hadn't died, as if he hadn't had to spend the past fortnight dealing with vicars, registrars, estate clearers, and worst of all, bloody solicitors.

Rosie returned, finally rid of the clients.

"They've gone. I think they'll be back though. There was definitely more to that story than you got. I think her parents have been paying the mortgage so there may be a counter claim." She moved smoothly round the office, replacing a file and straightening things up. He watched her, suddenly overcome with gratitude.

"Thanks so much, Rosie. Go home now, you've done

enough for today."

"It's fine. I just want to get tomorrow's court schedule up and then I'll be off."

Rosie knew she could have left a good hour ago. It
wasn't necessary for her to hang around to escort clients
out of the building, even if she was good at putting up
with the ones that babbled. It wasn't essential for her to
get the court schedules up, when the same task could be
done first thing tomorrow, and make no difference. She
could have been at home, with a meal in the oven and a
film downloaded by now. But she knew she had a responsibility. The issue had only risen today, and now
was first chance she'd had. It couldn't drag on. She was
unsure of course. If she proceeded with what she had to
say, she could be crossing a line. Would this go so well?
She'd always had a better insight than most into Stewart
Grady's private life. From managing him at work as well
as taking charge of his laundry, his online groceries, and
even having to buy presents for the occasional girlfriend
along the way, she knew the man as well as anyone. But
this was different. She couldn't predict how he'd react.
Yet that was no reason to shy away from what needed
to be done. It had to be mentioned.

"Stewart?"

"Hmmm?" He was browsing his laptop, and didn't
look up.

"Phil from the house clearance came by earlier. He
says the attic is all done now."

"Great. Thanks for telling me." His eyes remained
occupied on the screen.

"But they found some things in there, that they
weren't sure about, amongst the old files. Some things
that didn't fit any of the categories you'd outlined."

"Right." He looked up. Possibly because he'd heard

the hesitation in her voice. "Anything interesting?"

Rosie walked slowly out of the office and towards her own desk outside. He could see her reaching underneath her seat and lifting a box. Not especially large in size, it still filled her arms as she walked back towards his room. He stood to help her, but she was back before he'd left his desk. She placed the box down in front of him.

"There. It's just old stuff, but you might want to have a look."

Stewart looked understandably confused. There had been a ton of old stuff in the loft. Papers, files, books, broken furniture. Why would this have been saved, when none of that had?

He prised the faded cardboard flaps open, and looked inside.

Still worrying she was speaking out of turn, Rosie started to babble herself.

"When I say *just old stuff*, I don't mean any disrespect. I just mean its stuff from the past. But I did have a look, you know, in case I didn't need to bother you with it and it could just go straight in the bin, but it's quite *important* stuff, I think."

She paused again, wishing she could stop referring to this precious cargo as *stuff*. She managed to control the verbal diarrhoea as Stewart pulled out the first item on top - a newspaper clipping. That had been the first thing she'd read too. The story of the tragic, accidental death of the son of one of York's leading businessmen. Then the photo. A smiling teenager, bright eyed and innocent, the promise of the man he would become, shining out under the dark hair. Rosie watched as Stewart picked out each document, a school report, photos, a home made Christmas card, a watercolour painting and half finished sketch. The memories of John, the essence of who he had been, all boxed up and very nearly discarded. He remained stony faced for the most part. Once or twice he glanced up at Rosie, to find out if she'd seen that particular piece of his brother's life too. The pieces of evidence that proved he'd once lived. It was clear that she had seen them all. She'd gone through it earlier, and her eyes were now working their hardest not to blink. She needed the gathering pools to stay where they were and not run down her face. That wouldn't be professional at all.

He was nearly done. Just the plastic bag at the bottom - she'd assumed from it's squish that it was clothes and she'd been right, it was a coat - and he'd have seen everything.

He pulled out the last photo from the pile. Two little boys, who apart from a slight height difference could have passed easily as identical twins. Wearing matching Spiderman pyjamas and grinning into the camera, they sat on the top bunk of the bed. The faded biro on the back was unnecessary.

Stewart and John - the Grady boys 1978

His little brother, his spitting image, his happy place.

"Oh God."

Stewart let the photo fall on to the desk, as his voice cracked and he looked up at Rosie. Professional or not, she moved towards him, letting his arms grasp her waist as the tears fell. It was only a for a brief moment, they would never talk about this again, but Stewart Grady felt free to grieve the brother he'd lost. The brother he'd been forced to forget by their father, the father that had treated them both so badly, in such differing ways.

Twenty years late, but it was finally time.

Stewart released Rosie from his grip.

"I'm so sorry, I don't know what came over me.

Please, go home. I'm quite all right. I apologise for making such a fool of myself. It will never happen again."

He rummaged for his hanky, eventually blowing his nose, presumably to distract from the discomfort of the moment.

Rosie looked straight at her boss. He'd let his guard down for the first time since she'd known him. Rather than being embarrassed she found herself feeling relieved. It was time to take advantage of this momentary lapse in his armour. She took a deep breath. This opportunity would never happen again. She *must* speak.

"Stewart, before I go, I'm going to take this rather unique occasion to say something, and then, as you say, we'll never speak of it again."

Stewart blew his nose once more and stared into the computer screen, eyes straight ahead.

"I've watched you live your life the way you do for some time now. Always courteous and generous with the staff, you were a welcome change when your father retired, and we all appreciated it. A lot. But you are drinking yourself to death. You have no friends, your girlfriends never stay around for long and in recent months, even work is affecting your health. You have *got* to get yourself together. Now that Mr. Grady has died, you've got an excuse to take some leave without looking like you're actually cracking up." She paused. She *had* to say it.

"Even though, Stewart, you actually ARE cracking up. You're a mess. It's important to do something about it sooner rather than later, because..."

Rosie paused, trying to find the words.

"...because the way you're going, you'll end up exactly like him. A sad, bitter old man with nothing in his life other than this office. You deserve more than that. You are NOT him. You need to do something about it

NOW."

Rosie stopped speaking, and looked around. She saw where she was - standing in front of the boss' desk, as he sat studying his schedule for the following day. What on earth was she thinking? *Jesus Christ.* That was likely the last sentence she would ever have the chance to say to him. Time to grovel.

"God, I'm so sorry. I shouldn't have said any of that. Really, I don't know what came over me. I'm mortified. I'll understand if you want me to resign, or if you want me to move to another department. I'll go wherever you want to put me. I'm so sorry. Stewart? I'm sorry."

Stewart continued to scroll the cursor over his meetings tomorrow. He highlighted the early morning one, mentally checking he had the files he needed to hand.

"I'll see you tomorrow morning, at 8am as normal, and we won't say anymore about it. Just go home now."

She didn't need any more encouragement. She fled the scene of her outburst, pausing only to grab her coat and bag as she passed her desk outside. Relief flooded her body as she left the building. What had she been thinking? She shook her head as her heartbeat slowed to it's more usual pace, and raced home to a much-needed gin and tonic.

Inside the building of Grady and Son, a silent darkness was gradually descending. Everyone had left except for Stewart. He'd stared at his screen for some time after Rosie's outburst. Then he'd attempted to look through the box again, but stopped. That was a job that needed an alcohol accompaniment. He'd do that at home.

Finally he stood, groaning as the physical effects of the last fortnight took their toll. He stretched, and allowed the aches to intensify before relaxing back to his hunched state. He logged out of the network, switched off his office light, and shuffled into the foyer to find his coat. The coat stand was next to Rosie's desk.

Rosie. What to do about Rosie.

He'd known her almost as long as he'd worked here. Coming in as the boss' son, he'd never been treated as one of the gang. His early court losses, as he learnt on the job, were never the subject of gentle office teasing as they might be with another employee. Laughter stopped as he walked into the room, private jokes remained private. He had colleagues but not work friends.

And Rosie was a good employee. She'd always helped him since the start. Every time a new computer system was installed or when it was decided to change from PCs to Macs, Rosie had always been the one to show him what was what. She had patience with his inadequacies and didn't seem to resent the nepotism that had led to his employment. As soon as he had any real status in his career, he'd requested her as his PA and they'd always had a successful, professional relationship.

Which begged the question, *what to do about Rosie?*

Several miles away, curled up on a sofa with an empty glass and a blaring television, Rosie was blocking out all thoughts of work. The film wasn't helping though. Whilst Meryl Streep was one of her favourite actresses, watching her terrorise Emily Blunt as the boss from hell merely reinforced the point that her behaviour that afternoon had gone too far.

Stewart was a good boss. A great boss. He didn't always say the right thing, and he could certainly be tactless at times. She'd lost count of the number of times she'd had to smooth over someone's feelings because of his mis-choice of words. But deep down, she knew that he meant well. He wasn't a cruel bully like his father. Inside all that expensive bluster, was a lonely yet potentially honorable man. She was far too young to be his mother, but felt a maternal instinct nonetheless. He was still the lanky, insecure boy that had started in his Dad's firm all those years ago. Time had only hidden his insecurities behind posher suits and expensive whiskey. It hadn't eradicated them. She could only hope her next boss would be half as decent.

It was a shame that Rosie had persevered with the film. If she had returned to the office at that moment, she'd have witnessed her boss place a little square of yellow paper on her desk, just as he might leave a reminder or phone message. This one contained two words.

Thank you.

Tilda. Monday 24th October 2016. Stockport.

The living room was pristine, as was the rest of the house. She'd spent the morning hovering, dusting and polishing. The steam clean she had eventually booked, had worked it's magic a few days earlier, and every surface sparkled. A guilty conscience? Perhaps. But even though she was embarking upon a whole new outlook on life, she still had standards. She couldn't leave Mike with a dirty house.

And she was definitely leaving Mike.

It still didn't feel fair to him. He'd done nothing wrong at all. A few too many nights out with his mates without a phone call. An unspoken expectation that she'd be the one to organise his lunches and his washing and a Christmas present to his sister. There was nothing terrible that deserved the end of the marriage, nothing that bad at all. But it was now obvious to Tilda Rudd, soon to be reborn as Tilda Willoughby, that having your husband *not* do anything terrible, was no reason to stay when you were desperately unhappy and wanting more. It was time to go.

She placed the note by the darts trophy.

He'd see it as soon as he came in, what with it having pride of place on their mantelpiece. The weekend she had returned from York it was there. A lump of gold covered tin, impossibly gaudy and standing out like a sore thumb amongst her cream and pastel green décor. Her worries about hiding her anguish from her husband had been unfounded. He hadn't commented on her distress, perhaps not even noticed it. Her rehearsed monologues about the cause of her upset slipped away as it had dawned on her, he didn't care.

He hadn't asked about her weekend. He didn't enquire about the cause of her red eyes and occasional sobs. What he *did* do all Sunday was describe a variety of dart throws either performed or witnessed by him. At times there was video footage on his phone that he would hold towards her. She'd snap back into the room as she squinted at the screen in wonder that he was actually behaving like this. Did he really think she wanted to see these clips? To hear these stories? To talk about a topic in which she had never shown an interest, in nineteen years of knowing him? Her mind was a mess and there was a lot she couldn't process, but her feelings about Mike seemed to change that day. It had made writing the note much easier than she thought it would be.

It was far briefer than Bea's email, but she'd managed to say how she felt. He wouldn't understand, that went without saying. But no amount of words could ever explain that to him. There was really no point in the attempt. As a coincidental nod to her past, she'd filled the freezer with as many pre-made meals as she could, the irony of history repeating itself not lost on her in the slightest. Back then she'd returned home with her tail between her legs. This time she would not be coming back.

The bags were packed and waiting by the door. There was a little time before she was planning to leave. She had to wait for the tumble dryer to finish the towels and the kindest thing she could do in the circumstances, would be to empty the dishwasher when it had finished.

He'd get used to it soon enough, but it was only fair to leave everything clean for him. From her armchair, she sat and looked out of the window. The space in front of the house - what she had already begun to consider her ex-home - was filled with a new purchase. The single most expensive item Tilda had ever bought for herself. It would certainly take some getting used to - driving it and sleeping in it as well. The man that delivered it had given her a basic crash course in how it all worked. But after five years of saving her Dad's money, she had decided it was time to use some of it for a good reason. For an adventure. The campervan had fitted the bill exactly. By the time she hit her first bit of coast, she'd have it sussed with no worries.

She was Tilda Willoughby. She could do anything she put her mind to.

The knock disturbed her. Now wasn't the time for the neighbours to moan. She'd be moving it soon enough. She heaved herself out of the chair and opened the door.

"Morning, love. Parcel for you - needs a signature."

Tilda sighed with relief. Any other conversation was beyond her right now. Today was a day of reflection and new beginnings. Having to make small talk and pretend she was still the person she used to be, was unlikely to be possible.

"Right, thanks." She took the package from the postman, and shut the door. Usually parcels were for Mike. His eBay fixation meant a regular stream of comics, gadgets and once - for some unfathomable reason – a vintage Atari computer, turning up at varying intervals throughout the week. This delivery, however, was for her.

She sat back in her chair and peeled away the tape that was neatly sealing both ends. It was large and squishy. Tilda had no clue what it was.

The card fell out first. A white envelope labelled 'Tilda' that contained a generic greeting card - left blank for your message. There was indeed a message. An unfamiliar scrawl, yet reminiscent of Grady's in so many ways. The T of Tilda, and the loops on the Gs were exact copies.

> *Tilda,*
>
> *I thought you might like something to remember John by. I have a few bits and pieces but thought this might be appropriate.*
>
> *My father's funeral went well, I really appreciated your text that day. Thank you. It meant a lot.*
>
> *I know you have your own life and I don't want to cause any problems, but I was wondering if we could keep in touch? Only every so often, or maybe just once if you prefer. I'd really like to get to know my brother. I think you can help me.*
>
> *Best wishes*
> *Stewart*

Tilda opened the rest of the parcel, and found a tissue-paper clad gift. Marvelling at the precise nature of the wrapping - she couldn't imagine the crumbling Stewart doing this - she opened it up to see what he'd sent.

Her throat swelled as the tears pricked.

No Tilda, not today. Today is a happy day. You're leaving sadness behind. Time to be the star of your own show.

Her mental pep talk did the trick as she shook out the garment. Pulling each sleeve on, over her shirt, she stood in front of the mirror and inspected herself. She looked great. She felt invincible.

The towels could whistle. The dishwasher could stay loaded. It was time to go. Wearing Grady's khaki coat, Tilda Willoughby picked up her bags, and the box containing a never-been-used leather journal, left the house, and walked towards her new home.

In the distance, she could hear the hum of a lawnmower as someone else took advantage of this beautiful day.

ACKNOWLEDGEMENTS

As solitary as writing can seem at times, it is never a wholly individual endeavour. Back in *Carry the Beautiful*'s infancy, Helen Stalker was an excellent sounding board about all things Local Council related. Ste Rew provided his knowledge about private palliative care, and I made up the rest. Anything inaccurate is my own doing - they know their stuff.

Claire Dyer from Fresh Eyes was the perfect editor. Very encouraging, very detailed in her feedback and happy to point out the places I'd started to ramble. Her early support helped shape the end result enormously.

My man at Portal - Design & Illustration was invaluable with both his creative *and* technical skills, of which I have neither. I am happy for the world to defy conventional wisdom and judge *this* book by its cover.

My mum proof-read with her beady eye and I got detailed feedback from various family members. Thank you to Mary Bond, Frank Bond, Lucy Keavy, Monica Bartley Bond, Gav Bartley and Ashley Preston. Thanks also to the online friends that read my blog and offered support and encouragement along the way. A special shout out goes to Lisa McMullin, who reminded me at regular intervals that it's perfectly sane and not at all ridiculous, to want to do this for a living.

NB

Nicky Bond worked in Education for twelve years before discovering her inner Jessica Fletcher and writing a book in her kitchen. She is a Liverpool Ladies FC season ticket holder, relaxes by cooking and is passionately left-handed.

Carry the Beautiful is her first novel.